Mr. Wizard

A Novel

Jeff Wallach

PRAISE FOR *Mr. Wizard*

"Jeff Wallach's novel is about two brothers on a search for their bio-logical father after the unexpected death of their globe-trotting and colorful mother invites such an investigation. They find answers on an Irish golf course and in a familiar Long Island neighborhood. The writing is knowing and engaging, wise about its cultural orientations, and driven to discoveries both reassuring and life-enhancing."

—Michael Curtis, Fiction Editor Emeritus, *The Atlantic*

"Jeff Wallach is a prodigiously gifted writer—insightful, funny, and always surprising. *Mr. Wizard* twists and turns like a double helix. When you finish, you'll want to go back to the very first page and experience it all over again, just to see how Wallach pulled it off."

—Terri Cheney, author of
New York Times bestseller, *Manic: A Memoir*

"*Mr. Wizard* takes us on a genetic treasure hunt in which the characters learn much more about themselves than any DNA test could ever reveal. A hilarious and heartwarming novel about what it means to be brothers."

—Dan Pope, author of *Housebreaking*

"With *Mr. Wizard*, Jeff Wallach joins the likes of Michael Murphy, John Updike, and P.G. Wodehouse in writing wonderfully about golf in his fiction. It's a great read for anyone who loves golf and a good mystery. Family relationships swerve and dip like a double-breaking downhill putt but in the end everything drops into place with that pleasing sound of a golf ball falling into the cup. Not since *Golf in the Kingdom* has a fiction writer captured the mystical, bonding qual-ities of our game— and the mysteries of the human heart. Wallach's book brings to mind a rollicking round played with quirky, hilarious companions who love the game, and each other."

—Robert Trent Jones, Jr., author, musician, poet,
and renowned architect of more than
275 golf courses in more than 40 countries on six continents

"In the months after the death of the eccentric single mother who raised them, a pair of middle-aged New York-based brothers set out to discover the truth of their paternity. Cracking apart the fable their mother concocted to hold their curiosity at bay, they find themselves heading for the west coast of Ireland. In *Mr. Wizard*, Jeff Wallach draws on his decades as a travel journalist to add authenticity to his tale of the brothers' Celtic quest. Mining gems from the rich comic ore of his own New York boyhood, fashioning a narrative loaded with wisecracks, Wallach has crafted a novel that lets mystery embrace tenderness with its touching climax."

—Larry Colton has explored American cultural change in a series of best-selling non-fiction books, including *Goat Brothers, Counting Coup* and *Southern League*

"You'll enjoy the funny, vivid writing and fast-paced plot in Jeff Wallach's beguiling new novel, *Mr. Wizard*."

—Curt Sampson is the best-selling author of a shelf of golf-themed books, from *The Eternal Summer* to *Hogan* to his latest, *Roaring Back, the Fall and Rise of Tiger Woods*

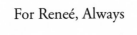

For Reneé, Always

"In all cases however, entering the past is a precarious business, since the past strives but always half fails to make us who we are."

—Richard Ford

"Understanding how DNA transmits all it knows about cancer, physics, dreaming and love will keep man searching for some time."

—David Brower

Prologue
Jenny

JENNY ELLIOT INSISTED SHE had to get her hair done; Robert Stack was coming to pick her up in his Bel Air convertible.

"He has a tiny prick," she told her son Phillip.

"Robert Stack? The actor?" Phillip said.

Jenny perched on the edge of the sea-foam sofa, her Velcro tennis shoes fastened tight as if she were about to make a run for it.

"Yep. Little pencil dick," she said.

Phillip took a long sip of his grapefruit sparkling water, trying not to laugh.

"And *you* should watch your drinking," Jenny said. "Being half Irish."

His orthodontured smile broke open like a whacked piñata. "Irish Jews? Is that what we are now?"

"Ballydraiocht," she said, cryptically. "A golf pro."

And two days later she was dead.

Part One

Chapter One
Phillip

THE NIGHT AFTER JENNY's funeral, Phillip mentioned the Ballydraiocht business to his brother Spencer. They were sitting in a dark drinker's bar on Columbus Avenue toasting their mom with twenty-three-dollar glasses of Macallan.

"Chalk that up to the dementia," Spencer said. "Or to the fact that she was always batshit crazy." He raised his tumbler in the air.

"I'm not so sure," Phillip said, clacking glasses. Meaning: was this a clue—whether inadvertent or intentional—to the mystery the boys had been trying to solve their whole lives: who, exactly, was their father?

Around midnight, unable to sleep, Phillip went online at the desk in his home library overlooking a currently leafless chestnut tree and a triptych of pre-war brownstones. The Upper West side was nearly quiet, the street pixelated with rain through the leaded glass. He ordered one of those DNA kits that you spit into and then send off to some lab.

Three weeks later he received more personal information about his own history than their mom had parceled out to him and Spencer in fifty years. Phillip found comfort in the charts and graphs and percentages, the links that revealed the coded structure of his own chemistry—whether he was likely to contract colon cancer or live past ninety, what his chances were of being a carrier of Autosomal Polycystic Kidney disease despite not having either gene variant; what percentage of Neanderthal ancestry he possessed; the probability that he'd develop age-related macular degeneration; his odds for getting Parkinson's, Celiac, or Canavan diseases; if he was a candidate for hereditary thrombophilia or hereditary fructose intolerance; the

3

likelihood of his coming down with Nijmegen Breakdown Syndrome; or if he might be the rare person to suffer from Photic Sneeze Reflex; and on and on, decoding the mysteries, focusing on what was undeniably, quantifiably real.

The test indicated that Phillip was forty-six percent Ashkenazi Jew but also identified a strong Northern European gene strain: forty percent of his DNA originated in the British Isles.

He called his brother.

"The Irish thing makes sense," Spencer said. "I've always loved the steak and ale pie. And *Riverdance*. That Michael Flatley sure is something!"

Phillip pictured his brother three miles away on the same crowded island between the Hudson and East Rivers, lying on the thick rug on the wide-planked oak floor of his loft.

"Don't you think it's strange, even for Mom, to have hidden this, if it's true? So what, we're half Irish?" Phillip asked.

"It wouldn't surprise me if Mom hid that we're half *Klingon*," Spencer said. "That was her peculiar charm: she hid things."

"I might not have cared if I'd known sooner," Phillip said. "But now it's disturbing. I've gone through my whole life thinking I'm a full-fledged Jew."

"You haven't done anything Jewy since your bar-mitzvah."

"It's still part of my identity. I'm one of the chosen people—I've just chosen to ignore it."

"Okay," Spencer said. "But don't reverse your circumcision yet. Why don't we think about this for a few days? See how we feel."

Phillip took a deep breath. Was his *brother* talking sense?

"Meanwhile, I've gotta go tend the potatoes," Spencer said. "Oh, and my Guinness is getting warm. Er, I mean it's getting cold."

CHAPTER TWO

Spencer

A FEW WEEKS LATER it was Spencer's turn to surprise Phillip.

"I took the test," Spencer said on the phone.

Phillip sounded out of breath. Spencer pictured him on a walk in Central Park, swinging his long arms—up at the northern end where the crowds dropped off, the oaks and maples ready to leaf. As if their turning red and yellow and orange back in November had been the end of it, but now here it was again: spring.

"What test?" Phillip asked, half listening.

Spencer knew what his brother was thinking: that earlier in life, before Spencer's unexpected success, he was always taking some test—a bartender's exam; for a license to perform weddings, to attend electrician's school.

"The DNA test, dum-dum. I studied for weeks. I have one variant of the APOE gene. Did you have that, too?"

"I have no idea what you're talking about," Phillip said.

"APOE predicts the possibility of late-onset Alzheimer's. Having one variant increases your risk for developing the disease. It might explain what happened to Mom. And what might happen to us. This is important shit: don't you care whether you're going to end up a drooling imbecile? Or if there's some way to prevent it?"

"Not sure," Phillip said. "What else did you learn?"

"I started reading about Mendel and the pea plants."

"Mendel? Didn't we go to elementary school with him?"

"That was Robert Mendel. I'm talking about Gregor Mendel, a nineteenth century monk. The father of genetics. Which is funny if you think about it. He figured out how characteristics are passed from one generation to the next."

"Anything of interest other than peas?"

"I'm about half Ashkenazi Jew, just like you," Spencer said. "But Irish ancestry . . . ? That doesn't show up at all."

He waited a few beats. As a drummer, Spencer's timing was spot on. Outside his window a rising blue-gray cloud of pigeons flapped their wings in polite applause.

"But *Southern European* . . . ? That I have," he continued. "I'm most likely descended from Spanish kings, although the test doesn't exactly specify."

"Wait, what are you saying?" Phillip asked.

"You tell me, half bro," Spencer said.

CHAPTER THREE

Irish Dustin Hoffman

As KIDS GROWING UP in North Woodmere, on Long Island, they'd joked about one of them having been adopted, so extremely opposite were their personalities. At Ogden Elementary School outsiders could see the brothers' different trajectories—Phillip helping out in the principal's office after class, Spencer being sent there on a weekly basis for misbehaving: injecting 7 Up into the gym volleyballs, or applying itching powder to the shorts of the bully who'd covered Phillip's locker with chewed gum.

In return for occasional muscle from his fearless younger brother, Phillip "edited" Spencer's assignments—the term they used for plagiarism—and drilled him with flashcards and mnemonic devices before math and history tests, sitting at the kitchen table by the bay windows overlooking the yard. They each protected the other in the way they were capable of.

It wasn't that Spencer was dumb; as one teacher put it to Jenny in a parental conference, "He just doesn't seem to give two shits."

"Sneaky smart," another teacher called him.

Phillip, fifteen months older, was the studious achiever, the science fair savant who corrected his brother's grammar and tried to enforce the rules of the many board games they played. He was tall and thin and sandy-haired, a favorite of smart, proper girls who would go on to become lawyers and publicists. He'd inherited his mother's orderliness, her obsession with numbers, logic, organizational systems—traits that contradicted her wacky, unpredictable side.

Spencer was the rebel, the cynic, a natural athlete who got kicked off the varsity basketball team because he wouldn't cut his thick, black, curly hair. The weed-smoking drummer beloved by bad girls, in his tight black jeans and band tee shirts with the sleeves hacked off. He received Jenny's irreverence, independence, and the ability not to give a high-flying fuck what other people thought of him.

What the *boys* thought—and often they thought the same thing simultaneously—was that their dad, Jack Elliot, had disappeared over the jungles of Vietnam in the 1960s, an Army pilot whose smiling photo taken beside his helicopter sat on the mantle of the split-level on Long Island all those years, next to their school photos, between two cedar-scented candles that no one ever lit.

Jenny had described Jack to her sons as "the funniest serious man I ever met." In the photo, he had the lean muscularity of an out-door gear model, with dark, smoky eyes crowned by delicate black eyebrows. Like a Jewish Colin Farrell, Spencer had always thought. Or—now—an Irish Dustin Hoffman.

Jenny implied that their father had been on a secret mission when he disappeared, but would never clarify the details.

"I'm not at liberty to speak about that," she would say. As if that phraseology had come to her directly from the Joint Chiefs. But when convenient she'd summon Jack Elliot's ghost.

In the third grade Spencer got sent home from school for farting his way through the Pledge of Allegiance.

Jenny said, "Your father got shot out of the sky protecting our country. Maybe a week without watching *F Troop* will teach you more respect . . . ?"

All they knew was that their dad was a Jewish war hero—an only child whose own parents had also died young. Phillip's sworn purpose early in life was to learn all he could about their father—despite that Jenny barely ever gave up any details. Although he couldn't have ar-ticulated it, he felt that knowing about his father was a pre-requisite to knowing himself.

While Spencer didn't care about the details, he thought *having* a father would have allowed him to belong to something larger than their tiny, incomplete family. He was driven by the notion of not being an outsider, which explained his propensity to play on sports teams and join a band. At the same time, he sought to portray himself as an iconoclast, a rugged individualist, so it wouldn't hurt as much if he *was* excluded from things.

They also knew that their mom wasn't normal: rather than packing their superhero lunchboxes with peanut butter sandwiches she sent them off with pâtés and soft cheeses, baguettes poking out of their book bags. She might drag them to a weekend EST retreat or cook organic snails for dinner. She exuded a petite Jackie O' self-confidence that caused men to follow after her like the tiny Shriners' cars at the back of a parade. She was the suburban mom that the boys' friends would develop crushes on, coming around the house in the hope of seeing Jenny stretched on the couch in hot pants reading a French novel.

Jenny had gone to junior college—she wanted to be a librarian or a writer of children's books—but dropped out when Jack Elliot proposed, or so the story went, and then grew mysterious, like a river that drops underground before reappearing with its downstream flow clearly established. She became a travel agent instead: In the opposite way that books became some people's travel, travel became Jenny's books.

Once, when he was a teenager, Phillip had done the 'maths' as he called it, and figured out that there were two narrow windows of time in which Jack Elliot could possibly have fathered him before heading off to war and then, just over a year later, fathered Spencer. Jack reportedly left for Southeast Asia in 1962. Phillip was born in 1963 and his brother arrived just over a year later, in 1965. Soon after drawing this out on graph paper, Phillip asked his mom whether Jack had come home for a visit at some point after shipping out.

They were in the backyard. Phillip was grilling hamburgers—one of his jobs at home—and wearing a white chef's apron with the U.S. Army insignia. The air smelled juicily charbroiled. The crab apple trees were in full bloom like pink umbrellas floating over the green lawn.

"Of course he came home," Jenny said. "Your brother is one-of-a-kind, but he was no immaculate conception." They looked over at Spencer, squirting lighter fluid onto the coals.

Phillip was partly satisfied with the timeline; he and Spencer *wanted* to believe that the brave, commie-fighting Jew was their dad.

And now . . .

Phillip said, "All these years I tried so hard to know more about who our father *was*—the kind of person, what he was like. His history. Now I see we didn't even know who *was* our father. Meaning the specific person."

"That's very confusing," Spencer said.

"Was the portrait on the mantle just a prop for a story mom invented?" Phillip asked. "Is that even the right guy?"

"I think it's possible that photo came with the picture frame," Spencer said.

Chapter Four

The Great Spencerino

In junior high Spencer found something to focus on for the first time; he was going to be a magician: The Great Spencerino. He would learn to produce unexpected things out of thin air—doves, women's underwear. He would choose his own path so that he didn't feel left out of other things.

Jenny bought him a boxed magic kit with fake-bottom coins and little silver cups and red foam balls and trick decks of playing cards. Phillip stood in as his lovely assistant, in taupe chinos, white button-down shirt, and topsiders. The Great Spencerino wore only black—except for a red silk scarf.

Spencer perfected the basics of the French Drop and some other skills—practicing in the mirror alone in the tiny guest bathroom downstairs.

One day Jenny said, "I'm going to teach you both a trick."

She rolled up her sleeves and shuffled the cards like a croupier. Her thin gold bangles spun on her slight wrists. She flipped her long, perfect hair out of her face with a little twist of her smooth, muscled neck.

"It's a party trick I learned from, . . . well . . . I can't tell you who I learned it from. It's all about misdirection."

The boys looked at each other as if she'd been drinking.

"Misdirection is when you get your audience to focus on something irrelevant so you can execute the trick," Jenny explained. "Distract them with one hand waving a wand so they don't notice the other hand performing the real befuckery, like slipping a rabbit out of your pocket, or stealing your subject's watch."

They were dazzled by her use of the word 'befuckery.' At the time they didn't realize that their mother had already mastered the art of misdirection herself.

"In this trick you want your audience to focus on what you're *saying*," she explained in a quiet, throaty voice.

She turned to Phillip. "Pick a card," she told him, fanning out the deck. "Any card."

He chose a card from the left edge of the pack, so as not to appear the rube.

"Now show it to me," she said.

He held the card close to his chest—covering the alligator on his polo shirt—so that not even his brother could see it.

"I'm not going to show it to you. What kind of a trick is that?"

Jenny rolled her speckled brown eyes.

He turned around the seven of spades.

She went to the phone and dialed a number. She held up one palm like a traffic cop. Her polished nails refracted light like tiny disco balls. She smiled, revealing perfect Chiclet teeth.

She said, "Hello, may I speak with Mr. Wizard . . . ? . . . Sure, I can hold."

Her blonde eyebrows arched high in surprise. "Hello, Mr. Wizard?!" she said. "Would you tell Phillip his card?"

She held the phone out so the boys could each put an ear to the receiver.

A deep male voice—a stranger's voice—said, "Phillip: your card is the seven of spades."

They started screaming. Phillip rolled back onto the floor, arms and legs in the air.

"That's fucking diabolical!" Spencer yelled.

"Hey! Language!" Jenny said. "Can't you think of another word for diabolical?"

Afterwards, 'diabolical' became Elliot family code for when you'd been totally bamboozled.

———

That evening, while the boys were helping with the dinner dishes, Phillip asked: "Mom . . . ? Is Mr. Wizard . . . our father?" He was half wondering if this were possible, half fishing for information.

Jenny put down the pot she was scrubbing and wrapped her arms around him, her rubber dish gloves warm on his neck. She smelled like waterfalls and grapefruit.

"Oh, sweetie," she said. "I wish! Your father's only trick was his vanishing act."

CHAPTER FIVE
Aunt Phyllis, Cousin Leah

A WEEK AFTER THEY'D compared DNA tests, Phillip phoned his brother again. "I'm going to call Aunt Phyllis. To see if she knows about this whole Irish thing."

"Sure," Spencer said. "Or why not just go see her in rehab. I think she's established permanent residency there. The big fat liar."

Phyllis was Jenny's only sister. They'd been cool toward each other since some childhood incident nobody ever talked about. Discovering the true story of *their* relationship was another archaeological expedition Phillip had always hoped to undertake.

The girls had grown up in a two-family house in Prospect Park, near the Brooklyn Museum. Jenny spent her spare time at the museum memorizing information placards on the exhibits, especially the Egyptian artifacts, or reading novels by the muted light filtering in through the big windows. Phyllis mostly strategized about her wardrobe and which parties to attend.

When Spencer was five, Aunt Phyllis promised to take him horseback riding to shut him up about something, although everyone present recognized she had no intention of ever doing so; she had no connection to horseback riding or to people who rode horses or anyone who might even know where to find one. The Bernsteins were not horse people—unless you went back a few generations to the Russian/Polish border, where family lore suggested their ancestors had trained stallions for the Czar's army.

After that, Spencer referred to Aunt Phyllis as a big fat liar because she hadn't fulfilled the promise. Jenny defended her sister by saying, "She's not a liar. She just hasn't kept her promise . . . *yet*." This family joke persisted to the current day.

"She's got to know something," Phillip said.

"Her biggest secret is a recipe for Cosmopolitans. She stole it from the Communists. Tell her hello for me. Tell her I'm looking forward to her upcoming appearance on Animal Planet."

Spencer didn't talk to their aunt directly because of the decades-old incident with Phyllis's daughter, Leah. Their cousin.

Spencer and Leah were latchkey kids who started hanging out in tenth grade, although they went to different schools—Leah at Woodmere Academy, Spencer and Phillip navigating public school in Hewlett.

Spencer would drop over at Leah's house because Aunt Phyllis was never home. They smoked a lot of weed and took Quaaludes or whatever their friends had found for sale in Washington Square Park. Leah was a year younger, but Spencer was her wingman. She was the alpha.

They sat close together on the lumpy couch in the basement, although the entire house stood empty. Posters of Prince and Queen hung on the paneled walls. Leah's short haircut may have been modeled after Joan Jett.

It was her idea to play Twister, which she called "Twisted." She put a Bowie album on the stereo and they used the album cover to separate the seeds out of a sandwich bag full of Acapulco Gold, which they rolled into a fat, stubby joint using cherry flavored Zigzag papers from the Pagoda head shop in the Green Acres mall. They smoked it in the yard as Leah's dog, Twixt, sniffed at the shrubbery.

They huddled in the cold air sharing a single, long New York Jets scarf. Leah pulled on her end to draw Spencer closer, then blew a lungful of weed smoke into his mouth. She followed it with her tongue. Spencer felt a wave of stoner bliss breaking over him. He was a sea wall. The salty spray was bracing.

"Let's go back inside," his cousin said when they'd smoked the joint to a burnt nub.

She spread the Twister board on the cold linoleum floor.

"I have an idea," Leah said.

It seemed like hours before she finished the thought.

"Let's change the names of the body parts on the spinner."

"You mean, like, left foot to right foot?" Spencer asked.

He recognized this as something *he* might have thought up. He felt close to his cousin.

"No. Different parts. Like elbow. Or ass cheek."

"Thigh," Spencer added. "Mouth."

"Tits," Leah giggled. "Zipper."

"That's not a body part," Spencer said.

"I'm super stoned," Leah explained.

"What if we change the names of the colored circles, too?"

"Penis," Leah said.

"Left ear," Spencer laughed, trying to neutralize this, just in case. Leah took the first spin.

"Mouth on penis," she said.

She kissed him again while he was practicing a one-armed back bend with his right foot on a green circle, his left arm on yellow. She tasted like cherry candy and charcoal. Her short black hair moved across her forehead.

She pulled his zipper down with one hand. Her feet weren't even on the board. The saxophone on *Young Americans* drowned out the sound of Aunt Phyllis's key in the kitchen door lock on the floor above them. When she came down the basement stairs Leah was on her knees. Spencer's overalls gathered at his ankles.

Phyllis dropped her Gucci purse and screamed, "You little barbarian! That's your . . . first cousin!"

A moment of stunned stoner silence elapsed—like sound waves rippling across the basement and rebounding off the wall and back to them before Spencer said, "Hey, it's not like we're planning to have retarded kids together," while pulling on his pants.

Sure, getting a blowjob from his cousin wasn't acceptable behavior, but then neither was being raised by a golden retriever, which was what he'd said back to his aunt about the way she left Leah home alone in the afternoons with Twixt the dog for years.

"I was working," Phyllis shouted, by which, according to Spencer, she meant: day-drinking with strangers. Her 'work' was another kind of mystery—she was a realtor, but Spencer believed this was her way of justifying meeting with rich men in empty houses all over the Five Towns.

Phyllis's husband, Uncle Jerry, had stepped in shortly after the blowjob episode. He was a dark, tall, well-muscled Sephardic, intimidating, with a rumbling voice that echoed eons of Jewish suffering and complaint. He drove up to the boys' house in his Lincoln Town

Car. Jenny was off on a business trip to the Netherlands at the time.

"You are no longer welcome in our home!" he'd shouted when Spencer opened the front door. "Your aunt won't even tell me what you did, so it must be terrible! Your father would be ashamed," Uncle Jerry concluded, before turning away and driving back out of their lives.

The boys understood there could be no negotiating with Uncle Jerry. He didn't find them to be entertaining little imps. He was the first adult they'd encountered who they couldn't game with their boyish charms.

"I don't know anything about a golf pro," Aunt Phyllis told Phillip on the phone. "Not that it would surprise me if Jenny dated one. She took golf lessons once. At the Lawrence Country Club. She thought she'd meet an eligible man but discovered they all looked like Jackie Gleason. That's when she switched to tennis. Then jogging. She loved the little Dior track suits—she always wore the short jackets unzipped to her navel. You boys were already junior fucking Cossacks by then."

"But you *knew* our father? Before he died in the war?"

"Died in the war?" she screeched in her nicotine voice. "Oh, that's still a good one, honey."

CHAPTER SIX

Richard

AT PHILLIP'S INSISTENCE, THE boys tracked down their birth certificates, which as expected listed Jack Elliot as their father. Phillip found his in the teak file drawers where he kept all of his important papers: closing statements from real estate deals; bank loan information; a signed letter from former New York Mets shortstop Bud Harrelson answering Phillip's Bar Mitzvah invitation. Spencer tore apart the cartons he was storing in the garage of his most recent ex-girlfriend Mirabel's house in Long Island City to find his.

Was Jack Elliot's name on their birth certificates something their mother could have orchestrated even if it wasn't true?

Yep, both brothers agreed. No doubt.

Phillip got down to business. "I did a little research," he said over the phone. "I found thousands of men with the name James Elliot in genealogical registries. Also a fuck-ton of Elliot Jameses. Hundreds of the first type might fit the age and geographical requirements to be *our* James Elliot."

"I know. I talked to the Mormons," Spencer said.

"The Mormons?"

"They have a death grip—literally—on these kinds of records. They were nice enough to offer to convert our dead ancestors stretching all the way back to Poland. Or in your case, Ireland. Would that make them latter day saints, or more recent day saints, do you think? Papa would have fecking loved that!"

Papa was their grandfather, Sam Bernstein.

Phillip noted that his brother said "fecking" the way the Irish do.

"I thought of one more person we could call. About the father question," Spencer went on. "I can't make that call myself, either. It's not lost on me that I bolloxed a lot of early relationships."

18

"Let me guess," Phillip said.

"It's Richard Linkletter," Spencer said.

"I wouldn't have guessed that. But I see where you're going."

Richard had been their next-door neighbor growing up in North Woodmere. As kids they'd made fun of him for not being very bright, though he was an engineer. They'd joked that this meant he drove a train. He was a handsome, awkward man who'd once drunkenly confessed to their mother at a neighborhood party, "You're the most exquisite creature I've ever seen." When he'd tried to touch her hair, Jenny slapped down his hand like a Kung Fu fighter.

"Richard, this is Phillip Elliot—Jenny Elliot's son," Phillip began on the phone.

"I heard your mother finally died," the old man croaked. "I'm sorry. For you, I mean—she was your mother. But holy hell, that woman . . ."

"It's actually my dad I wanted to talk about," Phillip said.

"I'm too old. I'm forgetful. I don't remember anything. Where are my car keys?"

"I'm coming to see you," Phillip said.

"Don't bring your idiot of a brother. I won't answer the door."

The boys long suspected that Richard Linkletter had an affair with their mother—Spencer used to say he was too lazy to go farther than across the front yard for extramarital sex. Then Spencer walked in on them one day in the garage when he and Phillip were supposed to be off with their cameras on a Cub Scout photography outing— although they'd secretly quit the Cub Scouts a year earlier. Spencer snapped a Polaroid of Richard and his mother in the back seat of the Elliots' Buick Electra. The windows were rolled down. Jenny was astride him, facing out the back.

Pulling his pants on, Richard yelled, "I'm coming after you, you little bastard!"

Spencer stood on the cement shaking the picture, waiting for it to expose.

"Don't worry, Richard," Jenny said, loud enough for Spencer to hear. "His photography is always blurry."

Spencer claimed to have hidden the photo in a secret location, which gave him a rare kind of power in the Elliot family. He argued to Phillip that the Cub Scouts ought to offer a merit badge for the skills he displayed. "The befuckery patch," he called it. "It's decorated with two Webelos screwing in a lean-to they built."

Nearly the whole neighborhood knew about the affair, including Richard's wife; but not their daughter, Barbara, a hapless, plain-looking girl who Spencer claimed was destined to become a bookkeeper and marry an actuary, whatever that "actuary" was. Spencer began acting nice toward Barbara, which alarmed everyone. He carried her books to school in the mornings and anonymously sent pint cartons of chocolate milk to her table at lunch.

"What do you want," Richard asked Spencer when this had been going on for weeks. He cornered him in the Elliot yard late one afternoon. Spencer was lying in a plastic hammock that Jenny had brought back from Thailand on one of her travel agent familiarization trips. He was flipping through her copy of *Lady Chatterley's Lover*—the 1962 edition with a bare breast on the cover—hoping to find pornographic passages.

Spencer shook his head as if he didn't know what Richard was talking about. "I'd like to be an astronaut," Spencer said, "but I don't see how that's relevant." He swung down from the hammock. At age thirteen he was taller than Richard. He drummed the paperback against the palm of one hand.

"Have you ever been paid for any of your photos?" Richard tried.

"Nah. I'm more of an amateur," Spencer said. "It's my passion. Like yours is fucking your neighbors." He stood close until Richard just shook his head and sidled back home.

Spencer never let anyone see the photo. It kept their mother just a little bit in line. She might have perfected a few guerrilla tactics, but they all recognized that Spencer was becoming a formidable force as well.

When Phillip arrived at the assisted living facility in Cedarhurst, Richard was pacing the lobby in the requisite white Velcro tennis shoes. His still-strong jaw line was stubbled white.

"Your brother ruined my marriage," he told Phillip.

"I can't really speak to that," Phillip responded.

"What do you want from me, anyway? I'm practically dead, too."

"We're just trying to get some information about our father."

"Your father? And I would help you why?" Richard flicked at the front of his plaid shirt, buttoned all the way to the collar. He was a bonier version of the attractive knucklehead he'd been when the boys were growing up.

"I was always a good neighbor to you, Richard. I cut your lawn every week. I painted your house. I helped Barbara study for her SATs. I know you were fond of my mother."

"Yeah, so were a lot of men. A *lot*."

"She never told you anything about our dad . . . ?"

"There were plenty of rumors," Richard said. "That he was killed in a secret military mission. That he still worked for the government in some covert location overseas. But he could have been just about anyone with a cock in the tri-state area. Check with the census bureau. Under penises!" Richard yelled.

Phillip nodded. "You've been very helpful, Richard."

"And tell your brother to go fuck himself backwards," the old man added as Phillip headed out the door.

Later, when Spencer asked him how it had gone, Phillip simply told him he hadn't learned anything new.

Chapter Seven

The Cottage

The boys travelled to their mother's house to sort through the chaos she'd left behind when she moved to the memory care center a few months before her death. The final sign of her decline had appeared to Spencer when he went to see her for dinner one night. She was working on the *Times* crossword when he arrived—a ritual of her daily life for decades. When Spencer picked up the neatly folded page to see if he could fill in any unanswered clues, the boxes were filled randomly with letters that didn't form words.

Phillip asked Aunt Phyllis to join them on their post-mortem search mission to Jenny's house and was surprised when she agreed.

"Of course she agreed," Spencer said. "She's still hoping to find a smoking gun. Something that connects Mom to the Lufthansa heist, or the sinking of the Edmund Fitzgerald."

"The Edmund Fitzgerald?" Phillip said.

"'All that remains are the faces and names of the wives and the sons and the daughters,'" Spencer said.

Jenny had lived alone in the small, elegant house—she called it 'the cottage'—in walking distance of the village of Larchmont, north of Manhattan. In forty-five minutes on Metro North she could be at Grand Central, a short subway ride on the shuttle and the 1,2,3 uptown to see Phillip or the Number 6 downtown to Spring Street to see Spencer. She insisted on riding the subway, or walking, even into her seventies, though the boys offered to pay her taxi fares.

Phyllis had aged less well than their mother due to a lifetime of smoking and drinking. Recently she had warmed to the boys, although they didn't know why. Spencer observed that the lower her voice dropped, the friendlier she became. Sometimes he referred to her as their evil stepmother. Phillip noticed that she seemed pained by Jenny's death, despite having had few good things to say about her sister when she'd been alive.

Their aunt showed up in a black Town Car driven by a rangy Sikh who kissed her hand before departing. She wore leopard print capris and a white silk shirt. She exuded a sophisticated, runway-model beauty, in contrast to their mother, the stunning Bohemian princess.

"Hello, you little animals," she said when they opened the door. She air-kissed them both and gave Spencer the usual admonishing scowl.

"We missed you too," Spencer said.

They began their mission by each taking a room, plodding through boxes of tax returns, drawers full of soft Hermes scarves and tie-dyed bell bottoms from upscale couture houses, files from Jenny's travel agency business, books, manila envelopes stuffed full of phone bills, receipts from restaurants that had served their last meal twenty years ago.

They organized art in the living room, financial info in the extra bedroom that Jenny had used as an office, personal items in the bedroom where their mom had slept. They chose items they might each want to keep. Phyllis set aside a gold locket that had belonged to her and Jenny's mom that she wished to pass along to her daughter Leah. Spencer picked a framed print of an ocean scene signed by a renowned California artist. Phillip said he didn't know what he wanted yet so they couldn't get rid of anything. He wouldn't even let them take out the trash.

Phillip remembered how when he was a child their mom's closet was a periscope into her ocean of contradictions—an ordered chaos of boas and long strings of beads, slinky cocktail dresses and hippie mu-mus, leather pants and high-waisted jeans and cropped khakis, mini skirts and proper pleated seersucker shorts, blouses that were cut low or buttoned all the way to the collar, old sneakers and black stilettos and mules and flats, an infinite variety of costumes for occasions ranging from corporate dinners for travel agents to adults-only swim parties where a few keys might get exchanged via a bowl on the glass-topped table in someone's backyard. She was an enigma to them, wrapped in a mystery, wrapped in Drake's cakes.

Spencer yelled from the spare bedroom. "I've got something!"

As Phyllis and Phillip came down the hall Spencer spread a folder of photos on the desk where their mother used to pay bills and do her paperwork.

The boys were hoping for snapshots of their father. Something from his childhood, a photo of him and their mother together, proof that they'd existed in the same corporeal plane. They each knew this about the other without speaking of it.

But these photos were older—from Jenny's own childhood: Jenny and Phyllis in front of their own parents' fruit warehouse in Manhattan. Another of them standing by their old truck, which they used to transport produce from the farms of New Jersey and Long Island. In many of the shots a young boy stood between the girls.

They flipped through the stack together in silence. Their aunt looked out the window.

"Hey, maybe that's Mr. Wizard," Spencer said, joking.

But Aunt Phyllis's turkey neck jerked in tiny spasms. She started weeping. The boys had never seen anything like it. Her mascara ran until she looked like Carrie at the high school dance, Spencer thought.

"How do you know about Mr. Wizard?" Phyllis choked.

"The card trick?" Spencer said.

"Was he our real father?" Phillip asked.

"Oh, sweetheart," his aunt choked out. "Look at the photo. How could he be your father? That boy was four years younger than your mom."

"Who is it, then?" Spencer asked. "Phileas Fogg? Houdini? The undiscovered Smothers brother?"

"That's *our* brother," Phyllis said.

Stunned silence. Possibly the first time Phillip ever saw Spencer surprised beyond a pithy rejoinder.

"You didn't have a brother," Phillip said flatly.

"Oh, for fuck's sake," Phyllis said.

She told them how Jenny had been driving the family produce truck on the New Jersey Turnpike at age fifteen with their younger brother in the back. Heading south to pick up a load of sweet corn.

"How could they let her drive at that age?" their aunt asked. "Why was he in the back of the truck instead of the cab, anyway?

"He was everyone's favorite. *He* was Mr. Wizard every day of his life. God, did he love that card trick! He double-dog swore us to secrecy when he finally showed us how it worked.

"He flew out of the back of the truck somehow, nobody knows what happened. We never mentioned him or the card trick again. He's buried in a plot two rows over from your grandparents because they'd only bought space enough for themselves at that point in their lives."

The brothers stood motionless, taking it all in. Taking solace in the fact that they were right about their mom having kept a dark secret. Phillip wondered if this was the thing that had stood between Phyllis and Jenny.

Spencer thought: now we know something that was hidden, but not what it means. He felt like Gregor Mendel comprehending how the pea plants reproduced, without seeing the powerful future implications—*On the Origin of Species*, the mapping of the human genome, CRISPR and the creation of creepy robot children with designer DNA.

"You look just like him," their aunt said to Phillip. And turning to Spencer she said, "And you practically *are* him. He was a lovable schmuck, too.

"All these years you've both been worrying about your father, always wanting to know more about your stupid father. But it's your mother who's the key to who you are—to why neither of you ever let yourselves get close to anyone. To why you're all so fucking frightening behind the wheel. She was right in front of you the whole time and you barely noticed, you were so busy trying to learn about your dad."

"Now *that's* fecking diabolical," Spencer said.

Chapter Eight
Fribbles

THEIR POOR DEAD UNCLE falling out of the cabbage truck: that explained a lot about their mom. But still: their father. Phillip got back to work. Following a few days of Internet research he called Spencer to share what he had learned.

"There was a soldier," Phillip said. "From Rockville Centre. James Elliot. Enlisted in the Army Special Forces in 1961, shipped out to Vietnam a year later as an 'advisor.' Flew a helicopter. Never came home. That's got to be him!"

"He enlisted?" Spencer said. "For Vietnam? Wouldn't that make him too much of a moron to have reproduced?"

Even though they were on the telephone, Phillip gave his brother the sharp look he'd been perfecting since the day Spencer was born.

Rockville Centre was only a couple of towns over from where they'd gone to high school—a blue-collar neighborhood largely lacking in Jews. Lots of Irish, which wasn't lost on them given the results of Phillip's DNA test. When the boys were little, around the holidays, Jenny used to dress them in their pajamas after dinner and hustle them out to the Electra to drive through Rockville Centre to look at the Christmas lights. As a boy without a father, seeing how other families celebrated the holidays made Spencer feel excluded from one more thing.

The boys' high school teams played against Rockville Centre High, and Spencer had a theory (inaccurate, as all his friends told him, but he stuck to it anyway) that Rockville Centre always won in football because their team was full of Irish toughs who didn't think twice about getting a concussion, whereas the boys' own school always won in basketball because Jews learned to shoot from the outside to avoid the preponderance of physical blows.

"I'd really like to get this squared away," Phillip said. "It would be good to know if we're half Irish. I was thinking about going out to the Island. To sniff around."

"If you mean Long Island—not Ireland—we could have lunch at Juniors," Spencer said.

Juniors was the luncheonette they'd frequented in high school. When he was a sophomore, Spencer had a crush on a waitress with big hips and a Boston accent. He always wondered if the café's name referred to a person, or to the eleventh grade class.

"Then we could smoke a joint with the stoners out behind Mr. Fernando's wood shop, like old times," Spencer continued. "Then he can smash my head against the bulletin board, like he loved to do back in the day. Remember how he'd make like he was going to smash your head but then hold his hand back there to protect you, except he was so dumb he'd forget to put his hand there? Which is why he was a shop teacher to begin with?"

"I never took shop," Phillip said.

"No, of course you didn't," Spencer said. "You were probably in home ec sewing throw pillows and learning how to type. I took shop twice. Passed both times. I have the candlestick and the bathrobe hook to prove it."

Phillip drove downtown to pick Spencer up in Soho outside his giant, drafty loft that had once been part of a shirt factory and was now decorated in a style that not even social historians had yet figured out a way to describe. It was a warm spring Saturday. Spencer felt like he should be reporting for Little League tryouts.

Traffic was light and their route appeared much as it had decades previously, when they'd first begun traveling it in the opposite direction on their earliest weekend forays into the city—for the Italian festival of San Gennaro, around Mulberry Street, to eat sugar-dusted zeppoles and buy loose joints; or to see Patti Smith in a club in Hell's Kitchen.

The sky was a smoky blue, the air perfumed with salt air from the New York marshes and a hint of burning rubber. They could hear airplanes gearing down to land at Kennedy and La Guardia.

Near the old neighborhood, just off the Belt Parkway, they passed the Green Acres Mall, where their mother had taught them to drive in the vast parking lot. Spencer had nearly managed to accelerate through the exterior wall of the Dime Savings Bank, before they had a drive-through. Phillip remembered his sixth birthday party at the Steak Pub just outside the mall, which he'd loved because it was decorated with suits of armor in dark hallways. Jenny had secretly ordered Phillip a cake for the occasion, and when it came to their table with candles blazing Phillip couldn't figure out how the waiter had known it was his birthday! It was the kind of magic only his mother could conjure.

Now, when the boys went out to dinner together, Spencer might secretly tell the waiter it was Phillip's birthday and have them deliver the worst dessert on the menu—always flan, if they had it—and drag the staff over to sing. They'd be wearing silly party hats, or sombreros—something intended to make everyone in the room look over at the table. Spencer pulled this gag two or three times a year, and almost never on Phillip's actual birthday. Then he'd skip a year or two until he was confident Phillip had forgotten about the whole thing.

The boys' first stop on Long Island was the Five Towns Public Library, to access *The Nassau Chronicle*—the hometown newspaper—in search of an obituary for Jack Elliot. If they found one that meshed with the dates they had, would it offer up any other clues?

They pulled up to the modern, low-slung brick-and-glass building, which looked quaint to them now. Phillip retrieved a leather saddle-bag briefcase out of the back of his cloud-gray hybrid Toyota Rav4. "Didn't there used to be a Friendly's nearby?" he asked. "Mom used to take us after story time in the library basement. On the menu they called a hamburger a 'hamburg.'"

"They served them on toasted, buttered white bread," Spencer recalled. "The milkshakes had a funny name."

"Fribbles," Phillip said.

They walked across the dark macadam of the parking lot, as if they were sneaking up on something. They could smell new tar and distant French fries.

"I haven't been here since I penned my award-winning book report on *Winnie the Pooh*," Spencer said. "I referenced the surprise ending as a critique of the industrial revolution."

"I used to love this place," Phillip said. "I'd come home every week with a giant stack of books. I thought that every answer to every possible question was hidden inside. It was like a stadium for the world's greatest treasure hunt."

"I thought I could read through the whole collection alphabetically," Spencer said. "I was going to start with books on aardvarks and finish with zebras. I mostly ended up reading the *Alfred Hitchcock and the Three Investigators* series."

"I loved that," Phillip said. "Jupiter Jones. I remember one about pirates, and another with a stuttering parrot that provided the crucial clue."

"Yep. Jupiter lived in a junkyard and had a secret clubhouse under a bathtub," Spencer added.

"Not unlike where you live now," Phillip said. "Hey, Wayback Playback: remember the book fair at Ogden every year?"

Wayback Playback was a game Spencer invented when he was getting stoned a lot in high school. One of them would say, "Wayback Playback: remember when Stewart Silverman drank his own pee in elementary school because he thought it was lemonade," or "Wayback Playback: remember when the Good Humor man left the door to his freezer open and it rained cherry pops down the street?" and then the other would know the rest of the story and there'd be no need to even finish the thought.

Phillip recalled how Jenny had instilled an early love of reading in them both, how each year at the book fair he carried a pile of books to the register that was taller than he was—a mix of biographies of early presidents and patriots, how-to books about building things out of colorful pipe cleaners or popsicle sticks, and a series with maps on the covers where each book was the name of a country, followed by an exclamation point: *Turkey! Trinidad and Tobago!* He long wondered why *Austria* was only followed by a period. Was this a typo, or did it convey some hidden implication?

Inside the library, despite the musty smell of hardcovers and old chewing gum they found a modern facility with computers in place of the old card catalogues. A few kids in their Abercrombie and Fitch-wear tapped away at iPhones.

"We didn't have cushions on the chairs, back in the day," Phillip commented.

"No. We sat on rocks and stumps. The desks were made of antlers.

Why even come to the library if you have an iPhone?" Spencer asked. "Isn't the library already in there?

"For the really old stuff," Phillip said.

He approached the librarian—a teenager with a giant diamond stud in one ear. He was also tapping on his phone. He looked up, startled to see someone who wanted his help.

"We're looking for old copies of the *Nassau Chronicle*," Phillip said. "The newspaper?" He realized he sounded like he was one hundred. He wanted to yell at someone to get off his lawn.

"How old?"

"From the 1960s. Maybe '62-'66."

"Those would be downstairs," the librarian said. "They're actual *newspapers*. But I don't know if we have them back that far."

"Why does he say 'newspapers' like he means 'tyrannosaurs?'" Spencer whispered to his brother.

They went down the carpeted stairs and found the metal stacks full of periodicals boxed by years. The *Chronicle* was a small weekly paper so the boxes were small, too. Phillip took 1962 and 1963, Spencer the following three years. The papers were yellowed and brittle. Phillip felt a chilly draft of excitement to be looking for information that might take them closer to their father.

"Why didn't we do this decades ago?" Phillip asked.

"Because back then we weren't certain that Mom was a liar, too."

"You just can't let go of the horseback riding, can you?" Phillip said.

In flipping the newspaper pages toward the obituaries in the back, they encountered ads for stores and restaurants from their childhood: Morton's Army/Navy, where Jenny took them to buy camp clothes; the Cricket Shop, which was for dress clothes; Al Steiner's, the steakhouse that hosted awkward dinners before senior proms; Crazy Eddie's, where each of the boys got to choose a stereo as a bar mitzvah present.

Back in the early sixties Long Island was first expanding into a bedroom community. The newspaper made the Five Towns—collectively Hewlett, Woodmere, Cedarhurst, Inwood, and Lawrence—sound like a farming community in Indiana: wholesome, intimate, single-minded. It never referenced Manhattan, a mere twenty-five miles away.

They nearly lost track of their mission. They read stories about shows being performed by the drama clubs at the nearby high schools (they always seemed to be putting on *Bye Bye Birdie*); reviews of new restaurants; expansions at Kennedy Airport when it was still called Idlewild; construction along Sunrise Highway. They read profiles of residents who'd played for the New York Mets' farm club or moved to town all the way from Great Neck, or who'd taken a French cooking class in—get this—France!

After half an hour Phillip said, "We're never going to get through these if we keep stopping to read every article."

They began flipping pages like the giant cards on *What's My Line.*

Twenty minutes later Spencer said, "Holy shit, look at this!" But he read to himself, not letting Phillip look.

"Bingo!" he exclaimed, clapping his hands so loudly that an elderly woman dozing on a couch nearby knocked her copy of *Dianetics* to the floor.

"James William Elliot, Jr.," Spencer read. "Born June 11, 1941, died date unknown, circa 1964, an Army helicopter pilot, disappeared in Vietnam in Southeastern Asia. Known as Jack, a star athlete at Rockville Centre High School, enlisted in the U.S. Army in 1961. Survived by his parents, James, Sr. and Patricia, of Dublin, Ireland; his sisters, Katherine . . . Margaret . . . Deirdre . . .; his brothers Patrick . . . William . . . Sean. And his beloved wife, Jennifer P. Bernstein, of Hewlett, New York. Funeral services to be held Sunday April 14, St. Finbar's Church, Rockville Centre, interment to follow at Rockbrook Cemetery."

The boys stared at each other for a long moment, each waiting for his brother to speak first.

"Do you know many 'only' children who have six siblings?" Spencer asked.

"Do you know many Jews who name all their kids after saints?" Phillip said.

"And St. *Finbar's?*" Spencer said. "Really? Jay-zus Crisco, how many fecking saints do they have, anyway?"

"Why are you asking me?" Phillip said.

"Because you're the Irish son," Spencer said. "Well, at least we found something Mom wasn't lying about: her husband existed. And he was a war hero."

"Let's go see him."

"Who?"

"Dad," Phillip said.

Chapter Nine
We're the Jews

THEY HEADED TO ROCKBROOK Cemetery, navigating the illogical roads of Long Island, passing low-slung blocks of sixties architecture—strip malls and brick apartment buildings; and old Cape Cods and saltboxes and Dutch colonials with faded lap siding, or aluminum siding that now looked like faded lap siding, on the edges of some of the small villages. Spencer half expected to see kids they'd known—little Bob Levy, riding his Stingray with the giant sissy bar; Paul Kleinman carrying his rancid catcher's mitt; Melissa Berger with her hairy ape arms wrapped around a stack of textbooks.

The cemetery was located off Sunrise Highway, behind a Mattress Outlet and a Roy Rogers. The office was staffed by a nun in a light brown habit standing behind a granite counter.

Spencer gave her Jack Elliot's name and dates and she looked him up on a computer that appeared so old, Spencer whispered, that it printed on stone tablets. He was on his best behavior, charming and demure toward the nun, as if still grieving the death of his dad more than five decades ago. She gave them a map to help them find Jack Elliot's grave and they walked out into the sunlight and through a neat graveyard crowded with graying headstones and white stone crosses. The cemetery was compact and well cared for, with no fancy crypts or mausoleums. Working class all the way.

The boys followed the crushed gravel path to Section C. Their shoes crunched on the loose stones. They were as close to their history as they'd ever been. They were each, in their own way, afraid—Spencer of finding their father, and Phillip of not finding him.

Phillip felt a prickling of his skin—like the hives that bumped out after eating pineapple—when they reached the grave and stood before the headstone with Jack Elliot's name and dates of birth and

32

death. The stone was graying at the edges, almost black. Phillip did the maths: Jack was probably twenty-three years old when he died.

Spencer could think of nothing cynical to say. They stood shoulder to shoulder. Phillip took his digital camera out of his coat pocket and shot a photo of the grave.

"All these years, and we never even knew he was here," Phillip said.

Spencer stood at the foot of the marble rectangle with the etched cross at the top. He wiped his eyes on the sleeve of his coat.

"Hi, Dad," he said. "Sorry we're late. We're the Jews. At least one of us may be your son. Yeah, we're surprised, too."

CHAPTER TEN

Aunt Katherine

BACK IN THE CREAMY leather seats of Phillip's Rav4 they stared out at the cemetery wall. Clouds were gathering and breaking apart in the sky above the Mattress Outlet.

"If this isn't an occasion to drink coffee and eat a Dunkin' Donut, then I don't know anything," Spencer said.

So they drove to a nearby donut shop and stared at the sky from there. Spencer pointed out that the corporate office had changed the name of the chocolate honey dipped to 'glazed chocolate cake,' which he didn't prefer.

Trees were budding in front of the small houses in the neighborhood, the pink and red and white blossoms like clusters of tiny balloons, swaying in air that felt newly arrived from somewhere to the south—the Smoky Mountains or Virginia. Phillip thought about the crab apple trees on the front and back lawns of the house they grew up in—the boys could see them out their bedroom windows, especially when they exploded with tender petals that fell to carpet the overly-green grass. He remembered employing garbage can lids as shields and having crab apple fights with the Rosenthals across the street. The girl, Susan, had an arm like a laser and once knocked Phillip down with a direct hit to the side of his head. Spencer broke the Rosenthal's kitchen window with a barrage of crab apples in retaliation.

"What now?" Spencer said as they ate their sweet, delicious gut bombs and sipped their coffee.

"Let's look for one of our new aunts or uncles," Phillip replied.

"Oh, the new ones . . . I have no idea what you're talking about. But speaking of aunts, I'm worried about Aunt Phyllis . . . I think she's like a, what do you call it . . . Like a chocoholic . . .? . . . Except with alcohol."

"Dad's obituary," Phillip continued. "His parents can't still be alive—they'd be seven hundred years old. But the brothers or sisters might be in their seventies or eighties."

They both made note, separately and without acknowledging the probable error of it to the other, that Phillip was still referring to Jack Elliot as *their* dad.

"And you're going to find one of them how?" Spencer asked.

Phillip waggled his phone. "I have a library," he said.

Phillip turned up a Katherine Elliot with an address at the Majestic Manor retirement home in Lynbrook, just down the road. He called her number as they sat in a blue vinyl booth. She didn't answer but her voicemail message sounded spry and cogent. They decided to drop in for a visit.

They climbed back into the car.

"This is awesome. It's just like Mystery Date . . . only with fathers," Spencer said. Growing up, they'd been forced to play Mystery Date with cousin Leah when they visited Aunt Phyllis and Uncle Jerry's house. Leah had added her own figures to the ones that came with the board game—magazine photos of skinny models in mini skirts, women rugby players, and Janis Joplin, glued to cardboard. It made the boys uncomfortable, although at the time they couldn't say why. Phillip usually ended up with the hunky mystery date wearing the aloha shirt, a beach umbrella held jauntily over one shoulder like a lance. Which also felt weird.

At Majestic Manor—"It's really not either," Spencer said—they enquired about Katherine Elliot at the front desk. A group of residents were emerging from a conference room off the lobby carrying the sort of Styrofoam coffee cups that made Phillip's teeth ache. The receptionist indicated an attractive old lady with a nest of red hair, wearing a pair of running shoes and a skinny belt that nearly matched her coiffure. With her white track suit she looked like the cross section of a lasagna.

"There's Katherine now," the woman said, then pointed at her own ears and whispered, "hard of hearing." Spencer couldn't tell if she meant Katherine or herself.

The boys approached, smiling, and the old woman smiled back at them, waiting gamely for what they might be bringing.

Spencer bent down toward her and said loudly, "Does the name

Jack Elliot mean anything to you?" Phillip noticed his brother was speaking with the voice he once used to communicate with neighborhood cats. Spencer inexplicably loved cats. He said they 'got' him.

"You're not Jack Elliot," the old women shouted at him, laughing.

Yep, hard of hearing, Spencer thought. And possibly demented.

"Are you his sister?" Phillip interjected.

"Who are you?" Katherine Elliot asked, as if they were maybe playing a good-natured trick on her.

"I'm Phillip. Phillip Elliot. This is my brother Spencer Elliot." He paused to see if anything registered.

"Did you know someone named Jennifer Bernstein? It would have been a long time ago," Phillip asked. "We're her sons."

She made a face—of dismissal, or annoyance, or perhaps something was stuck in her dentures. "Of course I knew Jenny. The cheerleader. She married my brother Jack."

"The cheerleader?" Spencer repeated, raising his one eyebrow.

The old woman gripped Phillip's hand. He could feel her skin like dried leaves.

"She *was* a cheerleader," Katherine Elliot continued. "You must have known that about your mother! At the other high school, over in, um . . ."

"Hewlett?" Phillip suggested.

"Yes. In Hewlett. She'd just moved there. She cheered at the football games. But it didn't suit her. She was too independent for that. She was too much of a dippy," Katherine whispered.

The boys considered this for a moment.

"You mean hippie?" Spencer asked. Although 'dippy' might also have accurately described their mother.

"Yes. She was a hippie. But before there *were* hippies. She wore all those crazy, colorful clothes." She leaned close and in a hushed voice said, "I think they got married just so they could have sex. Jack was a strict Catholic. Very straight-laced. I think it was Jenny's idea!"

"That sounds like the kind of sensible decision our mother would have made," Spencer said.

"But I don't understand," Katherine Elliot said. "Why did you boys come looking for me? Jack wasn't your father, if that's what you're getting at. He and Jenny never had any children. My poor brother went into the army practically as a child himself."

"Didn't he ever have leave, or, what, R&R," Spencer asked. "You know, like how they were always going somewhere on *M*A*S*H*?"

"That was the Korean War," Phillip said, trying to shut his brother up.

Katherine Elliot continued. "I'm sorry to tell you if you didn't know already. It was a marriage of convenience. It was never going to last. Jack was a very focused boy. Young man. He was going to serve his country. Maybe become a senator some day. But your mother bewitched him. She was so beautiful. She was wild, and he was going off to war. They got married at the courthouse. He was gone later that summer. We never saw him again, except in a couple of photos he sent home, one with a helicopter. We all received that one."

Phillip and Spencer looked down at the floor.

"Are you sure he never came home for a visit? Or maybe our mother went and met him somewhere overseas? She traveled a lot back then," Phillip said.

"He was involved in some hush-hush secret program," Katherine Elliot said. "We received letters from him at first with half the words blacked out. Then the letters stopped. But no, he never came back. We only saw Jenny a couple of times after Jack shipped out—the last time at his funeral. She'd been saying for a long time that she could *feel* he was dead. Nobody would listen to her. We wanted to believe he was alive somewhere, maybe a prisoner, maybe in a Vietnamese hospital. We told ourselves those things but your mother said she *knew*. But nobody wanted to believe her.

"Eventually they found his remains and shipped them home and we were able to have a funeral. Some of my siblings didn't believe Jack was in the box. They ignored your mother, which wasn't right. Those were difficult times, and Jack had been gone a long while, and we just didn't know how to act."

Katherine Elliot asked them to wait in the lobby while she went to her apartment for something. She disappeared long enough for the boys to wonder if she'd forgotten they were visiting.

She returned with a bible. In the back was a family tree. On one branch someone had written the names James William Elliot and Jennifer P. Bernstein. After Jack's name, they had scribbled: *(b. 1941, d. 1964(?))*.

Most of the other branches of the tree branched further and further, a veritable Catholic downpour of names that were also saints' names;

and dates of births and deaths, of prodigious clusters of children and grandchildren going back generations. Many of the people had names like Patrick and Padraig and Patricia—it was like a Garcia-Marquez novel, except with Irishmen, Spencer thought. But the branch with their mom's name hadn't flowered at all.

They thanked Katherine Elliott and left her half napping in a chair. The manor was quiet at this hour before dinner except for the slow exhalations of the HVAC system.

As they headed out toward the car Phillip thought: if Jenny had lied about their father for so many years, it must have been to protect someone.

But who?

Herself? The boys? The wall-eyed mailman?

"I guess we can cross Aunt Katherine off the Christmas card list," his brother said in the parking lot.

When they climbed into the car Phillip said, "She seemed like a credible witness."

"More credible than Mom," Spencer said. "Although Pol Pot was more credible than Mom. And Pinocchio, as another example."

"I can't think of a reason Katherine Elliot would be lying." Phillip went over the math again and reached the same conclusion. Somewhere in his mind he'd known it for a long time: Jack Elliot wasn't their father. Definitely not Spencer's, probably not his. "Maybe Katherine's not lying. But maybe she was duped too?" Phillip said hopefully.

"Duped. It rhymes with 'stupid,'" Spencer said. "Which describes us. For believing Mom's bullshit story for the past half a century."

"It doesn't really rhyme. That's a stretch," Phillip said.

"Nonetheless," Spencer said.

"Yep. Nonetheless," Phillip agreed.

CHAPTER ELEVEN

The Game Closet

THEY SAT IN THE car outside the Majestic Manor.

"Detective work involves sitting around in the car a lot," Spencer commented. Evening was closing in. The sun was already moving briskly toward Pennsylvania, leaving an orange slick in its wake.

"I'm starving," Spencer said. "As Jews, I feel we're required, when met with disappointment, to eat Chinese food. Want to see if the Chang's is still in the old neighborhood?"

"You know you can't say that anymore?"

"What?"

"The Chang's. It's derogatory."

"It isn't. That was the name of the restaurant. But anyway, isn't it grandfathered in?" Spencer asked. "Because it was okay to say it when we were kids?"

"It wasn't," Phillip said.

"I'm just a product of my time," Spencer relented.

"Are you?" Phillip pulled out of the parking lot, swerved the wheel to avoid a squirrel crossing the street, changing its mind, crossing again, changing its mind again.

"Am I what?"

"A product of your time?"

"As opposed to . . . ?"

"A product of your genes?" Phillip asked.

Spencer sat up higher in the passenger seat. "Is this the part where we talk about nature versus nurture and try to figure out if we're such sensitive fellas because we inherited that from a wise old Irishman, or because one of us had a pee pee accident in nursery school and all the other kids laughed at us and we've never been the same since?"

"Don't patronize," Phillip said. "I'm trying to understand all of this."

"Why does it have to be such a strict dichotomy, anyway? Scientists are still working on the DNA question right now in their unfashionable white lab coats. Or in our case, the DadNA question. What makes you think you need to solve all the age-old mysteries just because you spit in a tube and someone suggested your ancestors got the fuck out of County Dodge during the potato famine?"

"That's a good question," was all Phillip could say.

"And what about the ever-underrated concept of vagaries. Randomness. Entropy. Kismet. That some things *can't* be explained rationally. They just happen. Like my extreme handsomeness. That Pierce Brosnan got to play James Bond."

"I was always a Sean Connery fan. So I see what you mean," Phillip said. He continued driving toward the old neighborhood, where the House of Chang had once sat on the opposite edge of the Green Acres Mall from the Steak Pub.

"Let's swing by the old house first," Spencer suggested as they passed the duck pond on Mill Road. "I haven't been there in years. Maybe we can throw some crab apples at the Rosenthals."

Phillip noted this additional example of his and Spencer's thoughts landing on the same frequency—he'd just been thinking about the Rosenthals and the crab apples—though whether this was due to DNA or having grown up in the same house, or was a conspiracy of coincidence, he couldn't say.

He drove them along the once-familiar roads. Lights were coming on in some of the houses and they could smell grilling meat and freshly-cut grass on the breeze. The Five Towns had been a fine place to grow up, although the boys had both lit out for Manhattan at the earliest opportunity—Spencer finding his first basement apartment on East 6th Street in Little India, which he shared with a few fellow band members out of high school, Phillip renting a condo on Third Avenue and 83rd after graduating from Vassar. Many years later he bought the building. He was sentimental that way.

Both the boys had proved successful, despite early indications that Spencer might be headed for trouble. He got kicked out of Hofstra and NYU film school but earned a degree from a SUNY school way upstate. He made a fortune betting on dot.com stocks and getting out before they became, as he called them, 'splat.com' stocks. He stashed the gains in bonds and index funds knowing he could live off the distributions until he was one hundred fifty.

Phillip got rich in real estate. While a sophomore he borrowed six thousand dollars from Jenny as down payment on a rental house on Raymond Avenue, across from the Vassar campus. He collected rent from four roommates and parlayed the house into a collection of student houses, then exchanged those into small plexes and apartment buildings that became the foundation for the small REIT he built, which attracted capital from friends and family, and which he grew into a multi-million dollar venture over twenty-five years.

Both brothers attributed their financial successes to 'The Game Closet'—the monumental collection of board games, puzzles, books of lateral thinking challenges, and other pastimes stacked on rough, unpainted shelves behind four hollow-core wooden bi-fold doors in the basement of the house on Long Island.

Playing Monopoly, Spencer might orchestrate the trade of a railroad and a utility for a downtrodden property like St. James Place because he'd already made a side deal to acquire Tennessee and New York Avenues. Then he'd invest the money stashed in his tube sock to build hotels on all three. A board game at the Elliot house could take days given the complexities of deal making and shifting alliances. Many neighborhood kids were scared off by the ferocity.

When the boys had learned the intricacies of the games Spencer would suggest swapping playing pieces or spinners or dice from one game and figuring a way to enlist them in an entirely different game. The hotels from Monopoly became impenetrable borders between countries on the Risk board. The tiny pink and blue children that rode in the backs of the cars in The Game of Life were deployed as military hostages in Stratego. Spencer invented a version of Sorry that they referred to as Not Sorry! in which certain dice throws allowed one player to punch another hard in the arm. Spencer was the creative genius behind these innovations; his enthusiasms overcame Phillip's conviction that the games should be played by the rules.

They motored down their old street: Harbor Stream Road—although there was no harbor and no stream. After all these years the tiny maples that had been planted when the houses were first built in 1960 now converged far overhead to create a shaded lane. Spencer wondered how kids could play Hit the Bat under the encroaching canopy.

When they were nearly at their old house Phillip slowed the car.

In front of Richard Linkletter's house—next door to the house the boys grew up in—a middle-aged woman was mowing the lawn.

"Holy shit, I swear to God that's Barbara Linkletter. Richard's homely daughter. Look at her, I think she still has her braces on!"

Phillip slowed the car to get a closer view.

"Don't stop! Keep driving," Spencer said. "Don't let her see us! She's going to want your help with her math homework! She'll make us eat brownies from her Easy Bake Oven that taste like bark. Maybe she finally figured out by now that Mom was sleeping with her father!"

"Do you still have the Polaroid?" Phillip asked.

Spencer smiled. "Brilliant, wasn't that?"

"In a way."

"It never came out," Spencer admitted.

"Whaaat? The photo?"

"I forgot to use the flash. But Richard and Mom never knew that. It was misdirection, just like Mom taught us. It was her super power. Everyone gets one."

Phillip mulled this. "What's your super power?"

"I remember even the minutest details from every book I've read and every movie I've seen. It's useless yet impressive. I'm like the Mr. Wizard of trivia. What about you?"

"I can make the phone ring by peeing," Phillip said.

"How is that helpful?"

"I haven't figured out how to apply it yet. But every time I start peeing at home, the phone rings in the other room. Ninety percent of the time."

"Don't take it too hard. Every super hero has a fatal flaw. I learned that in Mrs. Huttner's Shakespeare class. Just before she threw me out."

"Do you really think that's Barbara Linkletter?"

"Look at her," Spencer said. "But don't stop. She'll want to talk. She might try to kill me."

"Okay, okay," Phillip said. He sped up past the Linkletter's house, past their own house, which had been painted brown recently and didn't look like their house at all. It seemed bigger, not smaller, as they would have expected.

They realized simultaneously that the crab apple trees were gone, giving the house a stark, exposed feel. But the Japanese maple their mom had planted was thriving in the side yard. Its leaves were the faded red of an old barn.

Phillip continued down the block toward the Orthodox temple.

"Jeezly Crow, don't people move away from here?" Spencer said. "The Sawyers' name is still on their mailbox. I think I just saw Alan Goldstein delivering newspapers on that stupid three-wheeled bike with the wagon attached. The neighborhood is like one of those museums with sod houses and a blacksmith shop, where the women are filthy and churning butter and sewing clothes that still have animal heads attached."

Phillip pressed the gas pedal and they headed toward where the street widened, where the kids who'd gone to rival Lawrence High School lived.

"Did you ever think that maybe Richard Linkletter *was* our father?" Phillip asked. He drove past North Woodmere Park, sped up past the Sephardic Temple toward Peninsula Boulevard.

"No, but maybe Art Linkletter was our father."

"Who's Art Linkletter?"

"He hosted a TV show. 'Kids Say the Fucking Stupidest Things,' I think it was called."

"What if Richard's affair with Mom started much earlier than we thought?" Phillip said.

"That would make Barbara our sister. It's too sad to comprehend," Spencer said. He played with the car radio, looking for WNEW, the old rock station, as if he'd hear DJ Scott Muni's voice from 1975 introducing an Emerson, Lake, and Palmer song.

"It really *would* be too sad," Spencer continued. "That we lived next door to our father all those years without knowing it? That we were so mean to him? Not even Mom could have orchestrated something so devious. What would the point have been? Why the whole story about Jack Elliot if the mentally deficient neighbor was responsible for us? I'm sorry, I don't know why I'm so choked up."

Phillip turned to see that his brother was crying for the second time that day. Something he hadn't otherwise witnessed since the New York Islanders failed to win their fifth consecutive Stanley Cup in 1984.

"I'm *considering* entertaining the idea that we had two different fathers," Spencer said. "Neither of whom was the father we both thought we had. Which also makes me sad. Yours was an Irish golf pro. Mine was most likely a Spanish prince. A dark-skinned but hysterically funny gentleman who kept the palace in stitches. We're mongrels. I accept that. Maybe we're not even related. Maybe we had three fathers. Maybe Aunt Phyllis is your father. Maybe we were sired by hedgehogs."

Chapter Twelve

Marty

As SPENCER PUT IT a few days later, the father trail was "rightly bolloxed."

But Phillip was not one to give up easily. He packed an overnight bag and headed back to the cottage. He would pursue the mother trail to see if it might lead him back to the father trail. Plus there was still plenty he didn't know about *Jenny* too.

On his way to Westchester he stopped at H&H Bagels—the new one on Columbus Avenue that lacked the precious smell of decades of dough—to pick up breakfast, at least partly because as he drove past he spotted an open parking space and as a New Yorker he didn't want anyone else to have it.

He stood in line behind a typical variety of Upper West Side denizens—a couple of hipsters with their Trilby hats and plaid shirts, probably having breakfast after a long night out before taking the train back to Brooklyn; a young Indian mother wearing a sari and pushing a double stroller; and his own ex-wife, Marty, who still lived a few blocks north of him, at 96th Street over by Riverside Park.

Marty was standing at the marble counter talking to the clerk. Her arms flew around her like Joe Cocker dancing. Phillip knew her by the cascade of brown curls spilling out of a knit Peruvian cap that Jenny had given her many years ago. His heart skipped like a favorite, over-played record album: *Frampton Comes Alive*, or *Highway 61 Revisited*. One you've listened to so many times that you anticipate the skip, but continue playing the album because you love it, and it brings back a specific time and place in your life.

As much as his heart flexed at seeing Marty, he hoped she wasn't going to order a blueberry bagel; early in their relationship they'd discussed the implications of eating any bagel other than the accepted flavors of plain, salt, poppy, sesame, garlic, onion, and everything.

The everything bagel was the only acceptable recent innovation, since it combined already accepted flavors. Ordering blueberry—or even cinnamon raisin—marked you as a tourist who was probably visiting New York from Iowa. Which was where Marty had grown up. But she'd been in Manhattan long enough to know better.

Now, the common dilemma of whether to reach out first and catch your former lover off guard, thus establishing an advantage, or to lay back, staring intently at your phone in the hope that either the other person wouldn't notice you, or that they'd take the opportunity to walk past and ignore you, thinking you hadn't seen them first. It was exactly the kind of thing that led to the demise of their marriage: Phillip finding it easier to walk past Marty, rather than engaging her directly. She was a spontaneous free spirit, like his mother. Phillip wasn't able to let go of his rigidity—wherever that came from. Was it due to being fatherless? He considered that a lame excuse that didn't make it any easier for him to loosen up.

"Let's go somewhere we've never been before," Marty might have said on a sunny weekend morning, salt on the fresh breeze a reminder that Manhattan was close to the sea. "How about Staten Island? Or Coney Island? Or The Cloisters."

"We'd have to figure out the ferry schedule. Coney Island will be mobbed. And I was at The Cloisters last year," Phillip would respond.

"Something in Brooklyn then."

"Do you feel like sitting on a hot subway car?"

"We'll rent bikes."

"My back is killing me."

They'd end up at a movie that Marty loved and Phillip felt lukewarm about, in addition to feeling guilty over not being more open to Marty's playfulness.

They married when Phillip was thirty and Marty was twenty-eight and divorced ten years later. Neither of them loved children: that was never their issue, though it split many of their friends from those days—either too many or not enough kids. They always had fun—Marty could pull him out of himself, out of the deep funks he was prone to once or twice a year. She was a rope ladder unfurled from the deck railing of a burning building, but seeing it Phillip always ran back into the flames. She encouraged his rare spontaneity though it was like pulling splinters with a tweezers. They ultimately agreed that she couldn't help him until he was more committed to being rescued. He was like his brother in this way, too.

She wanted a partnership, full and unencumbered by stacks of unresolved familial baggage—she was honest to an unfathomable depth, without guile. She didn't understand subterfuge. She expected the same from Phillip and couldn't comprehend why his own background made this so difficult. She didn't get that Phillip couldn't know and love her fully because he didn't yet feel he fully knew and loved himself. She knew that growing up without a father had made intimacy difficult for Phillip, but she told him that at some stage he needed to move along. To her point, he found himself not trying very hard to be straightforward, or to share his inner life: it was easier being alone with his feelings than to allow someone to see the funhouse mirror version of yourself that might lie beneath your façade.

She'd told him, "You're really only half here—half a husband," which resonated newly now that he was also only half a brother.

They ended the marriage like adults. It was Phillip's idea to split. He couldn't live with the constant disappointment of not being the kind of partner he knew she deserved.

Marty moved out over a weekend when Phillip was in Boston for a bachelor's party, proving that cycles continued. Even as her possessions disappeared slowly over the next weeks—first her clothes, then the dining table and chairs that had belonged to her grandparents, then half the extra batteries, half the toilet paper—Phillip didn't believe they were necessarily through. A single lawyer drew up paperwork that they signed before going to dinner together at a favorite West Side bistro. Marty suggested they speak in three months: daily contact would be too painful as she tried to launch a new life. A year later she had a boyfriend and their contacts lessened, like childhood pals who've ended up on opposite coasts—though Marty was still only half a mile away, and Phillip never ceased taking comfort in this.

Marty spotted him and stopped as she was carrying her dozen bagels and containers of shmears toward the door. She still didn't know the protocol of avoiding former spouses even after having lived in Manhattan for more than twenty-five years. She was too nice. Plus, Phillip knew, she still loved him.

She was wearing yoga pants discreetly camouflaged by a long, gray V-necked sweatshirt with NYU Law printed in purple on the front. She carried enough food for a small breakfast party packed neatly into two woven bags. Imagining her preparing brunch in the kitchen at 96th Street for friends—or maybe a new lover—was like a serrated bread knife dragged across Phillip's heart.

"Phillip!" she more or less shouted. He feigned surprise, as required by local statute.

"Marty!" he said. "No way."

"I still live up the street," Marty said. "Don't pretend I hightailed it back to Cedar Rapids."

Cedar Rapids had been a code word between them, a dimension removed in time and space from New York consciousness. Marty had remained Cedar Rapids even while embracing the Upper West Side. That was her super power. She was lovely, kind, well read, a creative marathoner in bed, and knew everything about popular culture—a long-tressed, blue-eyed Shiksa goddess who used to look at him over the tops of her rectangular horn-rimmed reading glasses in a way that turned his legs to gummy bears. She worked as a publicist for a media company and got free tickets to all the shows and concerts people were talking about. Phillip couldn't justify a single reason they'd gotten divorced.

"What are you up to, anyway? I haven't run into you in months," Marty said.

Phillip grimaced. "My mother just passed away."

"Oh, no," she said. Jenny had loved Marty, who'd learned all the right Yiddish and Hebrew words to utter at Passover and Rosh Hashanah, charmingly mispronouncing them.

Jenny never cared that Marty wasn't Jewish, and the women forged a bond that excluded Phillip. He'd walk into his and Marty's bedroom and find them sitting close together, cross-legged on the bed. When he entered they'd grow quiet, then giggly, as if conspiring at their lockers together after homeroom. Marty was entirely transparent in her relationships, but Jenny's opacity would prevent the women from progressing deeper, Phillip knew: what they most had in common was him—their fierce, protective love.

"I'm so sorry, Phillip," Marty said, taking his hand despite being overloaded with bagels and cream cheese. She started tearing up a little, making Phillip tear up, too. What was with all the sudden crying?

"I'm looking for my father now," Phillip said without intending to.

"Your father?" The first time Marty had seen the iconic photo at Jenny's house she'd asked who the dreamy fly-boy was.

"My real father," Phillip continued. "As it turns out, he might not have been who we thought he was." It was all Phillip could muster by way of explanation.

"Oh, Philly," Marty said, and he wanted to surrender to her, to rest his head in the crook of her arms and eat seven layer salad and love her the way he imagined a farmer might—gruffly but deeply, ready to defend her to the death or complain about his coffee being cold. He wanted to hear her exaggerated "owwwie" as his fingers caught in the soft curls of her hair.

Marty shifted her weight from one leg to the other. Phillip could see her quadriceps clearly, one releasing, one tightening beneath the tight gray fabric of her yoga pants.

"Can I help you with anything? Will you call me if I can help you with anything?" she asked.

"I will," Phillip lied.

"You won't," she said. "But I'll call and ask again. Maybe you'll relent some day. Maybe things will be different for you with your mother gone."

When she hugged him Phillip smelled blueberries.

Chapter Thirteen

The Dwarf

PHILLIP LEFT THE BAGEL place for Jenny's cottage and cut through the park as the temperature climbed and the roadway became crowded with runners, bikers, skateboarders, the odd roller-blader who thought it was still 1981. When he arrived in Larchmont forty minutes later it felt like another land entirely. Phillip's eyes watered from the histamines.

The realtor whom Aunt Phyllis had recommended to sell their mother's house—Spencer referred to her as "The Raccoon" because she clearly went to a tanning booth but wore over-sized goggles during her sessions—had hung a tidy 'For Sale' sign out front. But Phillip had ignored her recent calls about prospective buyers. Her last message said she wouldn't show the house again until she heard from him, which suited Phillip perfectly.

It hadn't been very long since their mother passed, and Phillip was in no hurry to let go of the house. He thought of it as an archaeological site; given his mother's propensity for secrecy, he would be equally un-surprised to find a secret wall safe stuffed with Krugerands or Sasquatch living with D.B. Cooper in Amelia Earhart's airplane in the yard.

Phillip had started reading about DNA recently—Spencer recommended a couple of books—and he'd learned that when scientists were trying to figure out what DNA actually *looked* like, its physical shape and attributes, one researcher came upon the idea of bombarding the location they suspected where DNA lived with X-rays, and photographing the shadows cast by the light. Phillip hoped to accomplish a similarly indirect but comparable discovery by exposing his mother's belongings to a metaphorically powerful light. It occurred to him that he and Spencer were a double helix.

Jenny had taught the boys from an early age to think laterally, to look beyond surfaces to see what might lie underneath. Subtext, she called it. Something you could find in great books. Which they assumed she'd read all of. She trained them as investigators, whether to solve the secrets of books or puzzles or treasure hunts.

Phillip recalled how he and his brother would sit quietly at dinner in the house on Long Island, lost in daydreams. Phillip might have been pondering a math problem or thinking about his essay on John Fowles's *A Separate Peace*. He imagined his brother fantasizing about girls, motorcycles, how to run a profitable Las Vegas night in the garage the next time Jenny was away.

"A man who lives on the 10th floor of an apartment building gets on the elevator every morning to go to work," their mother might say. She'd stop talking until they looked up from their meatloaf, put down their Dixie cups full of Coke.

When she had their attention she nodded. "When he comes home, if he's alone in the elevator, he goes to the 6th floor and takes the stairs the rest of the way to his apartment. But on rainy days he goes directly to his floor."

She cleared their dishes. She turned on the water at the sink. Her apron, untied at the back, swished as she moved.

"That's it?" Spencer said. He shook his head dismissively, to indicate he wouldn't participate in such silliness. Phillip squinted into the distance to show he was thinking.

"Was it a fitness thing?" Spencer asked anyway. "He was trying to get back in shape?"

Now their mom shook her head.

"There was someone he didn't want to see on one of those other floors," Spencer said. "His ex-girlfriend. He was scared she was going to kill him. He owed money to a bookie. To a mob boss. There was a monster. The man knew that the Captain and Tennille were practicing on the seventh floor."

Jenny ignored him. Which Spencer always took as encouragement.

"Aliens," he said. "Spies. There's a bomb. The builders forgot to construct three floors. There was an earthquake. Wait—I've got it: it was raining, and his shoes were wet, and he didn't want to leave puddles on the stairs because he was afraid old Mrs. McGillicutty would come out of her apartment looking for her blind cat and slip on the wet stairs and break her stupid neck."

It went on like this for an hour. Spencer followed their Mom around the house as she picked clothes up off the floor, went through the mail. He peppered her with theories as she worked the crossword puzzle on the couch.

Phillip came into the living room from where he'd still been sitting at the kitchen table.

"He's a dwarf," Phillip said. "He can't reach the button for his floor."

Spencer made a face. "That's stupid. What about the rainy days, Einstein?"

Jenny waved for Phillip to come over to where she sat on the couch. "My little genius," she said, kissing the top of his head.

"What about a kiss for the developmentally disabled brother?" Spencer asked, and Jenny waved for him to come over to her, too. She put her arms around both boys.

"Umbrella," Phillip mouthed to Spencer so Jenny wouldn't see.

"Oh!" Spencer shouted. "And the dwarf carried an umbrella!"

"That's it!" Phillip said "On rainy days he used the umbrella to push the button for the tenth floor!" Phillip still couldn't tell whether his brother got the solution.

Jenny also reveled in creating treasure hunts for them on birthdays and holidays. She couldn't just give the boys a wrapped box—they had to put in some sleuthing, which made every gift more precious. This search for their father was no different, and it paid to have a strategy.

For Phillip's high school graduation the treasure hunt began with a square black envelope on the kitchen table. Inside, the card read: 'The hunt for your gift should go swimmingly.' Phillip jumped in the Buick with Spencer and drove to the high school, where he found another envelope taped to the door to the pool, where Phillip often worked out during his senior year.

In that envelope was a postcard with an image of the famous Edvard Munch painting, *Scream*. Which sent Phillip off to the Carvel shop where he and his friends went for cones and milkshakes on hot summer afternoons. I Scream = Ice Cream, he deduced. At Carvel he found a graduation cake in the freezer with his name written in chocolate icing, and a tiny chocolate-script note that read: "You'll be on the right track if this clue suits you." He also took the cake—which made him wonder if that was her intended message—'Phillip, you take the cake!' He drove home and opened the hall closet, where one of Jenny's track suits hung.

It went on like that for a couple of hours, Phillip and Spencer driving around town in the Electra chasing down solutions. The final note read: 'It will be easy for you to tackle this last clue. Just don't get boxed out.'

He thought these were sports references, and raced back to the house to look in the garage, where a set of football shoulders pads ("tackle") and a leather basketball (the 'boxing out' reference), and other gear were organized on shelves. It took awhile to realize she meant the fishing tackle box hidden under a loose floorboard in her bedroom, where she once showed him one thousand dollars in cash to be used for emergencies.

When he pulled up the tackle box Phillip found several fishing lures. One had a length of clear fishing line attached. He followed the line into another closet where a pair of Vassar sweatpants hung. He stared at them. He was already going to Vassar in the fall. A pair of sweatpants?

"Put them on," Jenny said.

He felt something against his leg in the pocket. A set of keys.

He sprinted to the garage.

Since he'd been there ten minutes ago, someone had pulled a beat-up Honda Accord into the spot where his mother usually parked the Electra.

He looked at his mom. Her face was scrunched up to hide her emotions over her eldest heading off to college.

"I'm sorry," she said, dabbing at the tears. "I just wish Spencer was moving out too."

"Don't cry, Mom," Spencer said, putting his arm around her as Phillip hopped in the car. "He'll give you the parking space back."

Chapter Fourteen

Colin

Phillip spent the first hours at Jenny's cottage in a room-by-room investigation, focusing on the largest items in the house. He moved the furniture, feeling underneath the sofa and the big cushioned loungers and the dining room table and chairs for concealed envelopes. He rolled up the rugs and took every photo and painting down from the walls. The cottage was filled with artwork and crafts—thick, tightly-knotted, colorful Turkish carpets Jenny had picked up in Istanbul, Oaxacan tapestries, an early twentieth-century painting of apple orchards she'd bought on a FAM trip in the south of France; mid-century black and white photos of lower Manhattan taken by a moderately well-known photographer that he and Spencer long suspected had been her lover.

In the kitchen Phillip opened boxes of granola and squeezed bags of gourmet pastas and considered cans of salmon packed in Spanish olive oil arranged in perfect rows on the carefully paper-lined shelves. He looked in the freezer, expecting what? He had no idea. But he was compelled to thoroughness.

While searching Jenny's bedroom he remembered how his mother had secreted another one thousand dollars in cash—in addition to the thousand dollars in the tackle box—in a drawer with a false back when they were kids.

He pushed on the wooden slat at the back of the drawer of her night table. It gave way as suspected, revealing: a packet of condoms, a tube of lubricant and a vibrator as large as a turkey leg.

Sheesh. Should he put this all back or carry it to the trash? He opted to put it back; he didn't want to disturb his mother's belongings even while reminding himself that she wouldn't be coming home again. But still: Yikes!

Phillip checked behind books on the bookshelves—and he checked the books to see whether any had been hollowed of interior pages and converted to jewelry boxes or cash repositories. He felt for packets taped underneath the desk. He pulled at the edges of the wall-to-wall carpets to make sure they were fully tacked down. He poked bags of mushroom compost and opened boxes in the garage labeled 'dishes' hoping they contained pirate treasure or old photo albums.

He took a break and poured a rare afternoon drink. Jenny's bar was stocked with top-shelf liquor, but Phillip usually passed on the rare añejo tequilas or the twenty-one-year-old peaty single malts in minor rebellion when his mom offered them. He was wary of her generosity, which might be meant to distract from something more essential.

He sat on a high-backed carved wooden bar stool at the kitchen pass-through and sipped Jameson Black Cask from a cut glass Waterford tumbler.

He and Spencer still had much work ahead of them sorting and dividing their mom's belongings despite their previous visit—another reason Phillip was glad not to be selling the house just yet; selling would force them to disassemble the personal artwork of their mother's life. Ending the excavations. Like removing an Anasazi pot out of some remote Utah canyon, destroying its context and a deeper understanding of the people and circumstances that put it there. Without a father, and with his mother now gone, Phillip clung to the historical references that her archive presented. All while allowing his brother to think the house was for sale—a tiny misdirection.

Phillip considered two cardboard file boxes filled with phone bills. Spencer and Phyllis had wanted to toss it all in the recycle bin on their previous visit but Phillip wouldn't allow it. He wanted a closer look. He hadn't known that you could still *get* an itemized phone bill, which was just like his mother to do.

He started with the bills from the end of Jenny's life and worked backward. He recognized his own and his brother's and Aunt Phyllis's numbers on the pages. Their mom had also made hundreds of domestic long distance calls to a wide variety of area codes, some Phillip didn't recognize, and many international calls, some that went on for as long as an hour or more. Jenny had made friends—perhaps boyfriends—in dozens of countries over a long period working as a travel agent. Phillip pictured her sitting at the kitchen bar with a chilled glass of white Cotes du Rhone, the phone pressed to her ear.

Phillip noted the prevalence of calls with the United Kingdom's 44 prefix. Wasn't Ireland part of the UK? Or was that just Northern Ireland? It was very confusing. Could he dial one of these numbers and find his father on the other end of the phone? One UK number repeated often. He scribbled this sequence on lined notebook paper inside a folder labeled: CONTACTS. This and several other international numbers reappeared often, while she'd called others only once or twice.

Phillip pulled a set of colored highlighter pens out of his saddlebag briefcase. He determined the most efficient way to organize the phone information was to give each country its own color (possibly relating to their flags, he thought at first? No—too many countries used only red, white and blue). As he went through the bills, he decided on blue for Britain, green for Germany. But his alphabetical plan soon gave way to randomness (hence orange for France, which he realized would have been a more appropriate color for either Holland—their national football team wore orange—or for Spain, where they actually grew oranges). But the system allowed Phillip to see which calls repeated most often.

While he sipped his drink Phillip thought: what the fuck. He dialed the first number on his list—with the 44 country code. He pictured a doughty English travel agent or a fat pub owner or an officious airline reservations representative in London or Dublin picking up the line. Or his father, if he was honest with himself.

He listened to the beeps and clicks as if he could hear the electricity of the call squeezing through cables on the sandy floor of the Atlantic Ocean, traveling through geography and time, past sunken shipwrecks and giant octopi. The ring tone was unfamiliar; he wasn't positive it *was* ringing. Maybe he was calling a fax machine.

After six long, flat, off-key tones, someone picked up.

The voice was gruff. "Yavriched thad unbearing en kerr igskellig," it said. Phillip pictured a hairy fat man in a wife-beater stained with Earl Gray, a week's beard sprouting beneath bloodshot eyes.

The words were a long growl. Phillip couldn't identify a single phrase from any known language.

"Do you speak English?" he asked, enunciating extra slowly.

The voice came back on the line, matching his exaggerated cadence.

"I said . . . 'You . . . have . . . reached . . . the Dunbarton Inn . . . in Kerrigskellig, Scotland,' ya stoopid American twat. It's fooking half eleven, ya punter, and the desk is open until tain. So ya woke me and the old lady and the baby. Call me again I'll give ya a skelp on the lug."

———————

In the morning Phillip looked at the phone bills afresh over his first cup of coffee. He was embarrassed to have called Scotland so late the previous evening without considering the time difference: a rookie mistake. He picked another country code unfamiliar to him and dialed.

He reached a recording in German; was it someone's answering machine or a recorded message informing him that his call couldn't be completed?

The next call reached a man who said, "Posada de Roja, Juan Carlos, Claro."

"Do you speak English?" Phillip asked. He was shouting into the phone.

"Yes, Señor. This is the Posada de Roja. How can I help you?"

"What's a posada?" Phillip asked.

"It is a significant historical building—in this case a former convent from the twelfth century—that has been converted into a hostelry. A hostelry, Señor, is another word for hotel."

Phillip refrained from mentioning that he knew what a hostelry was. He said, "Is there any way you can check to see whether my mother stayed at your hostelry? She was a travel agent. She passed away recently. On her last trip to Spain she stayed at a hotel that she wished to send all her surviving children to for a holiday in her memory. There are seven of us," Phillip lied. "We're calling numbers from her phone bill to see if we can find the right place."

Juan Carlos said, "I am sorry, Señor, but we are not entitled to share the names of our guests—we have many who are extremely protective of their privacy." His accent was as sonorous as flamenco guitar.

"But I can see from the number you are calling from that someone whom I cannot name often called us from that same number and stayed with us many times over the years. Let me say that I personally am very sorry for the loss of your mother. She was greatly revered here. Please, we would very much like for you and your many siblings to come stay with us here in Sevilla. I could then share some further information of a more personal nature. Please, call any time and ask for Juan Carlos. I will take very good care of you."

Next Phillip tried a phone prefix he'd never heard of before: 353. Were there prefixes of more than two digits, he wondered? Of course there were: since there were more than ninety-nine countries they'd need more than two-digit numbers.

The call rang four times before someone picked up and said, "Hallo, golf shop, Colin speaking."

"I'm sorry, who am I speaking with?" Phillip asked.

"This is Colin? In the golf shop?"

"Where are you speaking to me from, Colin?"

"In the golf shop?"

"And where is the golf shop?"

"Ballydraiocht Golf Club," Colin said. "County Kerry. Ireland. The world."

Chapter Fifteen

Goats

PHILLIP HUNG UP THE phone like it was on fire. His heart was hammering.

Jenny's phone bills indicated she'd been making calls to the Ballydraiocht Golf Club over the past year. He let this new clue settle out, like the cloudy, freshly poured Guinness he imagined being sipped by an ancient golf pro at the clubhouse bar. Whom he'd been too flustered to ask Colin about.

The best way to avoid thinking too deeply on this—and risking falling for something—was to continue with his strategy. He'd think about it later, when he was calmer. He reminded himself that even if there *was* a Ballydraiocht Golf Club, and Jenny had been calling there, that didn't mean her last utterance wasn't mixed up in the blender of her dementia. But at least this *was* a clue—which affirmed there *were* clues at all. Phillip returned the phone bills to a clean, crisp folder and moved it to the dining room table.

He spread Jenny's large manila envelopes of travel receipts on the white quartz countertop of the breakfast bar. Each envelope was labeled with the year in Jenny's flowy cursive, beneath which she'd written the destinations of each trip she'd taken that year. Inside were smaller letter-sized envelopes containing receipts and papers from each trip.

Phillip started again with the most recent envelopes and worked his way backward.

Jenny had retired and sold her travel agency to her employees in 2013, when she'd turned seventy, although she continued to travel, using her many contacts for cheap flights and sometimes free overnights at the kinds of small hotels she had specialized in. Many of these hotels had been under the same ownership for decades. They considered her a treasured resource.

The year before her death she took two trips—to Phoenix and New Orleans, each for one week. As she grew older she replaced her international destinations with domestic locations, filling gaps in her travel resume as if adding birds to a life list.

Phillip rifled through the receipts from the Phoenix trip and found: airfare vouchers, bills from the Scottsdale Princess and the Boulders Resort that included in-room movies and a veritable onslaught of the mini bars. Was this a sign of change? For most of her life Jenny drank in public places, where she could interact with people, many of whom turned out to be men.

He found a receipt for the rental of an electric car, a brochure from Taliesin West, and a dinner check and postcard from a biker bar in Cave Creek. He discovered an invoice from an Urgent Care office in Carefree. Under the heading for 'complaint' someone had scrawled: 'disorientation.'

The year before Phoenix Jenny visited Portland, Seattle, and Vancouver, British Columbia. Phillip remembered this trip because he later recognized the early signs of his mom's decline. She'd called him from the Canadian border station along Interstate 5 because she needed him to fax a copy of her passport. She'd confused Vancouver, British Columbia with the small city of the same name just outside Portland, Oregon. Her friends had traveled on ahead; although she reunited with them at their hotel overlooking Stanley Park that evening, Phillip felt she never fully caught back up.

In other envelopes Jenny had saved cash register receipts from museums and gift shops, postcards from restaurants, business cards from people she met along the way: some were self-explanatory, like one for a tour guide from Morocco in a Morocco envelope. Others were more curious—a wine-stained card for a psychoanalyst with a Munich address in the envelope for a trip to the Loire Valley; a thick paper square that said only 'actor'—no name—and sported a phone number with an LA prefix printed in American Typewriter font, this one in the envelope for a jaunt she'd taken to Dubrovnik not long after the Balkan wars concluded.

When the boys were kids, upon returning from a trip she would giddily describe to them some of what she'd experienced. "We stayed in the most beautiful little hacienda on a coffee plantation," or "we dove the famous Blue Hole," she'd say.

"Who's 'we,'" Spencer asked one time to show that he was on to her.

"Oh, a colleague," Jenny said.

Phillip recalled a trip when he and Spencer were in high school. Jenny had gone off to accompany a tour group to Egypt and Israel.

She'd been reading for months about the great religions as background for the trip. The morning before she left, Spencer asked at the breakfast table, "Did you study about Zoroastrianism? How about Rastafarianism? Have you considered Nuwabianism?"

Spencer, a freshman, was struggling to capture their mother's attention, to belong at the center of something—which the boys could always accomplish by knowing more about a subject than she did.

Jenny looked up at her younger son over the toaster waffles and glasses of orange juice.

"I had no idea you were so interested in religion," she'd said. "Are you thinking of becoming a clergyman? Would you like to discuss the finer points of Martin Luther's *Ninety-Five Theses*? Should we should sign you up for Hebrew high school?"

Spencer poured syrup on his waffles until they were floating in a sugary bog. Jenny hated when the boys wasted food.

"I prefer Luther's *On the Jews and Their Lies*," Spencer said. "But I'm more drawn toward the obscure eastern sects. I'm interested in the Russian Orthodox," he added, to goad her further. "It's a form of strict Christianity."

"I know what it is," Jenny had said. "But for that you'll have to wait until you can grow some facial hair." Which ended their discussion of the world's great religions and reminded Spencer that their mom wasn't easily trifled with.

Jenny's early trips that snapped most clearly to mind for Phillip were memorable for what happened at home in her absence. The boys enjoyed blocks of time without adult supervision, although Aunt Phyllis and Uncle Jerry were charged with dropping by to make sure they hadn't established a tavern in the garage or listed the house with a realtor.

Their one responsibility while she was gone on the trip to the Middle East was to clean up their yard, which was overgrown with weeds and blackberries. Jenny set the gardening tools outside the garage—rakes and clippers, shovels, refuse bins—so there could be no confusion about the assignment and how to accomplish it.

Spencer—already a master at avoiding labor—had read that in other countries people used goats to clear unwanted overgrowth. He found a company in Suffolk County that would drop off a small herd of goats and pick them up a week or two later, depending on the size of the job. It wasn't expensive, and anyway, Spencer had recently learned from his brother about the secret pile of cash in the back of their mom's bedside drawer. Jenny loved animals; feeding some hungry goats would appeal to her.

The goats—just four of them—arrived in the bed of a battered pickup reinforced with plywood sides. Spencer had the driver back up along the side of the house so as not to alert any neighbors, but the animals still made enough of a racket that Richard Linkletter called that afternoon. Spencer answered the phone.

"So, now you're a goat herder?" Richard asked.

"I don't know what you're talking about, Richard," Spencer said. "But I'll get out my Polaroid in case I see any goats. It never hurts to have direct evidence. If you know what I mean . . ."

Richard could have peered over the wooden fence separating their yards to see the animals munching like teenagers at a dessert buffet, but he was more averse to getting involved with Spencer than to having the animals next door.

Spencer tethered the goats to a tree on a rope that he measured carefully so that the animals would be able to reach the blackberry bushes but not the roses. By the third day, having devoured everything they could access, the goats ate the rope while the boys were at school. They chomped Jenny's beds of columbine and purple coneflowers, asters, black-eyed Susans, the potted sedges and blue oat grass. They were about to start on the holly trees and maples when Spencer came home and corralled them again.

The goats had cleared the yard of debris, grass, leaves, stems, stalks, flowers, and everything else Jenny had tended, replacing them with clusters of what Spencer referred to as "goat Milk Duds." They ate the rattan off the lawn furniture and chewed the wooden slats on the table next to the barbecue.

"Fuck a duck—or in this case a goat—those ungulate mofos can eat!" Spencer exclaimed. He called the rental company to come pick up the hungry troublemakers. He tied them to the pole for the basketball hoop in the driveway to prevent any further consumption and to protect the cedar siding on the house.

Aunt Phyllis pulled up in her red mustang convertible right about then. She got out and stood on the concrete with her arms folded, staring down the goats, who were unimpressed. She walked to the top of the driveway and peered over the fence into the back yard.

When she came into the house a few minutes later she said, "I see you got the blackberries cleared out."

Phillip returned to Jenny's cottage from lunch with a giant world map that he tacked up with white push pins on the wall of the living room. He intended to stick colored pins in all the destinations his mother had visited over the past five decades. He'd devised a plan that involved listing out phone numbers of museums, bars, hotels, and other verifiable destinations Jenny had visited in these various locales. He recognized that he was trying to get to know his mother better as much as to find something specific; but he reasoned that by getting to know Jenny, something specific would be revealed.

Before fully executing this plan, though, Phillip had a hunch: he flipped way back through to the envelopes for trips from the single years before he and his brother were each born.

The hand-written dates on these early envelopes had faded from a deep, bold blue to a pale denim. The handwriting seemed to grow more carelessly expressive as his mother regressed toward the free-wheeling personality of her youth—similar to what her Alzheimer's forced upon her at the other end of her life.

Phillip discovered that roughly nine months before Spencer's birth, Jenny had visited Barcelona and Seville. Eight months before Phillip came into the world, she'd taken a week-long trip to Ireland.

CHAPTER SIXTEEN

Longstreet

PHILLIP CALLED HIS BROTHER from the old French Princess phone in Jenny's cottage.

Spencer picked up after two rings. "Mom?! Holy shit, is that you?!" he yelled into the phone.

"It's Phillip," Phillip said.

"Oh no . . . are you dead now too?!"

"I'm calling from the cottage."

"Uh, yeah, I got that, actually. I have this new invention—caller ID . . ."

"I found some things," Phillip said. "You should come up here when you can get away for a few hours."

"Get away from what?" Spencer asked. "I don't have a job. My girlfriend moved to Portugal. My band may be splitting up. My cat hates me. You're all I've got."

"You don't have a cat. How about tomorrow first thing?"

"See you then."

Spencer pulled up to the cottage in his black Lexus GX SUV—he called it 'the getaway car'—as Phillip was finishing breakfast.

Phillip hadn't expected his brother so early. He was eating the granola from Jenny's pantry and watching CNN. He felt compelled to eat the leftover food rather than throw it out, because it was their mother's food, and she was dead, and it was the least he could do. He was surprised to feel emotionally tied to breakfast cereal. He made a mental note to retrieve the brisket in the freezer.

Spencer stood at the front door wearing his typical uniform: faded black jeans, a bright lumberjack shirt, black Aldo Merane shoes. As he stepped inside he looked around the living room.

"Great Googly Moogly, what is this, CSI Larchmont? What is going on in here, Chief Inspector Phillip?" He took in the neatly stacked folders, the envelopes of receipts, the map on the wall. "Oh, Mom would have friggin' *loved* this! It's like pyramids and Roman baths hidden under someone's rumpus room. But really—what the what?!"

"I've been following a few leads," Phillip explained.

"Leads to what? A serial killer? A plot to smuggle Canada geese into the country? Who are you, Longstreet?"

"Longstreet?" Phillip asked.

"Blind detective show in the early seventies. James Franciscus, I think. Bruce Lee was in it, too."

"Wait, the detective was blind?"

"Yeah, so he didn't really need the magnifying glass. He was lucky if he could uncover the location of the toilet paper. But what are you doing here? What is all this with the maps and the colors?"

"I've been looking at Mom's papers."

"I'll say! Did you find a written confession?"

"Listen. I'm on to something. Can you shut up and be serious for one fucking minute?"

Spencer considered being serious. He put down his overnight bag. "Got any coffee?" he asked.

Phillip went to make another pot of coffee while his brother took a bowl out of the cupboard and helped himself to granola, milk, some of the strawberries that Phillip had brought from the city.

Spencer said, "It's weird. I feel like we're supposed to eat all this food instead of tossing it in the trash."

Phillip shook his head. How could it be possible that Spencer wasn't his full brother?

"I've been going through some old boxes," Phillip said. "Here's what I figured out . . ."

He told Spencer about the trips Jenny had taken to Ireland and Spain roughly nine months before each of their births. He mentioned talking to Colin in Ballydraiocht.

"You are absolutely shitting me," Spencer said. "But I still have no clue what you're getting at. She travelled all the time. She probably travelled six months before our birth dates, too. And three months. I think she got up from the birthing room and flew to Reno for a night."

"She got pregnant on those two trips. I know it."

"How can you be so sure? And by the way: so what?"

"It melds with the DNA tests, right? Mine with the Northern European blood—and what she said about the Irish golf pro. Yours being Southern European. This gets us closer to our fathers!"

"What about Jack Elliot? What about all the new aunts and uncles and cousins?" Spencer was tapping a backbeat on the rich wooden grain of the sofa edge. It was something he did without realizing. Phillip once recognized it as—literally—the beat of Spencer's own drum.

"We ruled that out already, remember?"

"I know, but I really wanted to be part of a big family. Can't we just pretend? The same way we pretended that Jack Elliot was our father for the past fifty years?"

"Is that what you want?" Phillip asked.

"I was perfectly comfortable not knowing anything about our father," Spencer said. "I was happy with the story of Jewish heroism triumphing over the Viet Cong. I never wanted any of this." He swung his arm in an arc to indicate Phillip's war room.

"When you change one teeny tiny thing like who was your father, everything else changes, too," Spencer went on. "I'm adrift. I don't know who I am."

"You're the same person you've always been," Phillip said.

"My old girlfriend Mirabel used to ask me all the time: 'Who are you?' She meant underneath my hilarious façade. I told her there *wasn't* anything underneath. That I'm an empty comic husk. She thought I was still trying to be funny, but I was being honest."

"You know that's not true," Phillip said.

"No, it is. And it's *not* funny. There's nothing funny about it. I know I'm hiding a deep, gaping hole. A wound. A frigging Berkeley Pit strip mine of pain. I know it's there, it's just that I can't *feel* it. I can't feel anything. That's not new, but now I'm also no longer on solid ground in my lack of emotions. It's a not very good combination."

"Nothing's changed, bro," Phillip interrupted. "You're exactly who you've always been. You're just updating the label on a folder. Everything inside is still the same."

"That's a heartwarming analogy," Spencer said. "I'm a folder. I'm a manila envelope."

Phillip took his bowl from the counter and put it in the porcelain farm sink. Spencer got up from the couch and nested his bowl inside Phillip's. Phillip anticipated a battle of attrition to see who might wash the bowls and return them to the cupboard—a battle that had raged already for more than half a century.

"I've been reading more about DNA," Spencer said. "Here's an analogy: this doctor compares our DNA to like a dozen full sets of the *Encyclopedia Britannica*. That's one person's genetic code. If you took all those gazillions of pages that define one person, that person's sibling's entire library of DNA would have about four pages that are different. A total stranger might have seventy different pages."

"And?" Phillip asked.

"And nothing. All I'm saying is, we're not folder labels. We're four pages in a library. And those four pages, which might seem like nothing, totally define us. They make us different from all the other people in all the other libraries. And our parents determine those pages . . ."

"And?"

"So I don't know if I love playing the drums because my father played the drums," Spencer went on, "or I was drawn to basketball because my dad was a famous Spanish soccer player and I inherited a gene that tells me to run up and down chasing a stupid ball. How about my hair color, or my rapier wit?"

"What's the difference if it came from your father or from Mom or you love basketball because you saw the Harlem Globetrotters on TV as a kid?"

"That's just it. I don't know anymore what's mine and what belonged to someone else—someone else other than the someone I've at least been able to imagine all these years. Now I have to guess at everything all over again.

"Wayback playback," Spencer continued. "Remember when people used to ask me what our father did for work?"

"I remember," Phillip said.

What he remembered was parents' day at school one year. They'd all been assigned an essay about their parents' professions—and 'parents' in almost all cases ended up being fathers, most of whom rode the Long Island Railroad to white-collar office jobs in Manhattan. Spencer had written that his father was an astronaut who'd been chosen for a secret mission and was flying around Uranus.

Phillip recalled standing in the gym after the assembly in which half a dozen kids read their essays to an audience of parents, teachers, and other students. Spencer had not been chosen for that honor.

Jenny was there with them on the hardwood gym floor, dressed in bell-bottomed jeans and carrying a knit purse made from the wool of Tibetan yaks. A few other kids and their parents stood chatting.

When Billy Rothman's mother asked Spencer, "So, what does *your* father do?" Phillip and their mom waited in dread.

Spencer replied, "Well, he's like a composer. But the opposite."

Mrs. Rothman smiled. "What does the opposite of a composer do?" she asked, ready to laugh at the cute answer.

Spencer said, "He decomposes."

"I never wanted to be defined by who our father was," Spencer said now. "I finally accepted he was dead and never going to be a part of us. And it's been fine for more than five decades. Do I really want to launch that ship of pain all over again?"

Phillip shook his head. "I'm going to Ireland," he said. "I have a plan. And I'm bringing my golf clubs."

"Golf clubs?" Spencer said. "I am *so* going with you."

Chapter Seventeen
TOWER of Haggis

When Phillip was a freshman in high school Jenny convinced him to try out for the golf team. He'd shown little inclination to play team sports other than the pickup games—softball, roller hockey, capture the flag—that spontaneously occurred around the neighborhood. Phillip understood why Jenny chose golf for him: it was the most intellectual of athletic pursuits, not requiring speed or brute strength. She succeeded in finding a sport he was eventually good at—and golf was also something the boys could play together, possibly for the full course of their lives. Many of her efforts were designed to drive the boys together, even if that united them in constant wonder about her. But now Phillip considered whether Jenny's encouragement about golf was an early clue meant to lead him eventually to his father.

Phillip was tall and wiry and clumsy as a teen, but he compensated with studiousness—he scientifically observed the kids who could cross-over dribble a basketball or throw a perfect spiral, and was able to model them and develop adequate competence.

After a few lessons from the golf coach Phillip became a classic ball-striker with smooth, breezy form; his long arms fluidly delivered club head to ball in a way that made him a great iron player. He viewed putting as a math problem in which he had to balance speed, slope, distance, green surface, and other factors to find a solution, which deeply appealed to him. He was a lights-out putter.

Spencer was a blunt force at golf, a tornado of unconventional moving parts. If a phys ed teacher or some boy's father told him to keep his left elbow straight during takeaway, he bent it. If they said take the club back half way he extended the arc around his head.

On warm days when Phillip was a junior and senior the boys sometimes drove to the public course in Lido Beach with a couple of tightly-rolled joints stashed in their golf bags. When the course was otherwise empty they would play games, like "Crossover" which Spencer invented: they'd start on the first tee but whoever won that hole would pick the next green, sometimes choosing one on the opposite corner of the course, which might involve hitting over ponds and streams or even the clubhouse.

In another game—which Spencer called 'Boatshot'—they'd practice driving balls from the fifth tee into Reynolds Channel when rich folks from Hewlett Harbor went past in their yachts and catamarans. The boys would save a few ratty Top-Flites or pilfered range balls and try to hit the boats. Once, Spencer landed a seven iron with a loud 'kerpow' on the starboard hull of a cruising sailboat and a naked couple appeared from below and stood on the deck threatening them, and the boys fell down in the short, damp grass laughing.

Ireland would be the first overnight golf trip the boys had taken together since their twenties, when Spencer's band, TOWER of Haggis, played a gig at Kellerman's Hotel in the Catskills. When anyone asked Spencer how he'd named the band he'd say that Tower of Power was already taken.

Phillip drove up from the city to spend a long weekend, play a couple of rounds with his brother, and hear the band warm up for the headliners: a group of octogenarians so shriveled, Spencer observed, they could travel in their own instrument cases. Jenny had helped Spencer land the gig through her contacts at the resort. She'd been sending them steady streams of aging Jews for years.

This was in 1987, when the Catskills was trying to reinvent itself for a younger crowd; they hired bands like Spencer's in the hopes of attracting a new generation. TOWER of Haggis played two short sets each evening so Spencer had mornings and afternoons free to tour local golf courses at The Concord, Grossinger's, or The Nevele with his brother.

Before the trip, when Phillip and Spencer began talking about the upcoming weekend over dinner with their mom in an Indian restaurant that served the hottest vindaloo any of them had ever tasted, she volunteered to join them even though she hadn't been invited.

Jenny told them, "Aunt Phyllis and I used to go to Kellerman's back in the late fifties, with Nana and Papa. . . We had some wild times . . . " She trailed off with a smile Spencer knew was meant to look nostalgic.

"I danced with Sammy Davis, Jr.," she added. "*He* was a real gentleman. But very skinny for a Jew."

"And very black for a Jew," Spencer said.

Phillip recognized that Jenny was slow-playing details from her life so the boys would agree to have her along, but it still worked. He and Spencer nibbled at the bait of an opportunity to learn more about their mother's past. They didn't mind having her tag along because she added an additional layer of unpredictability to any escapade, and she wouldn't judge them if they got high or snuck off to some matron's room with an attractive daughter.

They rolled into the sprawling lobby with its brass and crystal chandeliers, its black and gold color themes, its unspoken tribute to the ancient Egypt that their ancestors had worked so hard to flee from.

Spencer said, "It's like Liberace had a baby with Phyllis Diller. And it's been shot in Panavision."

His junior suite sported a round bed with a mirror on the ceiling above it; Jenny's contained a plastic hot tub in the shape of a martini glass. Phillip was afraid to walk barefoot on the shag carpet in his room.

TOWER was scheduled to play from 5:30-7:00 in the lounge next to the dining room. They met for dinner at 4:00.

Spencer's childhood friend Max Feingold, who played bass in TOWER, joined them. He was tall and lean, with a nose big enough for two faces, Spencer used to say, but he could flash a smile that made all his other features disappear, the kind of polite kid who could talk his way into—or out of—any situation. He was the perfect cohort for Spencer, and the boys spent many afternoons during high school in Jenny's basement, practicing with the band, playing Biplanes and Invisible Tank on Spencer's Atari 2600, and devising schemes to procure extra cash—selling weed or running book on football games.

During the seventh grade Spencer began calling Max "The Factor," because whatever situation he found himself in, the boy exerted an influence—whether convincing a store clerk to let him borrow clothing for a gig, or devising a scheme to promote Girl Scout cookie sales on commuter trains for a small commission. You could never plan anything involving him without considering this.

At dinner at Kellerman's the waiter delivered their gin and tonics in glasses etched with mountains, as if the Catskills were the Himalayas. Their server was a young upstate hayseed who they caught staring down the open front of Jenny's low-slung gold dress—Jenny was in her early forties and her sons recognized that her self-confidence was as much of an aphrodisiac to men as her red lipstick or push-up bra.

Phillip noticed Jenny noticing The Factor passing Spencer a white pill under the table.

"What's that?" she asked, sliding her gold bracelets up one arm.

"Something to help inspire the music," The Factor said.

"Yes, Max, I get that part. But what is it?"

"Quaalude," said Max. "A mild relaxant. Totally legal—I have a prescription."

"Oh, methaqualone," Jenny said. "That's the technical name. It was originally developed to fight malaria. The name is supposed to reference a 'quiet interlude'—but in my experience it's anything but! Could I buy one from you?"

"You can *have* one, Mrs. E.," The Factor said. "If I can get one of your sons to sign a permission slip. But don't drink a lot if you take the whole thing. Half is probably better."

"You're sweet," Jenny said, swallowing the pill with her gin and tonic.

Before they headed to the buffet, The Factor reached into his backpack again and pulled out something else that he passed to Spencer under the table. It was round and wrapped in wax paper.

"What now?" Jenny asked.

"Cheeseburgers," The Factor whispered. "Sorry, I only got enough for the band."

"Preventive measures," Spencer explained. "I know about the food here. They make up in volume what they lack in quality."

"The kosher police will throw us in the brig if we're caught," The Factor said. "Mixing cheese and meat is worse than dropping a log in the swimming pool."

By the time they approached the Viennese Table loaded with desserts—something Spencer hadn't seen since his bar mitzvah—Jenny was getting a little loose. She let out a throaty giggle at something The Factor said. She played with the pearls clasped around her throat—a piece of jewelry she'd inherited from her mother but hardly ever wore.

Spencer and The Factor got up from the table when their other band members came in and they climbed onto the stage to warm up. Phillip was erecting complex architectural structures out of sugar cubes when they left him alone with Jenny at the table.

"I still love this old place even though it's from another decade long ago and far away," Jenny said. "It's where I first met Jack . . ."

She said it like a long-established fact but this was new information. Phillip knocked over his sugar cube condos and looked up, wary of getting played.

"And where Aunt Phyllis met Uncle Jerry," she continued, as if some part of her *wanted* to reveal the details she'd been holding back for so long. "I met Jerry first. I knew he was exactly what your Aunt was looking for. Which is why I kissed him in the hallway after he walked us back to our room. He was good looking! And successful, with his jewelry business on 47th Street. And a good kisser! I knew if Phyllis thought I wanted him then she would want him more. I didn't let her lay eyes on Jack until she'd already made a hard play for Jerry. She went for Jerry like a lion on a gazelle.

"Jack was a dishwasher," his mother slurred. "But a ladies' man even at that age. Not like the soft, rich Jewish boys. He was going to pay his way through St. John's working summers. It was the first time I ever defied my parents—don't get any ideas!—by dating a goy. That was the start of something . . . my own life . . . I . . . "

Jenny crossed her arms on the white tablecloth and rested her head on them. That was the end of her story.

As TOWER of Haggis finished their second set, Jenny was at the bar drinking seltzer and flirting with two men in Brooks Brothers suits. Phillip was fending off a middle-aged woman in a strappy black dress one seat away.

Spencer came up between his mother and the suits, edging the men further down the bar.

"I think I just saw Buddy Hackett in the bathroom," he said. "He was having some trouble peeing. Kojak was in there too, combing his hair." He turned to Phillip. "Don Rickles said to tell you you're a hockey puck."

Spencer noted a crowd was forming near the stage as the next band began playing Herb Alpert.

"It's the dance of the living dead," he said. "The zombie mambo."

Jenny shook her head exactly the way the boys would both begin to do later in their lives. "You can laugh at this place all you want, but it's part of my history. Part of your history," she said.

"Then I'm going to learn from history," Spencer said, not unkindly. "Because the last thing I want is to be doomed to repeat this, like Sisyphus pushing a matzo ball up a gefilte fish."

Across the room the bandleader stepped up to the microphone in his powder blue tux and said, "Ladies and Gentlemen, we have a very special guest in the house tonight . . ."

In the background Phillip could hear the first notes of the dreaded tune. When he looked up, a waitress was schlepping across the dance floor with a slice of chocolate cake with a candle in it.

"Let's hear it for Phillip Elliot, everybody . . ."

The room joined in to sing *Happy Birthday* to Phillip, although his birthday was still months away.

———————

The next morning Spencer canceled their scheduled tee time due to hangover. And the morning after that.

On their last day at Kellerman's the brothers played 18 holes on The Behemoth—the famous local course that billed itself as the longest ever built. Spencer insisted on playing from the back tees.

"Don't be a pussy," he said to Phillip.

"Don't lose all your golf balls on the front nine," Phillip said.

Spencer actually ran out of balls on the seventh hole and detoured their electric cart to the edge of the practice area, where he jumped out and stole a hatful of range balls. While he was dashing back to the cart, an errant shot from the driving range grazed him in the head.

They spent the remainder of the morning at the Sullivan County Hospital emergency room.

But it wasn't a total debacle, Spencer said later: at least the doctor prescribed him a vial of Vicodin.

Jenny pointed out that its real name was hydrocodone and told Spencer he shouldn't take it if he was breastfeeding.

Chapter Eighteen
Serape

Phillip and Spencer discovered Jenny had left them an estate. The cottage itself—which she'd paid cash for more than two decades ago—had appreciated substantially. She also owned a small stock portfolio, jewelry, some fine arts and antique furniture, and a safety deposit box with twenty-five thousand dollars in cash. They finally sold the cottage but Phillip surreptitiously rented a storage unit in Larchmont for Jenny's papers.

A week before their flight to Dublin Phillip called Spencer to discuss travel details.

"Claro, la chaqueta corta aqui," Spencer said when he picked up.

"Huh?" Phillip said.

"La chaqueta corta aqui," Spencer said again. Then added: "It's Spanish for 'a short close-fitting jacket' Apparently a Spencer is a short, close-fitting jacket."

"I see . . ."

"I figured since we're embarking on this voyage of fatherly discovery I'd try getting in touch with my own Southern European ancestry. I'm testing it out to see how it feels."

"Even though you could be Italian. Or Portuguese. Or from Malta," Phillip said. "But how does it feel?'

"Caliente!"

"It feels hot?"

"I don't really know that many words in Spanish," Spencer admitted. "Do you think I'll need a serape on this trip?"

"I'd be surprised. But you never know. But I think a serape is more Mexican than Spanish."

"I just like to say serape," Spencer said.

"I know you do," Phillip said.

"Hey, are we going to County Mayo at all?"

"I don't think so. Ballydraiocht is in County Kerry. And Dublin is in, I think, County Dublin. Why?"

"What about County Ketchup?" Spencer said.

"Um, no," Phillip answered him. "I think that's in Northern Ireland, which is actually another country."

"That's never made any sense to me," Spencer said. "Couldn't they come up with a more original name once 'Ireland' was already taken? People do it for twins, and they're a lot smaller. You wouldn't call your kids 'Bob' and 'Northern Bob.'"

"Are you done?" Phillip asked.

"I'm not sure. I'm just burning off nervous energy."

"Yep," Phillip said. "I'm nervous, too."

"Are we going to find anything?"

"I have no idea. I think so."

"But you'll still be my brother? Even if we discover you're heir to a kingdom of leprechauns?"

"Would you like the role of court jester? You've been training for it your whole life."

"I was thinking of something more dignified. I could be your taster, to make sure your whiskey hasn't been poisoned. Sometimes you have to test the whole bottle to be certain."

"I'll let you wear my tiny crown of four-leaf clovers when no one is looking."

"I'm your brother," Spencer said.

"No matter what," Phillip reassured him.

Part Two

Chapter Nineteen

Wolverines and Unicorns

For their flight to Dublin, the boys used airline certificates they'd found in Jenny's house, in a folder labeled 'Airline Certificates.' They flew standby, as required, which allowed them to book and change their reservations easily, even at the last minute. They sat in adjacent aisle seats in business class.

Phillip had dressed for travel in crisply-ironed khakis and a white shirt with a gray pullover. He sported noise-cancelling headphones and a black eye mask atop his head for later, hoping to catch a couple of hours of sleep.

Spencer wore faded black Prana jeans and a plaid shirt so soft it practically 'baaa-d,' and ear buds that he liked to think made him look like a spy. He planned to watch movies throughout the flight, hit the ground running upon arrival, and catch up on his sleep the following night with the lullaby of a couple of Ambien.

Phillip thought that a person walking down the aisle to the crowded gumball machine that constituted the back of the plane probably wouldn't have assumed they were flying together. And probably not that they were brothers.

He pretended for a moment that they *were* strangers, to imagine how Spencer might appear to other passengers who were banging their roller bags into the armrests and clocking the business class passengers in the face with their oversized backpacks as they maneuvered toward the back: he looked like a successful, confident middle-aged man, comfortable in his clothes, going gray in a slow, calm manner, freshly shaved so that you couldn't see the glint of white in his stubble. A slight bump in his Romanesque nose from a line drive he'd misjudged forty years earlier. You might assume he was a father, partly because of his age, and in part because he had that relaxed look of someone happy to have a reprieve from a clattering, boisterous, loving house. Someone looking forward to a night of uninterrupted slumber. But Phillip knew that *he* was the family Spencer loved, and he felt a swelling of affection for his brother.

Spencer was looking askance at the stocky, red-faced Irishman who seemed exhausted by the mere act of sitting down next to him. The man explained that he'd been in New York for a conference, his first trip, how could people live like that, all so close together and up in the air. But the pizza sure was good even though the beer was shite.

Once they were airborne, the man asked Spencer what was bringing him to Dublin. "Going to visit my da," he said.

When the woman sitting next to Phillip asked *him* the same question he answered, "I'm on a golf trip with my brother," and inclined his head toward Spencer, who was by then giggling at a Wes Anderson movie on his laptop.

Three hours into the flight a horrific sound emanated from somewhere behind Spencer. His first reaction: there's a wild animal imprisoned inside the drink cart. He looked back over his seat to see a topless toddler wearing only a diaper standing on the seat behind him, screaming.

The boy's mother was watching a movie with headphones on. She was clearly aware of her son's behaviour—bloody hell, Spencer thought, people on the ground below were probably aware of it—and equally clearly had no inclination to take any action.

The longer she ignored the child, the louder his volume ratcheted; when pure sound waves weren't enough to garner a reaction the boy began pounding with both hands on the back of Spencer's seat. Spencer stood up in the aisle to get a better vantage point to give them both the stink eye. But neither reacted.

Spencer reached over and tapped the mother on the shoulder but she just shook her head without looking up from the screen, as if in the middle of a dreadfully important phone call—talking to mission control, huddling on a conference with doctors from the hospital for pediatric neurosurgery—and couldn't possibly be disturbed.

Spencer tapped her again and this time she held up the palm of her hand. He reached over, smiling, and pulled one side of her headphones off her ear.

"If you don't discipline that child I'm going to do it myself," he said.

With a flicker of annoyance she paused her film and looked up. She was thirtyish, attractive except for dark circles under her eyes. She wore pearls and a low-cut charcoal gray cashmere sweater.

"That would be terrific," the woman said with a British accent. "Good luck with that." She turned back to her movie.

Spencer crouched so that his head was level with the child, who stopped screaming, apparently startled to see this strange man engaging him eye to eye. Spencer spoke in a hushed voice, making it difficult for Phillip, listening, to hear what his brother was saying.

After a moment the boy sat down in his seat. Spencer nodded his assurance. He held one finger to his lips and the boy smiled and mimicked the same action, and they didn't hear another peep out of him for the rest of the flight.

Phillip thought back to their mom traveling alone with her two boys with no husband to help corral them. She usually insisted on car trips for just this reason—she could always pull over at a rest area or an empty field, open the doors, and let the boys' burn off their relentless energy. She kept a Wiffle ball and bat handy, and she could throw a rising curve that not even Spencer could hit until he was thirteen.

On their first overseas trip, to England, when the boys were nine and seven years old, Spencer had been on the verge of a meltdown on the airplane. He couldn't sleep. He'd been through two coloring books and a Ray Bradbury novel. Jenny caught him instigating a slap fight with Phillip and intervened with what she promised was the most difficult game of Hangman ever played—choosing words like 'obfuscate' and 'psyllium'; obscure movie titles (*Throne of Blood, Kind Hearts and Coronets, Eyes Without a Face*) and the names of books that didn't exist (*Runaway Rabbit, The Culottes and Capris Caper*). She also slipped a little bourbon into their orange juice.

They fell asleep trying to solve a lateral thinking puzzle that was beyond their abilities. Jenny said, "A man walks into a bar. The bartender pulls out a gun and points it at the man. The man says 'thank you' and leaves the bar."

———————

Now, as Phillip leaned his seat back hoping that the passenger behind him wouldn't notice, he thought it was best that he and Spencer hadn't had children, although he believed that his brother would have been a terrific dad—he was still half a child himself and kids loved him. But Phillip recognized the anger in his brother at the little boy: was it aimed purely at the boy's behavior, or that he appeared fatherless?

Phillip felt pity toward the kid. And a sense of communion. He related to a child with no apparent father, yelling and banging his fists.

Spencer sat, rebuckled, and went back to his movie. Phillip fell asleep. When he woke the plane was descending into Dublin.

Rubbing silt from his eyes at the baggage carousel, Phillip said, "Hey, what did you say to the devil child on the plane?"

Spencer smiled. He clasped his hands behind his back and stretched his arms up in the air in a variation of uttanasana pose.

"I told him there would be a unicorn waiting for him at the airport that could fart rainbow sugar cookies. But only if he was good. Otherwise, only the other kids would be able to see the unicorn.

"I might have added that if he didn't shut his little mouth I was going to stuff him in the overhead rack."

Spencer bent at the waist, reaching for his toes to stretch his hammies. "Where they keep the wolverines."

They landed in Dublin to a gray morning with occasional flotillas of blue patches drifting past. They checked into their sleek-lobbied hotel just off Grafton Street with its bar full of sharply dressed breakfasters sitting at zinc-topped tables. They showered and changed and went out to walk around the city. Phillip wouldn't let his brother lay down on his bed—an oasis of beckoning softness after the flight—because if they fell asleep in daylight they'd take three times as long adjusting to the time change.

After passing the Oscar Wilde statue in Merrion Square, they spotted the hop-on, hop-off bus and hopped on, figuring it would provide the best overview of Dublin. They sat on the lower level rather than the uncovered deck to stay out of a cold drizzle. Phillip consulted the map that came with their fare, opened his pocket guide for cross – referencing, and tried to create an itinerary. Spencer watched girls passing by on the street. He looked for red hair beneath rain jacket hoods and under knit caps. He'd always loved the gingers, as he decided to think of them now.

"I want to see the Writers' Museum and the James Joyce Centre," Phillip said. "You'll be happy to know that they spell 'centre' with the 'r' and the 'e' reversed at the end."

"I'll be at the Guinness Storehouse."

"Before lunch?"

"And the Jameson distillery. At some point we should talk about your plan for the rest of the trip."

Phillip pulled at the leather zipper tab of his merino wool sweater under his rain jacket. He'd ordered it from a catalogue full of clever travel gadgets and expensive clothing.

"I don't have a plan," Phillip said.

Spencer shook his head. "Hang on: you said you had a plan. You used those exact words when you first mentioned this trip. You said, and I quote, 'I have a plan.'"

"A plan to come to Ireland."

"And then what?" Spencer said.

"Ballydraiocht. A golf pro," Phillip said, quoting the last words their mother had uttered to him. "That's my plan."

———

Phillip embraced touring around Dublin because it allowed him to feel that he was about to embark upon the effort to find his father, but hadn't really begun yet; there was no possibility of disappointment— aside from the familiar disappointment he'd already felt his whole life.

That first night the boys found a pub with help from a tourist they passed standing in the middle of an intersection trying to orient himself with a popular American guide book. Spencer approached the man, who was wearing scuffed hiking boots, a fanny pack and backpack, and carried ski poles, as if he'd gone missing hiking in the Karwendel Mountains in Austria in the 1970s.

Spencer said "Excuse me," and asked if the gentleman's book per- haps mentioned a certain pub they'd already passed?

The man was happy to talk with someone who shared his plight of not knowing where to go. He looked up the pub in the guidebook index. He spoke with an accent Spencer identified as coming from someplace in Delaware.

"I don't see it here," he said. "The book recommends the Brazen Head on Lower Bridge Street. Says it was founded in 1198. Can that be right?" He said 'the book' as if there was only one.

"Okey doke, thanks," Spencer said, interrupting. Then he turned to his brother and said, "It's not in the guide book. That's the one we want."

They ate at the bar. Spencer ordered a curry so hot he had to swirl creamy Guinness around on his tongue for relief. Sweat popped out in tiny pearls below his hairline and ran down his face. His olive complexion reddened. Phillip chose the fish and chips—crunchy, greasy tablets of golden-brown haddock and potato wedges deep fried to a luster. He covered them in malt vinegar, figuring that's how locals ate them.

They stayed out late, considering they'd flown most of the previous evening. Spencer was keen to listen to the Irish band that was warming up in the other room and linger long enough to hear the amateurs who would play afterwards for tips.

Phillip encouraged him to borrow a guitar and play something himself.

"What about a drum solo?" Spencer asked. "I could play the Keith Moon part from 'My Generation.' People love that. Or wait, I know: How about 'Father and Son'—the Cat Stevens song?"

"How about 'Mother and Child Reunion' by Simon and Garfunkle?" Phillip asked.

"'I would not give you false hope,'" Spencer quoted. "'On this strange and mournful day.' What about Keith Urban's 'Song for Dad'? Or I could do Sister Sledge's 'We Are Family.' Oh, no, wait, this is it! The Hollies' song! I'll dedicate it to you."

"Which Hollies song?" Phillip asked with dread.

"He's just heavy—he ain't my brother," Spencer said.

At midnight there was a gap in volunteers to perform. Spencer climbed onto the small stage, sat on the stool in front of the microphone. He cleared his throat. He held his hands and fingers in position to play a chord.

"I don't have a guitar," he said into the mic. The crowd laughed.

Someone shouted, "Give the American a guitar!"

And someone did.

Spencer tuned the instrument clumsily, setting them up. Phillip recognized the classic misdirection. People were talking. Phillip heard glasses clinking behind the bar.

Then Spencer leaned into it. He played a loud Spanish riff from the Gypsy Kings to get their attention. The room quieted. He transitioned through a clever bridge into the basic chord pattern for 'Miss Monaghan's'—an Irish reel—played slow. He worked through the opening twice, and when he saw they were following him he improvised a complicated melodic exploration of the song's basics. Someone started clapping to the beat and the rest joined in. Phillip was glad his brother chose a song with no words—it showed off his guitar chops without distracting with his not-great voice.

When Spencer finished the patrons stood up and roared. Spencer bowed his head and handed the guitar back into the crowd.

Phillip clapped wildly, standing, admiring his brother's talent. Where did it come from, he wondered.

They walked home through Temple Bar at one thirty in the morning, lightheaded and beery. The streets were humming with energy.

Phillip eavesdropped on tourists speaking five different languages, one of which he couldn't even identify. They passed a hen party—bachelorettes walking the bride around town; a group of older Brits following a tour guide who held a pink umbrella above her head; and various collections of men and women in twos and threes and fours, almost everyone talking and laughing at the same time.

"I just saw James Joyce talking to Oscar Wilde," Spencer said, "but I couldn't understand a fecking word."

"He must have been reciting *Ulysses*," Phillip said.

For someone who'd made his way through college as if classes were bridges between drug binges, Spencer knew literature—thanks to Jenny's frequent entreaties for them to read any time they claimed to be bored. And Spencer's penchant for remembering everything despite downplaying his mental abilities.

"'Mr. Leopold Bloom ate with relish the inner organs of beasts and fowls,'" Phillip added.

"Huh?"

"It's from the book. *Ulysses*."

"Wait, you *read Ulysses*?!"

"Don't talk crazy—nobody's actually read *Ulysses*. But I wrote a paper about it at Vassar. I focused on a deep analysis of the opening page, and how it resonates through the rest of the book."

"So you only read the first page, is what you're saying?" Spencer asked.

"I read the first page of *every chapter*. Or maybe it was the first sentence. The book was actually easier to understand that way than when I tried reading the whole thing. Apropos," Phillip continued, "you probably know that 'all happy families are alike, but each unhappy family is unhappy in its own way.'"

Spencer recognized the first line from *Anna Karenina*.

"Touché," Spencer said. He shot his cuffs, which Jenny had taught him as an effective means of showing off without saying anything. "'I wish either my father or my mother, or indeed both of them, had minded what they were about when they got me,'" he said.

They sidestepped a puddle in the street, Phillip executing a little hop that Spencer thought would make a fine old-guy dance move.

"That's from *Tristram Shandy*—or some other unreadable nineteenth century British novel, if I remember right." Spencer added.

They were making their way through narrow, cobbled lanes. The crowds had dissipated street by street until they were the only people in view as they approached their hotel.

"I am the steel of my father, but tempered by my mother," Spencer said then. He blew on his hands as if it were actually much colder. It was a tell he sometimes displayed in poker games, although only Jenny and Phillip had figured this out. They never mentioned it to him.

"What's that from?" Phillip asked.

"I just made it up," Spencer said. "But it would be a great first line, wouldn't it?"

Back at their hotel they paused outside their separate rooms—Phillip was a light sleeper and Spencer snored, so when planning the trip they'd agreed to spend the extra money for privacy. Also, Spencer's room would look like a plane crash after a few hours, while Phillip would unpack his clothes into drawers and stow his suitcase in the closet.

"Fun day, bro," Phillip said. He put out his clenched hand for a fist bump but Spencer grabbed it and pulled him close. Phillip could smell a sweet breath of curry. And beer. And whiskey. And the simultaneously stale and fresh air of travel.

"Hey, I love you, man," Spencer said, clapping Phillip repeatedly on the back.

Phillip couldn't tell if this was a heartfelt moment or if his brother was quoting an old television beer commercial that parodied the way men express intimacy.

Chapter Twenty

Papa

THEY'D PLANNED TO PLAY golf that second afternoon at the Royal Dublin Golf Club—one of Phillip's real estate fund investors was a member and had set them up—but in the morning a deluge fell from the tin sky. Like the ocean was coming down on them, drop by drop, Spencer said. He could taste the salt.

An inveterate gym rat who played squash and tennis and pickup basketball at home, Spencer jumped on the elliptical trainer in the fitness center. He took a swim and had a hot stone massage and then read James Watson's *The Double Helix* in the wingback chair by the lobby fireplace.

Phillip spent the day exploring the city. The worst of the weather passed through by lunch, leaving an overcast afternoon that dropped patches of light rain but was still fine for walking in a fleece, Gore-Tex shell, and golf cap. He visited Dublin Castle and wandered along Grafton Street and around St. Stephen's Green and saw the *Book of Kells* at Trinity College. He ambled along the River Liffey from the shipyards to Phoenix Park, and then back along the opposite shore. He walked off nearly twenty-three thousand steps on his Fitbit. He successfully avoided thinking about what lay ahead, except in a vague way, as if he was squinting into the future and everything was blurry. Like one of his brother's early Polaroids.

They went for dinner at a restaurant recommended by the concierge. They sat in the boisterous dining room full of locals and ordered a bottle of Portuguese vinho verde with their oysters and moved to a tempranillo with their main courses of lamb for Phillip, gigantic sea scallops for Spencer. The meal was a slow progression of simple pleasures, from the warm bread slathered with Irish butter to the berry crumble they shared for dessert, each of them trying to spoon more of the ice cream before his brother could.

Over a post-prandial glass of Dead Rabbit whiskey, Spencer said, "Wayback playback: remember that trip to Miami to visit Nana and Papa, when we were supposed to play putt-putt golf but a force three hurricane blew in and it rained all week?"

Phillip recognized the segue: golf, rain and travel. His brother was free-associating. Phillip rode with it as if this were logical. Like they were piloting parallel motorcycles in the same lane of traffic.

Spencer reminded him about a day on that trip when their grandfather, Sam Bernstein, was supposed to entertain them while Jenny and Aunt Phyllis and Leah and their grandmother shopped at Bal Harbour and Aventura.

Their grandfather had promised a day of mini golf, but thick clouds pressed down. The sky was a light shade of black, and the ocean—which they could see out the window of their grandparents' fifth-floor condo along Collins Avenue—was a bruised blue color capped by white mist.

Phyllis and Leah were staying nearby at the Diplomat Hotel—with a working father at the head of their family, they had financial advantages that Jenny and her sons didn't enjoy. Jenny slept in the tiny guest room/office in the condo. The boys camped on the floor—because they could not agree who should get the couch, their grandfather's Solomonic decree was for neither to get it.

Uncle Jerry hadn't come with them on this visit. He never came with them. He was a stoic Jew who wouldn't travel on the Sabbath, but the boys made him out to be a spy. Any adult they couldn't figure out was a spy. Jerry was Jewish in a way that suburban American children could never be Jewish, and the boys felt he resented that they didn't take their heritage more seriously.

The day that mini-golf was cancelled, Sam Bernstein called the brothers into his bedroom. He was putting on his tefillin for morning prayers. He wanted the boys to participate. The women had all gone out for breakfast at Pumpernik's, where their grandmother would fill her purse from the basket of free rolls. She might hoard sugar packets too. Their grandfather once explained this was a common behavior among people who'd been through the Holocaust.

Sam sat on the hard bed with the white tufted bedspread. He wrapped his forearms with the leather straps of the tefillin and placed the black box containing verses from the *Old Testament* on his upper arms. Then he wrapped his head, placing another box above his one prodigious eyebrow.

"You look like a Jewish coal miner," Spencer said.

Sam grabbed him by the forearm with a bony hand. "There is nothing funny about this," their grandfather said. "Many Jews died for these beliefs. You may not care right now about your heritage but you must always remember that you are Jewish. No matter what anyone else says."

"Why would anyone say we weren't Jewish?" Spencer asked. He also thought: why would anyone care?

He and Phillip exchanged glances that said: humor the old man. Get this over with as soon as possible, maybe there'll be time to go to the Seaquarium.

"Nobody is saying that," Sam said. "But if it happens someday you will need to be clear. Your mother is Jewish dating back centuries. In our religion, heritage follows the mother. You should always know who you are and where you came from: a Jew, from a long line of Jews."

"Okay, Papa," Spencer said.

After a lunch of pastrami sandwiches their grandfather took them bowling and read a book while they bowled. He didn't understand why they had to rent shoes when the boys already had shoes. He would have preferred staying home and reading, he'd told them, and Phillip knew he meant so they could all be together without needing to interact.

When they got back to the condo, the women were in the living room drinking tea and eating chocolate-covered coconut patties. Boxes and bags from the mall lay scattered on the white carpet.

Leah jumped up, eager to show off her purchases. She danced around the living room in her new swimsuit, singing, "The bastards are home, the bastards are home!"

"Leah! That's not nice," Phyllis shouted.

Leah was alarmed. "But it's what daddy says," she cried. "I'm not being mean."

"I hadn't remembered that," Phillip said.

"I don't think she meant anything by it," Spencer said. "There's no way she knew what it meant. She was nine or ten years old. *We* didn't know what it meant—I thought she was saying 'bastards' as if she meant we were big meanies."

"Which wasn't true either," Phillip said.

"You're right. Maybe it didn't even mean that to her. Maybe she thought it was a pet name, a twisted endearment. Like saying, 'Could you pass the sugar, cocksucker'. But I think it's something she probably *did* hear her father say."

"So you think everybody knew. Way back then?"

"Of course they knew. They figured out what we're figuring out now. That Mom had two kids, and neither one of them could have been fathered by her husband. It had to be obvious."

"Maybe that's why Uncle Jerry never liked us. Not because we weren't Jewish enough. But because to him our bloodline was diluted with Guinness."

"Or in my case, Rioja," Spencer said. "And maybe he didn't approve of the way mom conducted her life."

"I don't blame Leah for the whole 'bastards' episode. She wasn't well socialized. She was an only child."

"She had a silent film star for a father, and Godzilla for a mother," Spencer said.

"Our mom was an only parent—which you don't hear about nearly as often. She did the best she could."

"Did she?" Spencer asked.

"I have no idea," Phillip said.

Chapter Twenty-One
Limerick

AT BREAKFAST THE BOYS sat among well-dressed hipsters and the usual coterie of stoic French families, jeans-wearing Americans in ball caps, and a group of Japanese tourists who carefully picked at the strange food on their plates.

The waiter, a tall Somali with a soft beautiful accent and a nametag that said 'Siobhan,' came over to see if everything was all right.

"All good, Siobhan," Spencer said. But he pronounced the man's name Sigh-O-Bonn.

"You know that's pronounced Shiv-on?" Phillip said. "Accent on the on."

The waiter nodded. His gold earrings shone against his black skin.

"Whaaaat? That doesn't make any sense. Are you sure?" Spencer said.

"Pretty positive." Phillip said. "Shiv-on?"

"That is correct," Siobhan said. "In most cases it's the name of a woman. But not this time."

"Really? Shiv-on? How was I supposed to get to that? You might as well just spell the whole thing with question marks!"

"That, sir," Siobhan said, "is the first funny thing anyone has ever said about it." They would get to know Siobhan a little in their short time at the hotel. After breakfast, Spencer would ask him if they had any flan, and whether the waiter could bring it to his brother with a candle.

The coffee was strong, the brothers happily noticed, and they partook liberally. Phillip was avoiding discussion about heading for Ballydraiocht later that day.

"I want to ask you something," Spencer said. Despite a light stubble he had the confused early morning look of a little boy.

"Okay."

"The moustaches." He paused a beat. "And the beards?'

"Yeah?"

"I'm trying to figure out. Are they supposed to be ironic?'

"I don't understand," Phillip said. Spencer had sported a goatee, always trimmed short, for many years, but when it became a hipster marker he got rid of it.

Spencer glanced around the room—partly for effect, partly to see if there were any gingers nearby to admire.

"The young guys sitting at that table . . . " He inclined his head toward the corner, where two men were drinking Prosecco from a blue bottle. One had a handlebar moustache waxed to bayonet sharpness. The other boasted a crazy long red beard, like one of the wildings in *Game of Thrones*.

"Do they sport that absurd facial hair because they love it, or because they think that it looks great? Or are they trying to be funny? Like they're making fun of a time when that was in style—you know, like a hundred years ago? And that it's become so uncool that it's cool again in a retro way? Like women wearing high-waisted jeans from the seventies again? Like the return of vinyl records? Like trendy restaurants serving Brussels sprouts?"

Phillip was focused on the black pudding on his plate. What was it made of? Why did they call it black pudding? It wasn't pudding-like at all. "I have no idea what you're talking about. And no, I'm not being ironic," he said.

"Never mind then," Spencer said, turning back to his eggs and roasted sausage, his baked beans and his tiny cubes of potatoes. "So what about Ballydraiocht? Is today the day?"

"It is," Phillip said.

"But you're not happy about it."

"I'm not."

"Excited?"

"No"

"Terrified?"

Phillip nodded.

"Dark cloud of dread?"

"Yes."

"A little sick to your stomach?"

"Yep."

"Want to skip the whole thing? Just play some golf?"

"Yep. But I'm not going to."

"I know you're not. But you want to establish the baseline feelings."

"Yep."

"You're going on record."

"Uh-huh."

"You feel too old to be facing these emotions. You'd like to get them out in the open and move on."

"I'd like you to take a trip up Shut Fuck Mountain."

"Huh?"

"Could you please just shut the fuck up?" Phillip said.

Phillip had enjoyed their two days in Dublin but the prospect of a third felt like drudgery. Now that he was rested up from traveling and adjusted to the time change he'd become restless. When their rental car was delivered to the street out front of the hotel the brothers were packed and ready to go.

Neither he nor Spencer was a particularly good driver. Even worse, Spencer thought that he *was* good. At Phillip's suggestion they decided to alternate every hour or two. And each of them retained the right to call for the other to step aside.

Did the bad driving come from their mother, as Aunt Phyllis theorized? Spencer had been reading about emotional inheritance in his DNA studies. If they *had* inherited bad driving from Jenny, was it because the trauma of losing her brother out the back of the truck had imprinted on genes that she'd passed along to them? *Or,* since she was a lousy driver, and she'd taught them how to drive, had she merely set a bad example? Was there a gene that itself imparted compromised motor skills? Or did they all just *happen to be* lousy drivers as a matter of coincidence?

Spencer volunteered to get them out of the city. He climbed into the left side of the car, where he expected to find all the crucial machinery like the ignition and the gas pedal. Phillip stood on the curb watching with amusement.

Spencer climbed back out and said, "Okay, very funny," and then walked around the vehicle and climbed in on the driver's side. "Stupid British cars," he mumbled, even though it was a German car.

They followed the road out of Dublin, their GPS describing

upcoming turns with an Irish accent they could almost always understand. Spencer had reserved them a broad, muscular, low-slung
Mercedes that he described as the kind of car hit-men drove.

As they made their way to the M7 Spencer said, "What the feck?
The road ends in a big fecking circle?"

"It's a traffic circle. A roundabout," Phillip said.

"Which way am I supposed to go?"

"Go left!" Phillip said as Spencer started to go right.

"And look the *other* way. Traffic is *coming* from the right."

"That makes no fucking sense at all," Spencer said, and Phillip
knew that his brother was flustered, because he forgot to say 'fecking.'

Spencer swerved to avoid a car he didn't anticipate coming from
what he still considered the wrong direction. They entered the circle,
missed their exit, and went around again.

And again.

"I can't fucking get out of here," Spencer yelled. "I'm going around
again!"

"Go left up there." Phillip pointed. "But get in the *left* lane."

More swerving until they ended up on the motorway headed in
the correct direction.

"Do not even get me started about this," Spencer said. "Driving
on the other side of the road? For what fecking purpose? To what
end? Just to be different? If they want to be different let them grow
ironic beards and moustaches."

Spencer stuck to the right lane until he realized that was the faster,
passing lane, then shifted to the left.

"Did you ever think about this?" Spencer said. He was driving
comfortably now, one hand on the wheel. "You're walking down
the middle of a narrow sidewalk in Dublin and there's a fat guy
coming the other way. You know there isn't room for both of you in
the middle so you have to move over to one side. Since you're in a
British Commonwealth country—or at least a country that *used* to
be a British Commonwealth country; who can even keep track of
this shite?—where they drive on the wrong side for feck's sake, do
you move to the right or to the left so you can both pass?

"I always thought that moving to the right was the correct thing,"
he went on. "That all humans would understand this like it was part of
our genetic code. Like the thing that tells us not to breathe underwater.

Or put cheese on apple pie, although some idiots violate the rules.

"But maybe we do it because we also drive on the fecking correct side? So my question is: in countries where they don't know where to drive, how can they know the first thing about where to *walk*? I'm surprised there aren't more pedestrian accidents in the British Isles and Protectorates. Whatever a protectorate is. Someone should do a study."

They stopped at a gas station—which Spencer was calling 'a bloody petrol station'—in Limerick to stretch their legs. Spencer was eager to go inside the Quick Mart to see what kinds of treats were on offer. Did they have slushies? Corn dogs? Were these universal? What was the candy like? Would there be sports drinks the colors of urine and transmission fluid?

They detoured through Limerick to get a look at St. Johns Castle and St. Mary's Cathedral and all the other saintly shite, as Spencer put it.

As they drove alongside the River Shannon, Spencer said, "Why do they call it the River Shannon, instead of the Shannon River?"

"They were here first. Before we started naming things in America," Phillip said.

"Yeah, but the Romans were early too. Did they drive their chariots on the other side of the road? Why don't you ever hear anything about that? I just don't see Hadrian bowing down to all this Anglo-Saxon fuckery."

Phillip looked out the window at sheep and green hills and the river flowing out of those hills and past those sheep. He admired the architecture of stone walls.

"And hey, since we're in Limerick . . ." Spencer said, "Do you remember my friend Rod? From Nantucket . . . ?"

"I think I do," Phillip said. Then he said, "A wonderful bird is the Pelican. His bill can hold more than his belly can. He can take in his beak enough food for a week, but fuck me if I can see how the heli-can."

Spencer shifted in his seat, hoping that moving around would keep his back from hurting. "That's a classic. I've got one more. A theme Limerick for our trip."

"Okay."

"An amoeba named Phillip and his brother were sharing a dram with each other. In the midst of their quaffing they split themselves laughing. And each of them now is a mother."

"It would be more apt if there was something that rhymed with father," Phillip said.

"That depends on which parent you think we're really looking for."

———————

They arrived in Ballydraiocht in the evening, as the sun dipped toward the sea. The air was dead calm and smelled like bouillabaisse.

They checked into their bed and breakfast with its views over the beach and the golf course beyond. They ordered pints of Guinness at the small lobby bar and carried them out behind the building and sat in old wooden chairs facing the water. They lit cigars from Phillip's travel humidor. A three-quarter moon appeared through thin clouds, waiting for its chance to shine when the sun finally set.

"Do you want to go over and snoop around the golf club?" Spencer asked. "Get the lay of the land?" He licked creamy Guinness foam from his upper lip.

"I don't think so," Phillip said. "I'll be ready tomorrow, but I'm not ready now." He puffed on his stogie, a small Cohiba that tasted chocolaty.

"You need to drink a Guinness and smoke a Dominican cigar. I totally get that," Spencer said. "Any idea what might happen tomorrow?"

"Nothing. Nada. Bubkus. No idea," Phillip said.

"Well, all right then."

"I want it to happen organically."

"I get that. I feel you, my brother."

"You feel me?"

"I catch your drift. I'm picking up what you're laying down. I'm hip to your square."

"Nobody says any of those things," Phillip said.

"I read you like a book, bro."

"Okay. I get it."

"And just so you know," Spencer said, taking a long puff on his cigar and exhaling an atmosphere's worth of bluish smoke, "I'm fecking nervous, too—and he's not even going to turn out to be my father."

Chapter Twenty-Two

Padraig

After the full Irish breakfast in the sun room of their B&B, Spencer was ready to drive to the golf club but Phillip kept procrastinating. He changed from gray slacks to khakis to jeans and then carried his golf clubs out to the car and then put them back in his room, and then dragged them back out to the car again. He changed his clothes one more time back to khakis and his favorite golf shirt with the puffin logo from Bandon Dunes.

"I have no idea what we're doing here," he announced. "This is probably all a giant mistake."

"It's just a golf course," Spencer said. "The worst that can happen is you'll lose a few balls."

They drove to the club along narrow country lanes with hedges and stone walls seeming to wander right into the road. Sheep bleated in the fields and the brothers could taste brine on the breeze through the open car windows. Smoke wisped out of chimneys and, as Spencer observed, all that *David Copperfield* sort of crap.

They parked in the gravel lot close to the modern clubhouse. They'd decided to get coffee in the dining room—you could never have too much coffee, Spencer said—and get a feel for the place.

They sat at a small table between the long, worn bar and the giant plate glass window. While Phillip watched foursomes practicing on the putting green, Spencer admired two wooden boards on the wall, hung between oil paintings of the golf course—one listing the names of the captains of the club going back more than one hundred years, one with the names of former club champions.

As he scanned the lists he noted several Elliots. Padraig Elliot won the club championship in 2015, a year before he became club captain. He also won the championship in 2011, 2009, 2008, and 2006. Back in the seventies and eighties, Patrick Elliot won the championship six times and was captain for four years.

On another board on the wall opposite, he saw that the women's club championship—which only went back to 1930—had been won four times by Patricia Elliot.

Could this be wacky coincidence, as Spencer had been half advocating as an explanation for some of the current strangeness of their lives? But *this many* Elliots for feck's sake? And did everyone in the whole fecking country have a first name that was abbreviated as 'Pat'?

While Spencer pondered, Phillip got up and asked the barman if they happened to have an old golf pro who'd been at the club for a long time. A very long time. He said he knew it was a strange question.

Before the barkeep could answer, a well-dressed man standing at the end of the bar said, "Is it a golf lesson you're looking for, then?" He appeared to be a few years younger than Phillip, with short gray-black hair and a clear, healthy complexion. He was enormously fit, his tailored shirt outlining the kind of powerful forearms that could drive a golf ball a long way.

"I'm looking for a fellow who might have been a pro here in the 1960s or 1970s. We may have some friends in common," Phillip said.

"Ah, you're American," the man observed. "Well, that would have to be old Patrick you're looking for. He's a legend around here. Old as dirt. Worked at the club pretty much since time began." Then he added, "That would also be my da."

"I've heard he's a very good instructor," Phillip said. He stepped back and bumped into the bar stool behind him.

"Aye, and still a real student of the game. You can usually find him here in the bar around half four—he's out playing on the new course today." Which in Ireland, Phillip knew, could mean it was built in 1870.

He returned to the table like a man trying out new legs. His hand trembled as he picked up his coffee, then set it down again with a clatter.

"There's an old pro . . . " Phillip said. "Usually comes in around half four. That's four thirty."

"Yeah, I heard. I was sitting right here," he said.

"We could wait. Or come back tomorrow. Or never."

"There's something else you should know," Spencer said. He pointed at the club champions' board and the captains' board and the women's club championship board. "This place is silly with Elliots," he whispered.

CHAPTER TWENTY-THREE
Patrick

THEY RETURNED TO THEIR hotel for a few hours, then went back to the club at four. They'd come this far, Spencer reasoned. They were old and unlikely to return here. The old man was even older, if in fact he was the correct old man. Not going back, Spencer argued, would be like watching two hours of *The Crying Game* but skipping the ending.

The bar was crowded with golfers coming off their rounds—mostly loud Americans with Ryder Cup caps pulled low describing every shot they'd hit all day even though their companions had seen them hit every one of these shots the first time. Small packs of locals gathered close as if to shut out the noisy intruders. The brothers ordered pints of Guinness and waited.

Just before five, the man they'd seen at the bar that morning came in with six other men of various ages, including a well-groomed older gentleman in sporty Travis Mathews golf wear who, Spencer recognized immediately, had Phillip's own warm smile and deep-set green eyes. The shapes of their faces were the same. This might be what Phillip would look like in twenty-five years if his hair turned white and he spent most of that time out in the wind and the sun. Spencer felt sad seeing his brother as an old man.

"Ah, Da, here's the fellow who was looking for a golf lesson this morning," they heard the younger man say when he noticed the brothers at the bar. He pointed at Phillip then disappeared into another group of men sitting on the far side of the room.

"You're Patrick?" Phillip managed to choke out before tears began streaming down his face.

"Ah, son," the old man said. "It can't be that bad. Is it the shanks? The yips? I'm sure I can help you." He put a calloused hand on Phillip's shoulder.

It wasn't lost on Spencer that the first word they heard the man utter was 'son'.

"I'm from America," Phillip said, wiping at his eyes. Other Irishmen came closer to hear where this was going. They stood with their hands in their pockets or examined their cell phones.

"Yes. I might have guessed," the pro said.

"Did you happen to know a woman named Jenny Elliot? Jenny Bernstein?" Phillip asked, as if he and the pro were alone in the room. "I'm Phillip Elliot. Jenny was my mother."

The pro looked at Phillip intently, as if tracking back in his memory, searching for something he'd misplaced a long time ago. He looked tired, like his years had not always been easy ones. Like he was trying to work up the energy for something difficult.

"Jesus tap-dancing Christ, you must be Philly," the old man said, using the nickname Phillip had insisted his mother stop calling him by in the third grade. The pro's eyes pooled up and water began rolling down his weathered face and he put his head in his hands; a lifetime of tears began to fall through his fingers.

Chapter Twenty-Four

Keyser Söze

Patrick yelled, "It's my son! The boy's my *son!*"

He grasped Phillip's elbow and led him to the leather club chairs by the window. They sat close, facing each other. Somebody went to the bar calling for shots of Jameson for the house, which came back in crystal barware sporting the Ballydraiocht logo.

The older man held Phillip's hand in his own big mitt. He yelled, "Where's Padraig? Hey, Padraig! Come over here . . . and meet your brother!"

From somewhere down the bar they heard Padraig call back, "Ah, Da, not another one!" Then the graying, well-dressed man Phillip and Spencer had seen earlier in the day came over to where they gathered.

"It must be that you're Jenny's boy," Padraig said. He offered his hand and when Phillip reached to shake it Padraig pulled him out of his chair and put his arms around him.

"We've known about you for some time," Padraig said. "But we didn't think we'd ever see you."

Then he turned to Spencer, standing behind Phillip's chair. "And who's this one, then?" Padraig asked.

"I'm the half wit half brother," Spencer said.

Padraig turned to his father and their green eyes locked. "Are we related to this one, too, then?' Padraig asked. "We've almost enough for a rugby side with the others now, haven't we?"

"Your mother wrote me when you were born," Patrick said to Spencer. "It was the last time I heard from her, all those years ago. Until she started calling recently, that is. She also left a few phone messages here at the club, but she never picked up when I called back. How is she getting on now, anyway? And why d'you think she finally told you boys about me?"

"She's not great," Spencer said, and then Phillip added quickly that she was dead.

"She didn't tell us anything," Phillip continued, and then explained about her late senility, and how she inexplicably gave up 'Ballydraiocht' and 'a golf pro' near the end. "Or maybe she did reveal it intentionally. We don't know," Phillip said.

The old pro looked down at the weathered oak floor. "I'm sorry to hear it. I'd always hoped to see her again. I was surprised when she started calling after all those years. She told me she had the dementia and wasn't sure how long she'd remember things. She told me it was okay if I wanted to connect to you. On the last call she talked about coming over to see me. But I think she was confused and thought I was Jack. She asked why I'd never come back to her. From Vietnam. It was heartbreaking."

"Jack?" Phillip said. He turned to look at his brother, who arched his single dark eyebrow like a question mark. Then Phillip turned back to the old man. *His* old man, as it turned out. "You knew Jack? Jack Elliot? Our father? I mean, our mother's husband?"

"Did I know him?" Now Patrick looked confused. "Did you not know that he was *my* brother? That I'm Jack's brother?" He squinted his eyes in a way that Phillip sometimes did.

"Wait, let me make sure I've got this right," Spencer interjected. "It's not that we're totally unrelated to the man we thought our whole lives was our father—it's just that he was our uncle? Or at least Phillip's uncle?"

"Did you never hear the whole story from anyone, then?" Patrick asked.

Telling an Irishman you hadn't heard a story was like telling a Jewish grandmother you hadn't eaten all day, Spencer thought, but kept this to himself.

Phillip explained how Jack Elliot's photo had stood on the mantle through their childhoods and they'd always been told that he was their father. Father to both of them.

Spencer added, "Until Phillip basically started his own detective agency and we followed the trail to where we are now."

"She wanted it that way from the start," Patrick said. "For nobody to know. Of course her family knew that you weren't Jack's baby. But nobody knew *I* was your father, and she figured it best that everyone else thought her dead husband was your da.

"She did it to protect you, I suppose. Better to have a war hero than a disillusioned golf pro for a da. But when she called last year she'd changed her mind. After half a century. She broke my heart saying she wished she'd done it all differently. That she wished she'd let me be a father to you. I told her it wasn't too late. She didn't seem like herself there at the end. But I didn't want to appear to you out of nowhere—I thought I'd wait to see if you found me. And now here we are."

"Who was she?" Spencer said. "If she wasn't herself toward the end?"

When nobody answered he said, "I mean it: who *was* she? Even when she still *was* herself? The Mayor of Crazytown? Keyser Söze? It doesn't make any sense. Why would she lie to us about our own father?"

"Oh, Keyser Söze," Padraig said, breaking a smile. "That's a good one."

"Your mother loved Jack," Patrick continued. "And she must have loved you boys. She never loved me—there wasn't ever time for it.

"I loved him too, my brother Jack. We didn't intend for anything to happen between us, Jenny and me, but we were left comforting each other over the loss of him. We knew he was gone from us when he first went missing. Something felt broken and we were certain that's what it was. Nobody else in the family would consider it, which pushed us together. He was so young, that boy. He had a bright future. He was the best of us.

"That was a senseless war America was fighting. I was disillusioned and felt homesick for Ireland, though I'd never been. I moved over here and started working at the golf club right before Jenny learned she was pregnant. We thought our tryst was a one-time thing. A kind of send-off for someone we both loved.

"Then she flew over to see me, unannounced, to tell me about the baby coming," Patrick continued. "I offered to be a father to you in any way Jenny wanted. She was a different kind of girl, different for back then, anyway. She chose to raise you herself, among her own people. She didn't want money or support unless I was going to come back to America, and I just couldn't.

"Even though Long Island was my birthplace I never felt at home there. When I returned to Ireland after Jack was lost to us I knew I was meant to be here. I asked Jenny to stay. A child is something you can build a life around. But it wasn't what she wanted—although I don't think she knew what she wanted.

"That was a hard time for the lot of us. I'm glad she changed her mind before it was too late. It must've given her peace toward the end."

He wiped his eyes again and reached for his glass of Guinness and took a hearty draught.

———

They stayed late at the golf club drinking. Spencer noticed that the loud Americans had finished their early alcohol consumption and headed off to dinners and probably jokes about mushy peas and further talk about brilliant bunker shots and long putts made. The locals had left for home, to their wives and kids and football matches on the television.

After more Guinness, food appeared—plates of pasties and bangers and chips and other pub fare. Padraig, it turned out, was the club manager. They gathered around a table in the dining room, telling stories, which reminded them of other stories, which often recalled other stories yet still.

Patrick told them how beautiful and wild their mother was, and what a mismatch she first seemed with the serious and upright Jack. "I remember Jenny wearing his uniform jacket at a party back on Long Island and saluting a lot, before he went off to war," he recalled.

"She called him 'Senator,' because we all believed that's where he was headed some day—like Jack Kennedy. She joked that she'd be America's first beatnik first lady—they weren't using the word 'hippie' yet, I don't think—and that she would put banners against war on the White House lawn. It gives me a chill to remember Jack saying—only half kidding—'Over my dead body.' Not long after that he *was* dead."

Padraig, the pro's son, recalled the first time their father told them about Jenny and their brother in America. "We already had all the brothers we needed right here," he said. "We didn't pay it much mind. Our mother had always known. I remember asking Da one time if we were really all his children. He said, 'Well, you're certainly special, Padraig, but you were no immaculate conception.'"

Patrick and his wife Lorna raised five boys and a girl, but only Padraig and Patricia—whom they called Trisha—still lived in Bal-lydraiocht, hence their frequent appearance on the captains and champions boards at the club. The others had gone off to bigger cities around the UK and Europe, Padraig said.

With the beatnik first lady story in mind Phillip described the time that Jenny took Spencer and him out to Shoreham, on eastern Long Island, to protest nuclear power when they were kids, and how Spencer had been confused and upset by that. The boys knew that they didn't have a traditional family without a father, but Spencer was surprised that Jenny would want to march about it.

"I thought we were going there to protest against the nuclear *family*," Spencer explained.

When it finally grew dark, and the tide had come in, and they could hear the susurration of waves on the beach, Padraig said, "Where are you staying, then? We should move you over to Da's house. There are all those empty bedrooms."

"We're at The Golfside," Phillip said. While he wanted to give in to the invitation, to fall backward into their hospitality, he felt cautious. He wanted to look out for his brother. It was his lifelong job. He had no idea how Spencer was feeling about all this.

"Why don't we stay where we are for now," Phillip said. "There's a lot to think about. To process. But it's a kind offer."

"Bollox on thinking," Padraig boomed. "You're family now. Whether you like it or not."

"Yes, and we'll still be family in the morning," his father interrupted. "But you'll come over to the house tomorrow for supper when you've had a few hours to sort through things?"

Spencer shook his head and downed his shot of Jameson. "I can't come if there's going to be alcohol," he announced.

"Oh, I like this one," Padraig said. He put his arm around Spencer. "I've given up alcohol as well," he added, lifting his glass and draining the last of it. "At least until breakfast."

As they were breaking up the party, Patrick asked, "Hey, do you boys fancy a game of golf this week? Or perhaps a playing lesson with an aging pro?" and Phillip and Spencer both said, simultaneously, "Well, my brother probably does."

Chapter Twenty-Five
Rosalind

PHILLIP AND SPENCER MET down in the breakfast room. The innkeeper brought coffee and a small pitcher of hot milk, and then their full Irish breakfasts appeared.

"Fuck me in a bathtub, who ever decided it was a good idea to eat canned baked beans for breakfast?" Spencer asked. "And not just once in a while, but every fecking day?"

Phillip pushed a fatty sausage around on his plate, past the eggs and the black pudding, the beans and the sautéed mushrooms. He didn't look up at his brother. He said, "We should probably talk about yesterday."

"What happened yesterday?" Spencer asked.

"We can still call this whole thing off at any moment," Phillip said. "We could go home. I could fly back over here some other time. We could go to Spain—check into that posada Mom used to stay at and start looking for *your* father."

"No need to patronize the retard brother *now*," Spencer said. "You've got a whole new family to worry about."

"I don't have a new family. You're my family."

"No, you do. And I'm not mad—you've found exactly what you always wanted. If you could have used a sextant and a protractor and an Excel spreadsheet to pinpoint the exact coordinates of a father, that's all you ever needed your whole life. And you did it. You got the definitive answer you've been searching for. And it took some brilliant investigative work!"

"A sextant?" Phillip said.

"I don't even know what that is—but you get my point."

"And what do *you* need?" Phillip asked. "You volunteered for this trip—you weren't drafted. What did *you* want to happen?"

"This is one way we've always been different. For whatever reason—DNA or whatever—you've always needed to know about your father. I've preferred not to. That's part of what makes me the lovable, irreverent genius I am today. I tried to want it, but I just don't. I pictured this happening differently. I'm here mostly for you."

"How did you picture it?"

"I thought I was finally going to be at the center of something. Or we both were. But here I am, an outsider all over again. Like I've been my whole life. I thought I'd end up belonging to a clan, a crew. A posse. Something bigger than me. But now *you* belong to something and I still don't. I don't begrudge it, but I'm even more alone than I was before, and the one person I was in this with is now part of something I'm excluded from. I know I'm being selfish but I'm like the Rosalind Franklin of this whole story."

"I have no idea who that is."

The innkeeper delivered what Spencer thought of as a chrome mail sorter full of brown and white toast, and the boys slathered the slices with butter and jam. Two other couples entered the dining room and sat down at a nearby table. They were dressed for a golf expedition, in thick argyle sweaters and wool pants. Spencer wondered what they wore in winter.

"Rosalind Franklin was the villain in Watson's *The Double Helix*."

"The book about DNA has a villain?"

"She insisted Crick and Watson were wrong. She was a non-believer. She got left out of the whole thing. Nobody says 'Crick and Watson and Franklin.' There was no room for her."

"So you're a non-believer?"

"Not exactly. I don't doubt the science, or the structure they found. Or the adorable x-ray photos."

"What else is there?"

"That's the thing! We don't know what else! But whatever it is, I'm being left out!"

"Look, let's book a flight to Seville for tomorrow. We can work on that part of the equation."

Spencer dismissed his brother's offer with a shrug. "And what? Hang out in tapas bars asking if anyone knows a handsome, humorous Iberian man with one eyebrow? I really appreciate that. But I'm cool for now, big bro. You're the one who wanted to talk about it." He looked down at his food. "I'm just not sure how many more times I can bear someone saying 'Sláinte' and hoisting a glass of whisky in my face."

They drank more coffee. Spencer ate hungrily. Phillip played with his food some more.

Phillip said, "I'm angry at Mom at the same time that I'm grateful for all this. She worked hard protecting us all those years."

"Protecting us how?" Spencer asked. He'd decided he would be satisfied coming out of this with some better understanding of their mother. Her misdirection was working again, he recognized—she'd taken the spotlight off of herself without her sons noticing.

"I guess I don't even know if she *was* protecting us, or someone else," Phillip continued. "Or from what. Or who. We don't know anything about Patrick Elliot. Does it matter if he's my father? I don't need a new father. What's he going to do, give me an allowance and pay for college? Teach me to hit a golf ball? He already missed all that. What's the big deal about genetics if he wasn't there for the past fifty years? First he was a pilot who died in a fiery crash five decades ago, and now he's suddenly some drooling old golf pro? What am I supposed to do with that?"

"Which question should I answer first?" Spencer said. But his brother continued as if he wasn't there.

"And Padraig? Now he's my brother? What the fuck? *You're* my brother. He's not my brother. He doesn't know anything about me. He didn't teach me to ride a motorbike when I was too young and ended up breaking my leg. He didn't smoke weed with me for the first time and nearly get me arrested. He probably doesn't know who Agent 99 was, or Captain Parmenter, or . . . Broadstreet, was it? The blind detective?"

"Longstreet," Spencer said.

"Who needs a brother like that? Where's the fun in it? Is this really what we wanted all these years? An Irish golf pro?"

"You've been waiting for this opportunity for your whole life," Spencer said. "Like in a badly-written sports movie where you practice kicking field goals over the clothesline in some dirty urban back yard and now the coach is sending you in to win the big game and save the town. Why don't you just let this play out. You've solved a major clue. Why not see where it leads next?"

"I'm afraid," Phillip said. "What if finding my father doesn't change anything? You're right: I've achieved a life-long goal. But not having it change anything changes things."

"That sounds like something I would say," Spencer said. "Meaning it doesn't make sense. What's finding your father supposed to change?"

"Who I am?"

"Oh, Phillip," Spencer said. "Is that what you're after?"

"I wanted to be complete," Phillip explained. "I wanted to fill that empty spot where a father was supposed to be. But now suddenly it doesn't matter—even after all this effort. I made a giant tactical error. I've been looking in the wrong place! I've been saving myself for the wrong person. Maybe we should pack it in and go home before we make this worse."

"I don't know about you," Spencer said, "but I could really use the golf lesson."

Chapter Twenty-Six

Moors

AFTER BREAKFAST SPENCER SAID, "I'm going to hike around the moors for an hour or two. Get some exercise. Not that I know what a moor is, or if they have any here."

Not long after he disappeared over a rise heading toward the ocean in his shorts and low Feit hand-stitched boots and a fleece shirt, the phone rang in Phillip's room.

"Good morning to you, Phillip," Padraig said cheerily.

"Morning, Padraig." Phillip looked out over the calm sea, expecting what: A submarine to break the surface? A whale? It would take a lot to surprise him at this point.

"Quite a day it was yesterday, Phillip. Quite a day, no?"

"Yes, quite a day. My hangover has a hangover."

"I wanted to see how you're getting on this morning, and if you and your brother fancy that round of golf. Or maybe you want to come over to the club for lunch?"

"Spencer just left for a hike," Phillip said. "I don't know when he'll be back."

"I hope you're okay with how things went yesterday." Padraig said. "I know we can come on a bit strong sometimes. I hope we didn't offend you or Spencer in any way."

"Of course not," Phillip said. He was traversing unknown terrain between his brothers, the real one he'd had for so long, and the new one that he didn't fully believe in yet.

"Well, so you know. You're family to us now, and he is as well."

"That's a generous position. We appreciate it."

"It's not generous. It's how we are. But you boys do what you need to. As long as you both know that you're most welcome."

"Thank you," Phillip said.

"A word of warning, though," Padraig said.

Here it comes, Phillip thought.

"My da is vulnerable when it comes to sons. We lost one some years ago. My brother Devon. The youngest. He flew out the back of a truck that Da was driving and broke his neck. He was only fourteen. Da's been trying to replace him since—as if he ever could. Always inviting our friends in as if they were family. To fill the hole, you see. It's like he's trying to take a mulligan. A do-over, I think you Americans would say."

"I'm not trying to scare you away, Phillip. I thought you should know. If you were to start getting close and then left us, well, it might be hard on him. He's not as robust as he lets on."

"Thanks for telling me," Phillip said.

"You're most welcome," Padraig said, "my brother."

Chapter Twenty-Seven
Mick Jagger

PHILLIP SAT OUT BEHIND the hotel as the sun climbed against a backdrop of rolling green hills. He read *The New York Times* and answered email on his laptop.

His ex-wife Marty asked how his 'vacation' was. Marty had reached out via phone and email a couple of times since their bagel shop encounter: she knew that losing his mother loomed large for him.

Phillip had mentioned the trip to Ireland without disclosing its true purpose. Now he wrote back to say that they'd finished the Dublin part of their journey and were headed off into the golfing wilds.

But why be so secretive—so like his mother—Phillip thought? It hadn't served him well, particularly in his relationship with Marty. He sent another email explaining about finding his dad.

His computer pinged. Marty answered immediately.

"Details?!" she wrote.

"Too much to go into right now," Phillip typed back.

"I am giving you that *look*," Marty wrote. The look was her way of showing hurt, disappointment, hopelessness in their relationship. Marty had weaponized that look. It was a symbol of the failure of their marriage.

He wrote back, typing maniacally, explaining everything from his mother's cryptic clue about Ballydraiocht to his encounter with Patrick at the golf club. It was early morning in New York. Phillip imagined Marty wearing dark tailored suit pants—with subtle white stripes—and a long cream-colored silk shirt. Pearls. She was at her office before anyone else, with her feet on her desk, laptop propped on her thighs, promoting some actress or new band that everyone would be talking about shortly.

"That must be hard," Marty wrote back. "How does it *feel*?"

How do you fucking *think* it feels, he thought, but wrote: "Empty? Painful?" What answer could she be looking for?

"Can you give me an analogy? Angry pain? Sad Pain? More like *Kramer vs. Kramer* or *Sophie's Choice*?"

"Why the Meryl Streep movies?"

"I'm not letting you get sidetracked. Pick your own fucking movie analogy," she wrote.

"*Field of Dreams*?" Phillip wrote. "Where the dead father comes out of the cornfield and they play catch? Sappy, I know. But that's what it feels like to have a dead father."

"Except *your* father's not dead. You just met him. Anything's possible. What do you want from this?"

"I miss my mother," Phillip said for the first time, ever, to anyone. "I want to be close to just one person in this life. Is that so much to ask for? I wish we were still together."

"You and your mom?" Marty asked.

"You and me," Phillip wrote.

––––––––––––

When Spencer came back—glowing with endorphins and smelling of cigar smoke—he had the wild hair and wide eyes of a kid just off some ridiculous carnival ride.

"I was thinking we could head over to the golf club and hit a few balls," he said. "See if they can squeeze us in for a quick round? You know—brother vs. brother, with the fate of the free world hanging in the balance?"

Phillip didn't mention the phone call from Padraig. Why cause more strife for Spencer, which would in turn cause more strife for *him*.

They drove to the club with their golf gear in the trunk—or, 'the boot,' as Spencer was now calling it. They brought changes of clothes since they had no idea where this day might lead them. Supper at the Elliot house was set for seven thirty—half seven—after which they would all go to the pub together to hear live Irish music.

When Phillip pulled the Mercedes into the parking lot Padraig was out front in a pair of sharply creased corduroy slacks and a cashmere Ballydraiocht sweater talking with some of the caddies. In their stained white jump suits they looked like inmates getting ready to pick up trash along the highway.

Padraig greeted the brothers with warm handshakes, a palm on their shoulders. Spencer noted it was like waking up with a woman you didn't know well but had spent the night with. They were careful and polite around each other, uncertain of exactly how far their intimacies extended. It had been easier to navigate in a fog of Guinness and Jameson.

"Did you bring your golf clubs, then?" Padraig inquired. "Maybe you'd like some coffee and a ploughman's plate and we'll see where we can fit you in on the tee sheet?"

"We were thinking we'd hit a few balls. It's been a while for both of us," Phillip said.

"Not a problem at all. We've not a driving range as you know it in America. But there's a teaching area where you can warm up—just try not to hit any sheep."

The boys looked at each other.

"I'm joking about the sheep," Padraig said.

"Speaking of which," Spencer said. "I have to ask…"

"Go on then."

"We passed a fair number of sheep in the fields on the way over. They were all spray-painted with a colored dot. Different colors, too—blue, red, and green, mostly. My theory is the color represents the color of the sweater they're going to be made into?"

"It's not exactly like that," Padraig laughed. "But I'm glad you asked. It's because farmers share their grazing land. One farmer picks a color so he knows which sheep are his when it comes time to split them all up again, to shear, or to send to market. I suppose it's so the farmer doesn't need to get to know them as individuals—you know, like, there's Joe, there's Bobby.

"They also tie a bag of dye onto the rams in mating season. That way when the rams mount a ewe the farmers know which one was mounted by whose ram."

"That raises another question," Spencer said. "Do you know the difference between Mick Jagger and an Irishman?"

"I've no idea," Padraig said.

Phillip shook his head with trepidation.

"Well," Spencer said, "Mick Jagger sings, 'Hey, you, get off of my cloud . . . Whereas an Irishman says, 'Hey, MacCloud! Get off of my ewe!'"

"Oh, my," sighed Padraig, grinning with Phillip's own handsome smile.

———————

Padraig set them up in the clubhouse bar with bowls of cullen skink—a hearty smoked fish soup—a plate of sandwiches, and steaming mugs of coffee. He left them to dine alone because he had meetings to attend, but offered to join them if he could out on the practice tee or the golf course.

The boys watched club members in the bar who seemed so happy to see each other. It was like a small town in Iowa in 1950, Spencer said. Which reminded Phillip about Marty; could things be different? Could *he* be different? Now that his mother was dead and his father was a ruddy old Irishman? Could he alter his personality, or was he stuck with it? Could he let someone get close to him? And by someone, he meant Marty.

After lunch they unpacked their golf clubs from their travel bags and came back to the locker room to put their shoes on. Padraig had warned them that in Ireland you never changed shoes in the car park. And you never wore your hat in the clubhouse—it could cost you a round of drinks.

They loaded their clubs onto trolleys and followed the gravel path out to the practice area adjacent to the parking lot. It really *was* a stone-walled farmer's field, though the farmer had moved his sheep somewhere else.

Spencer lay down on one of the artificial grass mats for some yoga poses to warm up. He executed downward dogs and sun salutations. Phillip held three golf clubs together and swung them in various patterns like a major leaguer in the on-deck circle.

When he finished stretching Spencer reached for his driver and began spraying balls around the field—and beyond it, over the stone walls lining each side. He mishit a few that barely made it out of the teeing area, and connected on a couple of solid ones that seemed to disappear into the troposphere.

After a few static stretches of his own, Phillip started with his sand wedge with half swings and hit a few short, high-lofted shots, longer flop shots, and then full wedge shots. Then to his gap wedge, and pitching wedge, working his way one at a time through all the clubs, from shortest to longest, until he'd executed three good shots with each.

By the time Phillip got to his driver, Spencer was randomly pulling clubs out of his own bag and hitting balls in rapid succession, swinging hard, barely glancing at where the shots landed in the soft ground.

"Time to put the name of a new Elliot up in the clubhouse," Spencer said.

"Is there a wooden board for most erratic shotmakers?" Phillip asked.

Old Patrick Elliot wandered over from the clubhouse dressed in a pair of dark plaid slacks and the same deep blue cashmere sweater with the Ballydraiocht logo that Padraig had been wearing. His wing-tipped golf shoes were polished to a high sheen.

Spencer noted the preponderance of cashmere. And the likelihood of a lot of cold sheep.

After they'd all shaken hands Patrick said, "I heard you boys might be out here showing off. I thought I'd come see what kind of games you have."

Phillip and Spencer hit some more balls with the pro watching. Spencer whacked four or five drives as hard as he could in the time it took Phillip to choose a club (seven iron) and place one range ball on the plastic tee. He addressed the ball, bent his knees, waggled a bit, then backed away.

"It's odd hitting a golf shot in front of my father," he said. "Who's a golf pro."

"Not to worry, I'm not judging you," Patrick said. "Merely observing. As a certified instructor. That's all."

"It's still weird," Phillip said.

He addressed the ball again, took a slow breath, executed a smooth, sweeping, classic swing. The ball flew high and long, with a slight draw.

"Very nice," the old pro said.

Phillip teed up another ball and executed a perfect replica of the first swing, with the same result. He hit a few more identical shots, then switched to a five iron. Same meticulous swing, same high, long ball flight. Phillip felt great out there smacking balls into the blue Irish sky. With his father watching. His *father*. He'd imagined scenes like this often growing up.

But he became aware that he wanted to impress Patrick, and this made him self-conscious, then resentful, then sad, and then tired. He felt like a ten-year old playing Little League—back when the coach used to stick him out in right field and occasionally a ball would fly over in his general direction, waking him from whatever reverie a ten-year old was lost in.

Patrick stepped forward and stood close enough for Phillip to take in the cedary, sandalwood scent of his aftershave. The pro looked out into the sheep pasture and the sky above.

"That's a very pretty high shot for your American courses, you've been well coached," the old man said. "But our golf's different, what with the salt air and the wind and the fast, firm running ground. Mostly the wind. It blows all the time. Hard. It's like an invisible hazard."

Phillip nodded.

"So you need to be more creative and play to the conditions here. In general, you want to keep the ball low and capitalize on the extra roll the hard ground provides. It can amount to fifty or sixty yards on the right shot. On a windless day you could probably tear up our courses with your beautiful swing," Patrick said. "But when the wind blows you'll be chasing the heifer all day."

"Chasing the heifer?"

"You'll be wandering the countryside looking for balls. You'll be mowing the marram."

"The what?"

"The marram. It's the wild grass that grows up in the dunes. You'll never find your ball in it, but if you do you'll be sorry you looked. Thick stuff, that. You won't be harvesting potatoes."

He said it like 'po-day-does.'

"Okay, no potatoes," Phillip said.

"So it's about adapting. You'll need to master a low, boring shot. Not boring as in uninteresting. I mean one that bores into the wind."

"A worm burner. A low screamer. A gopher guillotine."

"Yes. Exactly that!"

"Play to the conditions."

"Yes, adjust as necessary, be agile and flexible."

Listening in, Spencer considered the concepts of agility and flexibility: kind of like when you think you have a father and then don't have one, then you have an entirely different one. And then none at all, again. You adjust. You remain agile.

Patrick spent the next few minutes showing Phillip how to alter his swing to produce a low trajectory. Spencer watched the old man's smooth, educated motion and recognized its similarity to

Phillip's—perhaps it was just the mechanics of two good golf swings, but could something else be at work, he wondered? Could there be a genetic component to the golf swing, a chain of proteins that dictated how someone might execute this complex muscular action?

After topping a few balls Phillip began to get the knack of what Patrick had showed him.

"You work on that for a little while and I'll have a look at your brother," Patrick said. He clapped his hands together and shuffled down the line.

Phillip, who knew his brother never responded well to being coached at anything, preferring to figure technique out on his own, thought: this ought to be interesting.

Patrick stood behind Spencer, who was pounding long, clean shots into the bright sky despite that none of his swings much resembled another. Phillip recalled some other boy's father saying Spencer swung his club like an argument.

"Ah, this one's got the creativity," the old pro said, smiling. He was a man who loved his work. "But not the discipline."

Phillip marveled at this characterization of his brother, which took most people years to figure out.

"Well, Spencer, you might want to start with a change to your grip," Patrick observed. "That baseball grip will only get you so far. There's hardly been a great player in history who used it. But your hand-eye coordination is brilliant. It's how you manage to hit the ball at all given your unconventional fundamentals."

"I've never planned to be a great player," Spencer responded.

"Still. You might try the interlocking. Or the Vardon. May I?"

Patrick pulled a club out of Spencer's bag and put his large, worn hands on the shaft. They looked as natural as if they'd grown there. He demonstrated both grips—one with the fingers interlocked, one in which the first two fingers of the left hand lay atop the bottom two of the right.

"I like the grip I have," Spencer said. "The others never felt comfortable."

"They're not meant for comfort. They're for efficiency. They allow the hands to hinge together, which is crucial. Listen to me."

"I'm listening," Spencer said. "Just disagreeing."

"I'll insist on this point," Patrick said. "Your baseball grip is just no good."

Spencer let go of the club and it dropped to the ground. He struggled to remain cordial, but then it was out of him before he realized . . .

"And I'll politely insist on you not acting like you're my father," Spencer said. Patrick stepped back. Spencer put a hand on the old man's forearm. "No, I'm joking," he said. Which was less than half true.

"I'm not your father, no," Patrick said. He took another step back, out of Spencer's reach, arms at his side.

"I don't need one right now, is the thing," Spencer said, more softly.

"Don't you, son?" Patrick said. He let this hang in the air. "Well, then, maybe the right golf pro will do. Let's begin over again, why don't we? Take a mulligan."

"Yep, that's a good idea," Spencer said. "Everyone needs a mulligan."

Patrick stepped away from the teeing area and headed back down the path toward the parking lot. The boys watched him go. Spencer thought he was storming off to the clubhouse. Lesson over. But when he reached the asphalt, Patrick turned around and ambled back toward them.

"Here comes Shivas Irons," Spencer said, mentioning the name of the mythical golf pro in a famous book.

"Which of you is having the golf lesson today, then," Patrick asked.

Spencer looked at Phillip. "I am," Spencer said.

"Why don't you hit a few balls and I'll watch you, to get us acquainted—golf wise, that is."

Spencer stepped back up to the tee with his seven iron and hit four low screamers—the shot that Patrick had been trying to teach his brother. "I can hit high ones, too," Spencer said. "I like to play to the conditions—you know: to be agile."

"Show me a few more. Hit a couple of different clubs," the pro said.

He did. He hit high floaters and low boring shots; some drew to the left, others sliced wildly, a few dribbled a dozen yards into the grass. He swung without thinking, without a whit of self-consciousness or technique, nearly every swing a unique expression of amped-up Spencer-ness.

"You're a fine player, truly. A natural athlete," Patrick said. "There's nothing I can say that would be of help to you. Unless you have questions, or there's something specific you're working on."

He smiled warmly. He looked at his watch—a Gruen Curvex from the 1930s—as if their lesson was nearly over.

"I was wondering if you could explain the different grips to me," Spencer said. "I like my baseball grip but I've been told I'll never be a great player with it. What might the other grips do for me that this one can't?"

"We can work on that," Patrick said. "That's a great place to start."

He took another club from Spencer's bag and laid his hands on the too-smooth surface, all the resistance rubbed flat.

"You might want to change the grips on these clubs, too. Even if you don't change your own grip upon them," he said.

Spencer tested the other grips—the Vardon and the overlap—that Patrick showed him. He hit a few balls with each. "I think I'm going to stick with my original grip, but thanks for the info."

"Aye, you'd take a few steps backward before a new grip worked for you, and that might not be worth it. So, of course, it's as you wish," Patrick said.

Phillip, watching the exchange, thought: yes . . . a mulligan.

Chapter Twenty-Eight
Bollox to That

"*THAT* WAS EMBARRASSING," SPENCER said, an hour later, as they stood on the first tee waiting for the fairway to clear in front of them. They were playing as a twosome, which was called a 'two-ball' here, which Spencer found amusing.

"What *was* that?" Phillip asked.

"I'd guess anger," Spencer said.

"You're angry at *Patrick*? What did he do, except try to improve your horrendous golf swing?"

"Why do I have to be angry *at* someone? Can't I just be angry in general?"

"Sure. But why take it out on the nicest man in the world. He's like the Mr. Rogers of golf instruction."

"I guess it was an irritable day in the neighborhood. You don't have to stick up for him just because he's your da."

"Is that what you think?"

"Not really. Anyway, he was the most convenient target."

"Why don't you aim it at that barber pole in the middle of the fairway instead?" Phillip said.

Spencer sliced two new Titleists into the cemetery off to the right of the first hole—he teed the second so quickly the first hadn't landed yet among the graying tombstones. "If you look for my golf balls tomorrow you will find them a grave man," he said.

On the second hole they hit out into a narrow causeway carved between mounds of waving marram. A savory wind brushed over them as they followed the ramp of short, immaculate grass toward the green. The greens were perfect—natural, rolling dance floors canted at slight angles like fescue-covered ocean waves. Phillip breathed deeply as if he could absorb all of Ireland into his lungs.

On number four Spencer knocked two balls into a tiny stream crossing the fairway. He wallowed in a bluish funk, kicking at tufts of grass.

Phillip knew his brother had been angry beneath the surface for most of his life—the kind of anger born of pain, which Phillip surmised bubbled underneath Spencer's anger. And underneath the pain, Phillip also knew as well as anyone, was growing up without a father. Having to go to Cub Scout meetings with their mom. Learning sports from gym teachers. Never operating power tools. Although Phillip believed Spencer was happy for him to have found his own father, this was one more thing Spencer was excluded from, which probably didn't help the anger issue. And put Phillip in the position of trying to protect his brother again.

On the back nine Spencer began cursing the game of golf itself.

"Jesus three-putting Christ," he said after missing a two-footer.

On number twelve he topped his drive forty yards.

"Have you thought about trying one of the grips Patrick recommended?" Phillip asked.

"I didn't much care for the lesson."

"He was just trying to help," Phillip reasoned.

"Yeah, well, I wasn't asking for help. Who does he think he is, giving me an unsolicited golf lesson?"

"I think he thinks he's a golf pro. And he saw a flaw he thought he could correct."

"Well, bollox to that," Spencer said. "It's like if I was at a concert and I went up to one of the musicians at the break and told him I thought he should maybe hold his guitar a little further up the neck. What the fuck?"

"It's not really like that at all. You're not a professional teacher of guitar, for one thing. That's a terrible analogy."

"Oh, that's rich. I'll tell you what it's really like. It's like if my brother, who is not a writer or literary critic or academic, started giving me lessons about how to make an analogy."

"Your brother is totally shutting up now," Phillip said.

Spencer paused. "What if it's *me* I'm angry at?" he asked.

"How's that?"

"What if I'm angry at myself? Disappointed. Anger caused by disappointment."

"About what?"

"About the cluster-fuck I've made of my life? That I'm acting like a big baby because I feel like these Irish strangers are taking you away from me?"

"How can you say that about your life?" Phillip asked. "You're successful by every measure. You're a self-made rich person. You're funny and smart and always win at board games. You're fit and handsome and not entirely gray. What else do you want?"

"I want a partner," Spencer said. "Someone to share it all with. Somebody who could take out the recycling once in a while. I've been alone my whole life. I don't give a rip about this 'find-the-father-in-the-pizza' contest. I'd like to have someone around me. Someone other than you—although I like you just fine."

"I thought you preferred it that way? The whole rugged individualist thing?"

Spencer pulled on his golf glove and teed up his ball. He hit a towering drive down the middle of the seventeenth fairway. "I'm over it," he said. "It was misdirection. It was so well executed I didn't even recognize it myself until now."

CHAPTER TWENTY-NINE
Trisha

THEY DROVE UP TO Patrick and Lorna's house a few minutes before seven thirty. The evening was light and fresh, with a cool tang to it, the way evening can only feel in latitudes where the sun doesn't set until late. The days were long and languid. Dusk was still a distant promise.

The pro and his wife lived in a large stone cottage built in the nineteenth century. Inside was clean and spacious, with wide-plank wooden floors polished to a shine and windows looking out in every direction over the water and fields and the golf course in the distance. The furniture was of decidedly sleek modern European styling—Danish, maybe, Phillip thought—and the overall vibe was of a historic building brought lovingly into the current era.

Lorna welcomed them with glasses of champagne at the door. She was a lithe, well-groomed beauty with red hair gone mostly gray, and gray-blue eyes that seemed quietly entertained. She hugged the boys with one arm as they all held their glasses aloft.

The brothers sat with Patrick and Padraig in a book-lined parlor while Lorna cooked. The long pine dining table by the fireplace was set for five—Trisha, the daughter, would meet them at the pub afterward.

"So, how'd you get on today?" Padraig asked.

Cheese and biscuits had been laid on a tray on the oversized tufted ottoman—covered in a tartan plaid—that also served as a coffee table. Phillip and Spencer fell back into the deep leather couch. Patrick and Padraig sat in French Bergere chairs arranged at opposite corners of the ottoman.

"Well," Spencer said, looking at his brother. "There was some—how did you put it—some mowing of the heifer? Some chasing of the marram?"

The two Irishmen hesitated before laughing. They were beginning to figure Spencer out.

"There was some gathering of potatoes as well," Phillip added.

This was an opportunity for Spencer to carry the theme forward and say something funny, but he withdrew into himself.

Patrick got up to help his wife in the kitchen, and the brothers—new and old—were left alone together.

"I heard Da gave you both a golf lesson today, I hope that was all right," Padraig said.

"He taught me how to hit a low running shot," Phillip said. "Which is very helpful."

Spencer said nothing. He examined a collection of golf books on the shelves against the wall.

"The thing about Da's lessons," Padraig continued. "Is they're almost never about the golf."

Spencer said, "He told Phillip he needs to be more agile and creative. Two things I've been saying to him his whole life."

"He told Spencer he needs to get a better grip," Phillip said, looking at his brother.

"Is that right?" Padraig asked, but before they could pursue this line of conversation Lorna announced that the lamb was being carved and they could come to table.

Over dinner they talked about family, mostly, and things people talk about to get to know each other. It was the oddest of first dates. Patrick asked what they'd chosen for their work. Lorna described how the house had been in her family for five generations—her great-great-grandfather had been a ship captain and built it so his wife could observe the weather out at sea and know when he'd return home.

Notably absent was any mention of Jenny, although she was the one who'd convened this gathering, who'd spun this weird double helix of connection. Her presence hovered there. Like the ghost of Gregor Mendel, Spencer thought to himself. Or Robert Mendel, he thought that his brother would have thought.

Halfway through the meal Spencer got up to use the facilities and was startled by a familiar photo hanging in the hall: Jack Elliot in his army uniform standing beside a helicopter. Farther down the hall hung a group photo that included Patrick, Jack, and their other siblings—including the old lady they'd gone to see at Majestic Manor—when they were all still young and vibrant. Jack was laughing with his head thrown back. One of the girls wore a plaid tam-o'-shanter.

Spencer realized in that instant that he wanted to leave Ireland as soon as possible—maybe tomorrow if he could work out the logistics. He was gumming up Phillip's trip with his anger and his dumb jokes. Sure, he'd loved the idea of belonging to a large Irish family; but he hadn't thought through that Phillip might belong to it and he wouldn't.

He was getting in the way of something Phillip had waited for his whole life. Spencer was tired of being selfish. He'd log onto the airline website first thing in the morning and see what he could arrange for a standby return flight. With luck he could be back home in two days, back to his routine of workouts and listening to music in clubs at night. And he could get some decent Italian food for fuck's sake. And not have to think at all about fathers—his, or anyone else's.

Back at the table Patrick described how he'd been employed by golf facilities throughout Europe to teach his signature exercise of having his students throw their clubs. He used the club toss as a metaphor for breaking rules and letting go, although he didn't encourage students to repeat the exercise anywhere but in his workshops.

"I've already got that move," Spencer said, and they laughed. He had to remind himself the Irishmen were not his new family. Though he felt they should be.

———————

At nine Padraig looked at his watch and announced they ought to head to the pub, the music would be starting. They piled into two cars—Padraig riding in the back seat with Phillip and Spencer, and Patrick and Lorna driving in their old Saab Turbo.

The pub—St. Urants—was one of three in the village, in addition to a fourth down the road a couple of miles at the Irish Heritage Center, where the town council had created a replica old-time Irish village where tourists could watch locals dressed in old-timey costumes spinning yarn and blacksmithing and shoeing horses. Tourists found the fake pub a little too fake; they craved a pub full of colorful Irishmen, so visitors began straying to one of the old pubs in town, which began catering to them, and attracting more of them, so the locals who'd frequented that pub switched allegiances and began frequenting the fake pub in the Irish Heritage village, which was cleaner and there were no tourists, and the food was better, though the Guinness was about the same.

"Just how many saints do you have around here, anyway?" Spencer asked, as they ducked into the pub beneath a logo depicting an ancient bartender with a halo pouring a draught from a tap. "I mean: St. Urant? Really?"

Patrick said, "The name actually came from the old 'restaurant' sign that hung on the place for years. Some of the letters burned out, until only 'st urant' was left. So without papal approval we recognized the patron saint of well-poured Guinness."

"Ah," Spencer said, smiling for the first time since he'd sunk a long, sloping putt on the seventeenth hole.

Inside, the bar was lined with locals of ages varying so widely it looked like some patrons were drinking next to their great-grandparents. The tables in the main room were filling with tattooed men in shirts representing local football teams, and old timers in herringbone and Harris tweed jackets, and women whose features looked beautifully carved and buffed by years of strong breezes.

Patrick introduced the brothers around as friends visiting from America and left it at that.

When Spencer's eyes became accustomed to the low lighting inside the pub the first thing he noticed was a musician messing with the band's set-up in a corner of the main room: a red-headed woman sitting on a stool at the drum kit, adjusting the heights. She wore a black western shirt with red piping with a couple of buttons undone in the front, the sleeves folded back on her fair-skinned arms. A short red skirt with a black leather motorcycle belt, and short black boots. Subtle red lipstick highlighted her full lips, accentuating finely drawn cheekbones sprinkled with freckles. Red hair styled short in a sort of punk/pixie cut that she might have just started growing out.

When she finished with the drums she performed mic checks and arranged the guitars and fiddle on the stage, as well as a contraption that Spencer would later learn was a set of Irish pipes—bagpipes, but played on the lap rather than standing.

Spencer felt a wave of nostalgia seeing the instruments spread across the small stage. His own band had performed many gigs in Irish pubs in New York. It reminded him he'd be going home soon. At the same time, he couldn't take his eyes off the girl.

While Padraig headed for the bar to gather drinks, Patrick led them to a table off to the side of the stage with a great view of the band and the 'ginger' woman, who turned out to be the drummer. There was something familiar about her: was it was possible the band had played in the tri-state area or someplace else he'd been?

"Ah, there's Trisha now," Patrick said. He climbed up onto the stage platform and put his arms around the girl.

"Hiya, Da," she said.

He took her hand and brought her over to their table and said, "Well, Trisha, meet Phillip and Spencer."

"Aye, the Americans," she said. "Well then, they look all right." Then she shook their hands firmly and looked them over, and when Spencer looked back he recognized the deep, speckled green eyes of his brother.

Spencer had seen a lot of bar bands but few exuded the rowdy enthusiasm of Gorsey Park. They played like nothing else mattered.

There were five of them—lead and bass guitar, drums, piper/fiddler, and a female singer who shook a tambourine and rang a cowbell. They played an eclectic set of Irish tunes—including some lesser-known Van Morrison like 'Street Choir' and 'Autumn Song'; a couple of sad, crooning ballads; as well as a few original compositions. The set list was cleverly crafted—they had codgers dancing and young toughs crooning on the slow songs, and girls swaying in the arms of whomever they were with.

Trisha played the drums and sang lead vocals on about half the numbers, backup vocals on the rest. Her voice had a range as wide as a clear western sky, a deep rumbling timbre on some tunes—like the voice that might result if Tom Waits had a love child with Cyndi Lauper—and a high, searching angelic tone like Sarah McLachlan on others. Spencer was mesmerized. Her voice cut into him like a favorite memory, like going to the beach as a young child with your mother when she was still the center of your world and eating a hot dog for the first time.

During the break Trisha sat with them. Spencer could feel the heat coming off of her. He recognized her exhilaration.

Phillip told her, "Spencer's a drummer, too."

They looked over at him, surprised.

"Yep. The rare singing percussionist," Spencer said.

"Ah, you, me, and Ringo," Trisha said.

Spencer wanted to communicate a humble sophistication, to imply something about his own character without seeming like a know-it-all. Which he knew he was. Particularly about music.

"I'm more of a Levon Helm," Spencer said.

"Would that be before or after the throat cancer?" Trisha said.

"A touch of 'Up on Cripple Creek,' a bit of 'The Dirt Farmer,'" Spencer said.

"Yeah, good. I'm more like Moe Tucker."

"Velvet Underground? Okay, I can see that," Spencer said. "The whole gothic thing . . ."

"Gothic with a hint of Dave Grohl, to modernize it."

"Does Dave Grohl count as a singing drummer? He drummed in Nirvana, but he played guitar and sang with Foo Fighters," Spencer said. "Two bands, two different roles."

She smiled. "Okay then, more like Don Henley—that whole soulful singer-songwriter thing. But energized. Maybe Grant Hart is a better example."

"Grant Hart?"

"Ah, I've stumped him," she said to the others. "Husker Du?"

"Husker Du? Really? What is that, a caffeinated Norwegian beverage? Now if you'd said, 'Don Brewer,' I could understand. Or Phil Collins crossed with Micky Dolenz."

"Now you're just trying to show off. Micky Dolenz? That wasn't even a real band. It was a show on the telly."

"Not real? 'Last Train to Clarksville'? 'I'm a Believer'? Total classics!"

"You might as well add Peter Criss, and Pete Rivera if all you're doing is naming singing drummers. And throw in Karen Carpenter and Roger Taylor, why don't you? Oh, and Marvin Gaye." She put her arms up in a victory sign.

Spencer shook his head like he'd just been clobbered. "We have a winner," was all he could think to say.

Phillip couldn't remember ever seeing someone outdo his brother in calling up useless trivia. When he looked around the bar he noticed a waiter headed toward their table with a bowl of dessert with a candle in it, but before he could say anything Padraig groaned audibly and muttered, "Oh for feck's sake, not again."

The waiter presented the dessert to Padraig, who forced a smile as the crowd broke into 'Happy Birthday.'"

"You should have told us," Phillip said.

"I would have. Except it's not my birthday. That's in November." He looked over at Trisha. "She does this all the time. She thinks it's the funniest thing.

"What's worse," Padraig continued, "it's sticky toffee pudding—not even a real dessert. It's what tourists order—they think it's an old Irish staple that our great-great-grandmothers made before the potato famine, or some such shite. But some hotelier invented it in the 1970s. I've heard rumors it's *Canadian*. Nobody here would ever order it." Padraig pushed it toward the middle of the table. "It's the flan of Ireland."

Phillip and Spencer exchanged glances. Spencer shook his head at the coincidence. It reaffirmed something. But what? He wondered at the feasibility of a gene that made you send your brother a lousy dessert in a restaurant on a day that wasn't his birthday. It seemed like a stretch. But pure coincidence? That felt unlikely, too.

When no one reached for the sticky toffee pudding Spencer pulled the bowl toward him and began eating, though his stomach was churning and he had that off-kilter feeling that, for him, preceded falling for a girl.

Chapter Thirty

The Great Migration

AT 11:00 THE LIGHTS came up and all the patrons abruptly rose from their tables and barstools and filed out the front door. Spencer thought it looked like an organized fire drill.

The brothers followed their hosts into the night, which smelled like warm bread. Most of the bar goers shuffled around the side of the building and queued up at another door that led back inside.

"What the what?" Spencer said when they gathered on the sidewalk.

Patrick explained, "The council requires everyone to leave pubs by 11:00 . . . But there's nothing to say they can't come right back in at 11:01, so . . . "He indicated the line with his hand. "They call it 'the great migration.' This is where us old folk call it a night."

"And some of us younger folk as well," Phillip said. "It's been a long day."

"Hey, bro," Spencer whispered. "I'm going to stay for another set if you don't mind driving back alone. Trisha asked if I might want to sit in with the band."

"You all right to get home by yourself?"

"She's going to drop me off," Spencer said.

"Of course she is," Phillip said, nodding like a bobble head doll.

The others—Padraig, Patrick, Lorna, and Phillip—headed home. Spencer relocated from their table to a high stool back by the bar. He sat between a geezer who smelled like apple pipe tobacco and a girl who looked too young to be in a pub. She was watching some shenanigans in the place that she found hysterical.

A series of adorable half shots of Jameson accompanied by short glasses of Guinness began appearing before Spencer on the bar top like an endless line of soldiers marching toward the front, and he drank them in turn. He had a high tolerance for alcohol from his earlier days as a drug user; but he felt a warm buzz from the drink and his surroundings and the Irish camaraderie as the crowd thinned but the band picked up tempo.

Toward midnight a more intimate collection of drinkers and die-hard band fans remained. Audience members talked to the musicians as if they were sitting around in someone's parlor, and the musicians spoke back between songs. The band worked skillfully through a rollicking version of 'All For Me Grog' with a few original verses and the remaining patrons singing along on the refrain.

Trisha pulled the mic close and announced—in a husky voice that sent Spencer reeling—"We have a special guest who's going to sit in on drums. He's never played or practiced with us but we'll beg forgiveness if he screws the pooch. Here he is, our American brother, Spencer Elliot."

He played drums along to a couple of standards—Mark Knopfler off the 'Local Hero' soundtrack, a song from The Decemberists. When the band recognized his competence they became more playful, riffing into a quick Irish reel he couldn't possibly be familiar with. He kept up admirably, and when the musicians stopped short during a bridge in one song, they hit Spencer with the spotlight. He performed a short solo that caused the other band members to bow in his direction.

When it was over, Trisha yelled, "Goodnight everybody, see you next week!"—even though 'everybody' was the bartender and a few rumpled drunks snoozing in the back beneath the framed rugby jerseys on the wall. Lights came on and the barkeep roused the remaining patrons and herded them toward the exit—the side exit this time.

"I can help you break down the drum kit," Spencer offered.

"Oh, no need, we don't have another gig, we'll leave this up all week and hope that nobody hurls on the amps. Or thinks they're Keith Moon."

"The dreaded 'My Generation' solo," Spencer said with a tired smile.

They passed out of the bar into the evening and headed toward Trisha's ancient two-door Mercedes coupe in the car park—Spencer forgot where he was again and held open the wrong door for her.

"You driving?" she said, amused.

She got in behind the wheel and they drove through the village past the bakery and the sporting goods store with green and yellow soccer balls hanging in the window. Lights shone in apartments above the shops, giving off a warm glow. Spencer recognized they were headed in the opposite direction of his hotel.

"Is this where you take the tourist out and murder him on the moors? Like something out of *American Werewolf in London?*"

"I thought I might show you the beach, one of my favorite spots," Trisha said. "If you're up for it. I don't have to be at work tomorrow . . ."

"Work?" Spencer said, as if she were suddenly speaking Gaelic. "What is this 'work' you speak of? What kind of 'work'?"

She shook her head, moonlight glinting off her red hair like firelight.

"You Americans are always asking that," she observed. "It's usually your first question. I can't figure why that is."

"Deep intellectual curiosity?"

"The dog's bollox. I think you want to know right off how much money we make. Where we fit. Isn't that it? To identify our social strata?"

"The dog's bollox? Really? But I couldn't be less interested in money," Spencer said.

"Well, aren't you the odd one?"

"Still," he said. "Let me guess at your employment. Are you a blacksmith by day? A superhero named Ginger Snap?"

"Ah, that's not bad," she said. "I'm with Irish Heritage. You know—'Preserving history, promoting the motherland, making the world safe for potatoes'. I've a degree in it. I love it." She said 'love' like 'loove.'

"I'm interested in Irish heritage myself," Spencer said, and when he realized it sounded like a come-on he added, "As you know, my brother recently came down with a half case of Irishness."

They clamored over the dunes and dropped to the strand. Spencer felt the wind freshening. The sand crunched under their feet. He smelled oysters, grass, the warm, savory-sweet scent of his new friend. Trisha took his arm in both of hers and leaned in to protect herself from the breeze.

"I think I just saw one of the golf balls I lost this afternoon," he said, having to raise his voice above the timpani of the breakers.

"It's weird, isn't it?' he added.

"About the golf ball?"

"About us. We just met three hours ago. You're my brother's sister—and that's a first. Which makes you, what, my half sister once removed? My step-step sister? I don't know whether to hug you or shake your hand or tell mom that you hit me first."

"Technically we're not related at all. I couldn't do this if you were my brother, even in Ireland." She stopped on the sand and pulled his face to hers and kissed him, like a lingering question that had been on her mind, and she was asking if he had a sensible answer.

"For feck's sake," he said after the kiss had gone on a little while.

"Oh, 'For feck's sake,' is it?" she said, laughing. "When did you pick that up, then?"

"Back when I thought I was going to turn out to be Irish, too."

"Your accent is terrible," she said. "Nobody would ever think you were Irish."

"I don't know what I am," he said. "I'm a mongrel. An unidentified half breed. Like if a monkey had a baby with a . . . donkey. I don't know what I'm doing here. Your dad's not my dad. I was thinking about going home tomorrow, until . . ."

"Until what . . .?"

"This," he said, and he kissed her this time. "I like that," he said. "It's not incest."

"You shouldn't joke about that in Ireland. It's a small island. We're all related somehow. Especially in the wee towns. And of course you like it. But that's all there is for now, except for the romantic strolling on the beach. We'll see how this sorts itself."

She pulled her boots off one at a time, standing on the opposite leg like a tipsy flamingo, holding onto Spencer with the other hand. She pulled off her socks, decorated with winged four-leaf clovers. She tiptoed into the swirling edge of the surf, her short red skirt flapping around athletic calves and thighs.

"Ah, it's fecking cold," she said, laughing.

"Fecking cold," he repeated.

"*Fecking* cold," she said again.

"Ah, feck it," he said, but not any better.

———

Trisha dropped him outside the bed and breakfast at three in the morning. He fumbled the front door keys, bumped into a lamp and a table in the hallway. He tried his hardest to be stealthy, though he was happy enough not to care. He quietly whistled an Irish reel.

When he made it inside his room and closed the door and fell back on the bed, he heard a low knocking. The wind banging a shutter outside? Trisha? It took on the beat of their secret family knock: ta ta, ta-ta-ta, ta-ta-ta. If Spencer could recognize anything, it was a beat.

He cracked the door to see Phillip standing in the hall in a pair of soccer shorts and an old Vassar tee shirt.

"Sorry, did I wake you?" Spencer asked without opening the door any further.

"Nah. Couldn't sleep. Heard you come in. Wanted to talk."

"Why are you speaking in sentence fragments?"

"No idea."

"You want to sit? I was going to bed but . . ."

"Nah, we should try to get some sleep," Phillip said. "I wanted to let you know. I'm leaving tomorrow if I can get a flight out."

"Ah, fight versus flight," Spencer said. "That's genetics, too. The so-called warrior gene. MAOA. Which we don't seem to possess."

Spencer was drunk but still sharp-witted enough to remember that until he met Trisha in the bar he'd been ready to flee, too.

"But why would *you* want to leave at this crucial moment in the story?" Spencer asked. "Just when you appear to have gotten what you always wanted?"

"I find it alarming," Phillip said. "Maybe I wanted this my whole life the way some kids want to be policemen. And then they become policemen and realize: holy shit, people are fucking *shooting* at me."

"Now *that* may not be the greatest analogy," Spencer said.

Chapter Thirty-One
Waffle

WHEN THEY SAT DOWN for breakfast in the dining room the next morning Spencer said, "I'm not going to eat baked beans again. They can't make me. Have they ever heard of a fucking pancake? Or a waffle? Those are from Belgium. It's not that far away. What about a croissant? It's from France. That's practically next door."

"Ask for some porridge," Phillip said, attempting to stop the tirade. "Tell them you're a vegan."

"Yeah, and they'll say, 'But first, a little Bunga Bunga!'" It was the punch line to an old joke. They'd reached a point a long time ago where they didn't need to tell the jokes to each other to get a laugh—just the punch lines. It was part of their silent, brotherly code, their common strands of humor proteins.

"So," Spencer said between sips of coffee. "You still thinking about leaving, or are you over that?"

"Not over it," Phillip said. "I feel strange here, even if Patrick is my father. I'm not ready for the next phase of that. Do I want to be part of this family that's gotten on perfectly well without me for so long? I don't want to rush into their arms and then have to tell them it wasn't the right thing."

"But you're just getting started on this whole paternal journey," Spencer said. "There's a lifetime to catch up on. Two lifetimes. Your whole world has cracked wonderfully open, like some delicious egg. Like a piñata full of fabulous candy—the little Ice Cube chocolates we had as kids. Or Mozartkugel. Or Swedish fish if you like that sort of thing. All raining down from the heavens. And now suddenly you don't like sweets?"

"I'm craving something more substantial suddenly," Phillip said. "Something meatier."

"This isn't really about your father, is it?"

"Not anymore," Phillip said. "I just figured that out."

"Okay, but hang on a second," Spencer said. "You should know: I'm staying,"

"Whaaat?"

"I'm not ready to go home. I've got it in mind to stay. I decided last night after I stumbled into bed. Maybe just a few days. I need a couple more full Irish breakfasts."

Phillip sipped the strong, earthy coffee. "It's the girl," he said.

"Of course it's the girl. It's always the girl," Spencer said.

"My sister," Phillip said. He said it to test it out, to see how it felt.

Spencer tilted his head to one side, wrinkled one side of his mouth the way Michael Kitchen does in *Foyle's War*. "Really? You're going to play the sister card? You just got her."

"I'm not playing it. I'm just looking at it as part of my overall hand. I don't know what it does—is it trump? Is it like a nine in Stratego? Is it a get out of jail free card?" Phillip knew that he sounded like his brother when he got wound up. It was another part of what made them brothers to begin with. Or maybe resulted from being brothers.

"Yeah, me either," Spencer said.

"I wanted to see what the sister card could do. And I like saying, 'my sister.'"

"I get it," Spencer said.

"Please be careful," Phillip said then. "Please don't fuck this up for everyone else if you stay."

"That makes me want to say 'bugger off,' when you say that. But I thought about this. I know you're right. But that's what Mom used to say before I went somewhere in the car—'Please be careful'. Even if I was going to the garage to get something out of the trunk. Like the trunk had malevolent intent and was looking for an opportunity to close and trap me in there.

"I'm not sure which part riles me more—the 'be careful' or the 'please'. It's probably the 'please'—because it implies that if you're polite you can say anything, like: 'Please don't molest any children on the playground.' It implies that if you hadn't asked so nicely I might go do the thing. Or not do it, in the case of being careful . . . "

"Does it seem strange that I'm going home and you're going to stay?" Phillip asked.

"Yep," Spencer said.

More coffee arrived, and Spencer nearly asked the waitress if he could have something different for breakfast—a popover, or a scone, a bowl of gruel, anything. But he didn't ask, and she poured more coffee nearly to the rim of their big white porcelain mugs and headed back toward what Spencer was thinking of as the 'full Irish breakfast factory.' Spencer hated when a server poured more coffee without asking, when you'd already established the perfect ratio of cream to coffee, and now with the addition of more coffee, you'd have to start all over again.

"I considered asking them if it's okay for me to stay," Spencer said. "But wouldn't that be even weirder? I'm already here—maybe you could say that you need to get home for some sort of business thingy and they'll say, 'Spencer, why don't you stay. You're already here.'"

"I don't know what to tell them either," Phillip said. "I want to say how much I like them, and how I'd like to come back. But then why leave in the first place?"

"'Why don't you stay, Spencer,'" Spencer said again, in his lousy Irish accent.

"'You're already here. You haven't even been to the leprechaun museum. You're always after me Lucky Charms.'"

"You might want to leave that one out. And drop the accent. It's terrible."

"So I've been told," Spencer said. "Christ on a bike, they're all so open and warm and fecking *likable*. They're the opposite of everything I represent. They feel like the family I never had. But they're not. I have to remember this: they're the family *you* never had. Except now you have them."

"I know it looks like I'm running away from all this," Phillip said. "Like I always do. But I want you to know: in this case it's more that I'm running *toward* something else."

CHAPTER THIRTY-TWO

Nescafe

THEY SAT OUT BACK of the hotel with their laptops. Phillip researched return flights while Spencer looked up slang Irish phrases. Now that he might be staying, they could come in handy. If nothing else, perhaps he would understand what those around him were saying more than only half the time.

He wondered when he might have occasion to say: 'I'm so hungry I could eat the twelve apostles.' He made a mental note to refer to someone as 'a wanker.' He thought of additional ways to exclaim something similar to his current favorite 'Christ on a bike!' 'Jesus Jim Caviezel' was a good one. He also liked 'Jiminy Christmas.'

"There's something out of Dublin tomorrow late afternoon," Phillip said. "I could drive to the airport after the baked beans in the morning. It makes sense for me to take the car, no?"

"That's fine," Spencer said. "Unless I end up going with you."

"I thought you were staying. You know, for the girl."

"I'd like to. But I should probably ask her."

"But it's settled then. I'm going to fly out tomorrow afternoon either way."

"Yep."

"I'm going to call and invite everyone out to dinner tonight."

"Yep."

"And you're going to check with the girl."

"Yep yep."

Spencer drove the rental car down the road through the village and beyond, winding alongside a clear, shallow river running over rounded stones. When he pulled up the gravel driveway Trisha was out front

140

of her cottage doing yard work in an old U2 tee shirt that looked even better for being nearly worn through. She wore a pair of denim shorts and colorful gardening boots decorated with blooming flowers, and matching gloves. She sported a little black watch cap that made her hair look like red-hot pewter.

The garden was wild and formal simultaneously—a wide mix of English plants and flowers architected tightly in perfect rows but overgrowing with exuberance, like a high school yearbook full of photos that fit into their same-sized little frames, but in which the students had crazy dreadlocks or giant afros or wore funny hats or flowing robes that extended beyond the visible areas of the compositions. Purple catamints exploded up from the ground; foxgloves stood in soldierly rows as if the soldiers were tired, or drunk; phlox and larkspur canted outward over the edges of the beds. Rambling roses rambled across the red brick borders.

He parked beside Trisha's old Mercedes and climbed out. She came over and put her bare, freckled arms around his waist. "Hey, brother," she said. "You found me okay?"

He smiled at that. It felt warm. "I find you much better than okay. And yep, it was easy. Like you said—a left, a right, two lefts, and Bob's your uncle."

"Bob's my uncle? And Fanny's your aunt!" she said. "Did you get that off the Internet?"

"Yep."

"Nobody really says that here."

"I do," he said. "Sorry, that's stupid. I'm fecking nervous—I wish I could just shut up."

"Speaking of which. I made you a cup of caw-fee. When you said you were coming right over. Caw-fee," she said again. She was drinking tea from a mug with an artist's rendering of Dublin Castle.

"That's not a half bad New York accent," he said. "Is that Brooklyn or the Bronx? Or a speech impediment?"

She held up her fists toward him in a sort of boxing stance—the kind of pose someone would strike if they'd never actually boxed. "You'se want one lump, or two?" she asked.

She sipped her tea while he marveled at possibly the worst cup of coffee he'd ever had. He might have to spit it out. He looked for a chance to dump it in the garden without her noticing, though he feared killing her plants.

"Wow, this is fantastic," he said.

"Truly?"

"No. Not even close. It tastes like New Jersey."

She laughed.

"Hey, here's a surprise," he said, with no segue. "Phillip is leaving. He moved his flight up. To tomorrow." He knew his timing wasn't perfect on this reveal. But he needed to get it out.

"Oh . . . "Trisha said. "So soon? We hardly knew ye."

"Yeah. Some top-secret spy stuff. He's an astronaut, you know? An astronaut hit man. Plus he doesn't want to intrude on your family."

Trisha swirled her tea in the mug, maybe looking for leaves in the bottom that would tell her what to say next, Spencer thought.

"And you?" she asked.

He took a sip of the bitter coffee, having already forgotten how awful it tasted. It *had* to be freeze-dried Nescafe, which he remembered from European trips decades ago. Maybe they hadn't used it all up yet.

"I *want* to intrude on your family. I like feeling as if I'm a part of something. And your brother—er, your other brother, Padraig: he *gets* me. I especially want to intrude on the part that contains you. But that might be weird being that my brother is your father's son. I know that sounds like an SAT question, although you probably have no idea what the SATs are. Anyway, I'm just the push-me, pull-you that's attached to Phillip. It doesn't make sense for me to stay if he goes home . . . Does it? Although I can keep my hotel room for another couple of nights. And I can get a flight whenever."

"It makes sense to me," she said. "I might like you."

"That's what I might have been hoping you'd say. I'll be alone if I stay. Can we hang out? Would you adopt me for a few days? Like when you take a kitten home from the animal shelter to see if you like it?"

She poured the dregs of her tea into the flower bed. Why hadn't he found the courage to do that with the coffee?

"Okay, then" she said. "But I hope you're not planning to poop in a box."

"Tally ho," Spencer said, for no apparent reason.

"It's settled," she said. "You'll stay. Though I have no idea what I'm doing. I'm sure it'll be great. Aren't I?"

"That's why we'll get along so well," he said. "You know what else would be pretty great?"

"Ah, we're not going there yet. Sorry, cowboy."

"No, not that. Although that would be great, too. It would be great if you could maybe say something to the others so it doesn't look like I stayed beyond my welcome."

"I can do that," she said.

"Like at dinner tonight. Phillip wants to take everyone out to dinner. He's trying to set it up right now."

"They won't care if you stay. They'll be happy to have you. They *do* seem to get you. I can't say why."

"It's my boyish charm. And that I'm an eejit. They feel sorry for the poor, half wit orphan boy. Wins them over every time."

Chapter Thirty-Three
Grand Central

THE HOSTESS SEATED THEM in a private room with old stone walls decorated with rich, clear black and white photos of the town—golfing scenes, fishing scenes, a shot of a dog sleeping among sheep, three old women sitting in a field laughing. A stunning young Irish girl with constellations of freckles. They were Trisha's photos, from an earlier artistic phase of her life.

They greeted each other with much hugging and back pounding and found their seats and the waiter brought out a bottle of champagne Phillip ordered in advance.

Patrick and Lorna had dressed for dinner—she in a long-flowered skirt that flattered her slim figure, he in a sport coat with a collared shirt. Trisha wore a black strappy thing that showed off her well-sculpted arms. Drummer's arms. And revealed a richly-colored jasmine flower tattoo on one shoulder, spreading to her back.

Lorna was the first to notice the gift box on her plate and looked around at the others, smiling. Maybe she thought it was another joke between the children.

"It's a thank you from me and Spencer," Phillip explained.

She untied the ribbon on the box—a long rectangle wrapped in striped paper. She wrinkled her brow when she opened the box itself—inside was a black and white photo of Times Square.

"Look on the back," Phillip said.

She turned the page over. She waited for him to explain.

"It's a voucher. For an airline ticket. To New York, if you like," Phillip said. "Or anywhere else you want to go."

He explained how their mother had been a travel agent and explored the world at every opportunity and instilled a love of travel in her boys. "I wanted to give you a chance to visit somewhere you've always wanted to go. I hope you'll consider coming to visit me and Spencer in Manhattan. It would be a great way for us to get to know each other better. You could see where we live and we could visit Jack's grave if you want," Phillip said. "Or drop in on Aunt Katherine in Lynbrook.

"The vouchers came from Jenny, our mom. This gives her a part in this ongoing story, since she was the cause of it to begin with," Phillip said.

The others opened their boxes to reveal photos of other New York icons—the Chrysler Building, a hot-dog vendor in Central Park, Grand Central Station at night.

"You boys live in the train station, then?" Padraig said.

"It's noisy, but convenient," Spencer said.

Phillip continued. "The reason we're giving these to you tonight is that I'm heading back to New York. There's something that I need to take care of there. I found a flight tomorrow afternoon."

"So you're leaving as well, Spencer?" Padraig said.

Before Spencer could answer Trisha broke in. "Spencer, you should stay. You're already here . . . If there's nothing calling you back home right away . . . "

Phillip thought: Oh, she's good.

"Stay as long as you like," Padraig said. "Play some more golf. We've got plenty of balls, even for you. We'll show you around. You haven't seen anything yet."

"I guess I *could* stay," Spencer said, staring at the ceiling to make it look as if he were trying to figure out if he could stay.

"You'll stay at our place," Patrick offered. "In one of the kids' rooms." He looked at Lorna. "We insist."

Spencer looked at Trisha. "That's nice of you, Da," she said.

They went about their meal like a family having dinner together in a small Irish town on a warm summer night. At the end of dinner they said their goodbyes.

"I'll miss you, my only brother," Phillip said, pulling Spencer close outside the restaurant as they stood in the misty coastal air.

"Don't be sad," Spencer said. "You'll still see me in the morning."

Part Three

CHAPTER THIRTY-FOUR

Bunga Bunga!

BACK IN NEW YORK a day after a day spent combatting jetlag, sorting through his mail and paying bills, and returning phone calls—all of which at first worked to anchor him to his previous life—Phillip felt adrift. Even among his own belongings, even in the king-sized bed with his Sonos speakers playing Rusted Root or the Mozart station on Pandora or the *All the Books* podcast. How was he to deal with the fact that his entire history had shifted wildly beneath him like an idiot cowboy riding a bull, for fuck's sake—yet nothing was really different at all?

Was he still the same person now that he was half Irish as he'd been as a full-on non-practicing Jew? What was he to make of all this? What did it even mean to be a Jew, a man, the person you thought yourself to be?

And a whole new family? What was he supposed to do with that? When he thought about his 'father' he still conjured the photo of Jack Elliot frozen in time at the age of twenty-three. He pictured the brave Jewish helicopter pilot who went down in flames protecting America from communism—even though that person never existed. The congenial golf pro he'd just met in Ireland barely registered.

And what would his mother have made of all this? Phillip was angry at Jenny while simultaneously impressed by her commitment to the creation myth she'd invented and protected until nearly the end. If he hadn't been so determined in his pursuit of the father issue, they all could have gone on—living and dead—maintaining their beliefs, and nothing would have changed.

And had it changed for the better? That much was unclear.

Did it even matter *why* Jenny had hidden his true lineage?

Phillip believed Jenny's "Ballydraiocht" utterance was a moment of

149

pure clarity. That wasn't Alzheimer's speaking. She knew her sons—which was why she'd said this to Phillip, not Spencer, correctly assuming he'd pursue it with his typical doggedness.

But Jesus on a pogo stick, what other shockers might be hurtling toward them down the pike?

Phillip recognized things were going to be different for him now. He just needed to figure out which things, and how they were going to be different. Was it a setback or an opportunity? He had his suspicions, but needed to test a few things out.

Phillip made a new plan—even if he knew it was a dumb one, the kind of thing his brother might have dreamt up.

———

On Sunday morning he woke early. While the streets of the Upper West Side filled with joggers heading for rare, coveted open spaces and tourists consulting their phone maps in the middle of intersections, he hurried past the familiar brownstone with the 'All Lives Matter' sign, and the one with the stained glass window hanging on the inside of the clear glass pane, and the one with a café table on the front landing, secured by chain to a bolt in the limestone.

He crossed the park just below the reservoir. He ambled down Fifth Avenue to Midtown, looking in the windows of the upscale clothing stores, and reached his destination: the noon mass at St. Patrick's Cathedral.

Phillip sat near the back. Each time a new worshipper entered the church he could hear the distant river flow of traffic out on Fifth Avenue, which tethered him to the New York he'd long known.

The service started with organ music, which Phillip found uplifting as he absorbed the stoic beauty of the marble and stained glass and gothic styling of the building, and the variety of New Yorkers who held these traditions in common, who were bound together beyond race and social class and economic status. They knelt together. They crossed themselves simultaneously. They mumbled in Latin.

He might as well have been wearing a yarmulke and a tallis, so sure was he that he stood out as a Jew masquerading as something else—although he was probably more Irish than half the people in the church.

Catholic wasn't Irish, per se, he knew that much, but the whole heritage thing was maddeningly opaque. What, exactly, made him who he was?

Genetics?

Belief?

God?

Luck?

Bunga bunga?

When the liturgy began Phillip closed his eyes and listened to the deep, sleepy voice of the priest, which at first was transporting—he could feel the weight of two thousand years of European history stitched together with gold thread and the blood of non-believers. He remembered a post-college backpacking trip he'd taken to Italy and pictured mosaic tiles and the wine shop where he'd tasted Barolo for the first time—a kind of spiritual awakening in itself.

The service wasn't so different from his own bar mitzvah, also performed in an ancient language he didn't speak or understand. How could he judge those around him for rote recitation of meaningless verbiage when his own so-called passage to manhood had required exactly the same thing?

At age thirteen he hadn't wanted the bar mitzvah. Jenny had told him it was his choice, but in a tone that communicated that there wasn't any choice at all. His friends were being bar mitzvahed—and enjoying lavish parties or trips or gifts meant to help pay for college.

Max 'The Factor' Feingold's family had taken their son's friends on a ski vacation to Killington to celebrate, although what a Scandinavian winter sport had to do with Judaism none of them had thought to ask. Phillip considered the whole thing a scam, but it was too difficult not to stand down. He did the opposite of the one thing that would have really made him a man at that early point in his development. He gave in.

The highlight of the whole bar mitzvah episode occurred at the house party following the service. A long-haired soft-rock band played in the yard, a magician performed (sadly, he did not execute the Mr. Wizard trick), and an artist drew caricatures of Phillip's friends and wrote pithy captions underneath ('Most Likely to Kvell'—written on his friend Brad Feldman's portrait—was one he remembered with embarrassment).

After cutting the giant sheet cake covered with iced Hebrew writing, Phillip went to his bedroom to retrieve a baseball signed by the New York Mets to show off to one of his pals. His cousin Leah followed him down the hall. She was already dressing in low-cut tops, wearing glittering neck jewelry and tight, clingy pencil skirts. Phillip slunk out of her presence whenever possible, fearing she'd spy his inevitable boner.

In his room Leah sat very close to him on the bed. He could smell the cinnamon gum on her warm breath. Without preamble she reached over and touched his penis through his bar mitzvah suit and said—in the accent of an old Jewish Rabbi—"So? Now you are a man?!" She gave his dick a good squeeze. And then she laughed.

While Phillip was both confused and also hoping this might progress further, Uncle Jerry charged into the room. He carried an old testament in a silver book jacket decorated with large imitation gemstones. He wore a dark blue custom-tailored suit with a light blue shirt, open at the collar, the collar set outside the collar of his jacket. Phillip knew that underneath his clothing Uncle Jerry wore a gold Star of David around his thick neck.

"This is the most important gift you'll ever receive," Uncle Jerry said, interrupting Phillip and Leah and handing over the book. "You'll read it when you're ready. Today you are a man!" He offered his giant hand for Phillip to shake.

"Thank you, Uncle Jerry," Phillip managed, while behind his Uncle Leah lifted her sheer blouse and flashed her tits at Phillip, which was the closest thing to a religious experience he encountered that entire day.

Two years later, when it was Spencer's turn to be bar mitzvahed—he'd already been threatened with expulsion from Hebrew school several times: he brought a BLT sandwich and ate it in class one afternoon—Jenny seemed oddly adamant that he should stand in the temple and read from the Torah.

It didn't make sense—they were barely Jewish, as far as the boys could tell. They ate ham and cheese sandwiches at home and treated the Sabbath no differently from any other day. Their strongest nod in the direction of the Holy Land was to attend temple on the high holidays. Reservations were required on those days, although the sanctuary was mostly empty the rest of the year.

"I got two seats in the velvet, two in the velvet," Spencer would joke every year at Yom Kippur—in a hoarse whisper meant to imitate a ticket scalper outside a Knicks game at Madison Square Garden—"C'mon, two in the velvet. Close to the rabbi. Kiddish passes!"

"This is your heritage," Jenny explained. "It's where you came from, dating back centuries. If you don't respect me, show some reverence for your ancestors."

Uncle Jerry inexplicably got involved in preparing Spencer for the bar mitzvah—perhaps he and Jenny feared Spencer was planning some nefarious act of rebellion.

"You are practicing your haftarah every night, yes?" Jerry asked during one of his now-frequent evening appearances. "Do not screw this up, Spencer. Do not embarrass your mother. Be a good Jew for once."

He would arrive just after dinner, when the boys were trying to sneak out with their baseball gloves or returning to a Risk game that had been ongoing for three days. When they spotted his Lincoln Town Car in the driveway they'd look hopefully for Leah in the back seat—this was after she'd grabbed Phillip's dick at *his* bar mitzvah but before the blow-job incident with Spencer. She was like a sexy guerrilla fighter the boys feared and admired. And lusted after.

"Let's hear what you've been practicing," Uncle Jerry would say, dropping a big paw on Spencer's shoulder and squeezing. As if this were the only form of affection he could summon.

"I'm going to sing like Jewy Armstrong," Spencer told Uncle Jerry, striding out of the room before he could respond. Later Spencer complained to Jenny and Phillip. Jerry's insistence about their religious education, given his otherwise total disregard for the boys, confused them.

"After all these years not giving a shit about us, now he's acting like the boss of me," Spencer commented. "Who does he think he is: the sheriff of Jewville? Schlomo Earp? My *father?*"

"I asked him to teach you some discipline," Jenny interrupted. "Since you don't listen to anything I say. You need the influence of a strong man in your life and Phillip is no Jack LaLanne. Your uncle just wants what's best for you."

At the bar mitzvah service the rabbi called Uncle Jerry up to the bema to read one of the blessings before Spencer's performance as 'the headliner,' as Spencer described it. Jerry sang the prayers with a braggy solemnity that reinforced Spencer's opinion that he was an unemotional jackass with a beautiful voice.

The memorable incident at Spencer's coming into manhood was his consumption of whiskey sours at the evening party at Leonard's of Great Neck, surreptitiously brought to him by the eighteen-year-old son of one of their neighbors who found the whole thing terribly good fun. Phillip remembered his brother downing one of the sugary cocktails in a long gulp and proclaiming to his friends, "Here's to putting the 'bar' in bar mitzvah!"

He passed out in the coatroom and had to be revived by Uncle Jerry in time to pull the curtain revealing the Viennese table, the requisite collection of too-sweet kosher deserts meant as encore to the over-salted kosher meal, which—their mother often reminded them, even years later—had been paid for by Uncle Jerry.

Now the bar mitzvahs seemed even more of a sham to Phillip, knowing that he was only half Jewish according to DNA, and no Jew at all based on the way he'd conducted his life. But still . . .

———

After a few minutes of listening to the service in St. Patrick's, and watching a couple of altar boys following the priest around the podium while he attended to what looked a lot like housework in a costume that looked a lot like a dress, the whole thing struck Phillip as over-the-top Jesus-y. He pondered the fantastical *New Testament* story but got hung up on the tenet that the earth was six thousand years old, and Jesus riding a triceratops, which brought to mind televangelists and anti-abortion rallies and the NRA, the crusades and persecution of the Jews. He left the sanctuary in a flop sweat, hoping he wouldn't run into anyone he knew on the way out.

Chapter Thirty-Five
McSorley's

After leaving St. Patrick's, Phillip made his way to the only other Manhattan location outside of a firehouse or police station that struck him as a symbol of his new Irish heritage.

He headed south down to East Seventh Street in the Village, toward Cooper Union, along gritty streets lined with tiny galleries and student coffee shops. The day was growing warm. Girls appeared in shorts and tiny dresses, in tank tops and halters, yoga pants and running tights, on roller skates and bicycles and pushing strollers. Phillip loved New York on a humid, overcast afternoon. He recalled navigating these streets with Marty. New York often reminded him of Marty, even years after they'd divorced.

Decades ago he and Spencer used to come to this hallowed place, which extolled a different aspect of Irish religion and culture: Mc-Sorley's Ale House. It looked exactly as it had in the 1980s—which was as it had looked in the 1880s—the clover-green sign with white lettering floating above a black façade the color of Irish stout. The view of the low-slung storefront beneath a red brick tenement ratcheted a nostalgic excitement—that feeling of getting ready to meet up with your friends in a bar when you were young and good looking and financially solvent and living in the greatest city in the world; when New York unfurled before you like a rich, embroidered carpet. When you could do anything—which they often did.

What Phillip did on a particular night at McSorley's in 1987 was meet Marty—although she wouldn't become his wife for some time. Was it coincidence that turning Irish had also turned Phillip back toward where he'd met Marty, or was something else at work?

Phillip had gone to McSorley's that evening with friends from the old neighborhood on Long Island who'd moved to Manhattan. Max

'The Factor' lived in a railroad flat just off East 15th Street; he'd taken a job with a Wall Street firm near Battery Park. Phillip's other friends toiled in advertising or sales, or for insurance companies, or waited tables while hoping to be discovered as musicians or writers. Spencer came out to meet them that night as well, before playing a gig, and the group procured a couple of big round tables close to the bar.

They were celebrating—a birthday or promotion, or someone's impending move to California or that someone else had just passed the bar exam. In those days they always had an event worth celebrating.

Spencer met Marty up at the bar first—he was gone a long time when it was his turn to haul back a dozen glass mugs foaming with dark mahogany beer. He waved for Phillip to help him carry them, and when Phillip rose and went to the bar, Spencer said: "This girl is fantastic, but she's going to friggin' *love* you!"

Phillip was never sure what his brother meant by that, but he was right nonetheless. He and Marty talked at the bar before he invited her to their table and she brought a few of her friends, which made her even more welcome.

She was an art student at Cooper Union. She wore a choker of tiny gray pearls and a motorcycle jacket and jeans the color of cigar ash. A sweet complicated breeze rose off of her—lilacs through smoke, warm doughnuts and bacon—he couldn't identify it other than to recognize it as a dangerous intoxicant.

"What do you do?" Phillip asked her above the noise of a few hundred other men asking other young women what they did without listening to the answers.

"I'm studying art," Marty said. "Why is that always the first question men ask in this city?"

"Where are you from?" Phillip followed with, thinking this was a pivot to a different topic, a segue spinning off of her clue that she wasn't from here.

"And that's always the second question. Iowa," she said.

Phillip felt stumped so he introduced himself and extended his hand.

"You have a very strong grip," he said. "Piglets or pigments?"

"I don't understand." Her smile was so innocent and uncomplicated he felt he'd never seen one like it on the Eastern Seaboard.

"Dumb joke. Not even a joke, really. Piglets, like you worked on

Old Macdonald's farm or something. In Iowa. It's stupid. Pigments, like you were crushing pigments to make your own paint. I don't even know what I mean. I'm nervous, you're beautiful."

"That's sweet," she said. "Very disarming. What do you do, Phillip? Where are you from? Can I see your resume, too?"

"I am totally unprepared for this interview," Phillip said. "But I want the job. I'll make up for any shortcomings with my passion for the work."

"I like you," she said. "You're odd."

"My brother told me you would. And he's never wrong—just ask him."

Despite the artiste persona Marty curated she came from money; her father owned acres of soybean and feed corn fields back in the Midwest. But beneath *that* ran the rebel streak of an artist, and under that, a phyllo layer of little-girl playfulness. She went on and on, like a pastry, and Phillip meant to get at the honeyed core of her—which not even ten years of marriage revealed. She remained an enigma to him to the end, when she claimed that the solid wall of his resistance to going deeper in their relationship was forcing her off in another direction, down some alternate hallway in the maze of finding what *she* wanted from life.

Phillip still missed her—if he was properly interpreting that hollow feeling in his solar plexus—as he entered McSorley's and sat in one of the old wobbly chairs at a small table. He ordered the corned beef sandwich and eavesdropped on two men at the bar speaking with—yep—Irish brogues.

Phillip drank the cool, bitter beer the waiter brought him in two glass mugs and listened to the men's thick accents. They could be from Dublin, he thought. They could be his cousins. He was tempted to talk with them. But what would he say: that he was Irish, too?

Weren't his memories of bar mitzvahs and drinking parties on Atlantic Beach and summer camp in the Catskills what made him who he really was—far more than invisible intertwined strands of deoxyribonucleic acid? Did he really have as much in common with two Irish strangers at a pub, or with a distant golf pro, as he did with the person he'd always thought himself to be?

Nah—he was a New York Jew, if not a very good one. Despite his newly-discovered lineage, regardless of what DNA had to say.

Phillip turned his attention back to his sandwich, and recognized

157

the perfect symbolism of his lunch—corned beef: he'd hit upon the thing his two cultures had in common—and laughed out loud, causing the men at the bar to move away from where he sat.

Chapter Thirty-Six

Danny

WHEN PHILLIP LEFT THEIR hotel to flee the country, Spencer decided to stay there one more night. Not knowing in advance how things might go in Ballydraiocht, they'd only booked the rooms for three days and were adding on to the reservation each day, so there was nothing to cancel.

After Spencer checked out he settled into Trisha's old room in the Elliot house—it was the largest among the children's bedrooms, and on the far side from Lorna and Patrick's room. The walls were hung with photos that Trisha had taken. There were several of the same girl whose photo hung on the wall of the Braden Arms, where they'd had their farewell dinner: the long-haired, freckled Irish princess—portraits, snapshots of her and Trisha with their arms around each other, a photo of a women's rugby team with the two of them, muddied and grass-stained, in striped uniforms, at the center.

Trisha picked him up after getting off work and they went for dinner in a pub in a neighboring town so they wouldn't be disturbed by the many folks Trisha knew in Ballydraiocht. They ran into the guitar player from Gorsey Park anyway—he'd come to the pub so nobody would see him with the sister of his former girlfriend.

"Things are going well with you two," he said.

Spencer wondered if it was a question or a statement—the Irish manner of speaking made it difficult to tell.

"I've no notion what you mean, Danny," Trisha said. "But how are things going with Shannon?"

"I've no notion what *you* mean," Danny said. He tilted his lager in their direction and went back to his table.

"Just so you know," Trisha said to Spencer. "I haven't uttered a peep to anyone about us. Not that there's much to peep about yet. But folks round here have an uncanny sense of other people's business. You'll be at the Tesco picking up some crisps and old Mrs. Waggoner will say, 'So, Trisha, how's the diarrhea, then?' or 'That Williams boy was always a creepy one,' and they'll smile and go on their way.

"Good to know," Spencer said. "I'll keep an eye out for them. The Williams boy *and* Mrs. Waggoner."

The next night Trisha seared tuna steaks and tossed a salad at her house. They talked about music and made out on the couch. She dropped him back at her parents place at eleven.

At midnight Spencer heard a commotion outside his window and when he pulled the curtain aside Trisha was climbing over the balcony railing. His room was on the second floor. He opened the sliding glass door.

"First time I've snuck *into* my parents house at night to meet a boy," she said, out of breath.

"Don't you have a key?" Spencer asked.

"Of course I have a key, but where's the fun in that? I want my parents to think I went home. Not that they would care. They've seen far worse from me. But why advertise. Especially since I'm not clear on your intentions. Or my own. It's early for that. But I wanted to see more of you."

"I'd like you to see all of me," Spencer said.

"There'll be plenty of time for that," Trisha said. "This isn't such a romantic setting then, is it? My old bedroom?"

"The golf trophies are a turn-on." Spencer said. "I also discovered that your clothes don't fit me."

"I've not made out with anyone in here," Trisha said. "For weeks . . ."
So they did.

"Let's try all the rooms," Spencer suggested.

"Not my parents' room," Trisha said. "That would be too weird."

"We could wait until they're not in there."

She hit him with a stuffed unicorn. "This is Riley," she said. "Riley got me through some difficult times."

"Padraig told us about your brother Devon and the accident," Spencer said.

"That's an odd thing to have shared with you. Probably he was trying to protect my da? So that he doesn't try to adopt you and Phillip both and leave you the house in his will?"

"What's even odder," Spencer said. "My mother lost a brother when she was young. He fell out of a truck, too. She was driving."

"What do you make of it?"

"I can't say," Spencer said. "Something's at work here."

"How's that?"

"I keep thinking of Zen koans—I studied them back when I was using a lot of drugs and looking for enlightenment. They're similar to the lateral thinking puzzles my mom used to throw at us. But freakier. I can't tell if this is more like *The Taste of Banzo's Sword* or *When the student is ready the teacher appears*."

"That's some mystical shite," Trisha said.

"I can't put my finger on it. I can't make it sound rational, or point to direct cause and effect. A lot of coincidences are swirling around. They're like tee-shirts, and I'm stuck in the washing machine with them. I can glimpse them flashing past me in the water and suds but I can't see them clearly. I can make out vague colors but not the designs. Is that a concert tee shirt? Does it have hearts and flowers? Does it depict the zombie apocalypse? Does it just say 'Budweiser'?"

"What does any of this have to do with Zen?"

"That's the part of the riddle I haven't solved yet," Spencer said.

———

On Spencer's third morning at Lorna and Patrick's house, Padraig picked him up to play golf. Trisha was at work. No one in the family acted like it was strange that Spencer remained in Ireland. He surmised they knew nothing about his courting Trisha. They weren't any less warm. They didn't look at him sideways. They made him feel like an intrinsic piece—if not an edge or a corner piece—of the jigsaw puzzle of their lives.

But during the golf round with Padraig, there it was.

The two men had seemed eager for some time together. Spencer thought they each saw in the other a quality they liked, or aspired to, or admired—though he couldn't have articulated what it was; the closest explanation was Spencer's notion that Padraig 'got' him.

As they were teeing up on the seventh hole of the Old Course at Ballydraiocht, Padraig observed—with no preamble—"So. You're getting on well with my sister."

Spencer couldn't tell if it was an inquiry or an accusation.

"I am," he said warily.

He admired the Irishman's slow playing of the sister card, waiting until more than a third of the way through their round. He wondered if Padraig was so methodical as to have done the math.

"She's a cracker, that one," Padraig added.

"That means something very different in the U.S.," Spencer said.

"What does it mean?"

"A toothless redneck. A banjo-strumming racist."

"Yeah, that's not what I mean about Trisha."

"I figured."

"She's a stand-up girl, is what I mean. A treasure. A real corker."

"She is," Spencer said. "I totally get that."

"But not as tough as she'd like you to think."

"No?"

Padraig stepped up and hit a low running draw that shaped itself to the edge of the fairway and then careened off a slope that gave it a bobsled kick farther down and into the middle of the runway of shorter grass.

"Speed slot," Padraig explained. "James McKenna, the golf architect, put it there in 1897. With maybe a little help from God."

"That was good of him," Spencer said. "Of both of them." He executed a blacksmith's swing, making up with sheer force what he lacked in technique. His ball towered into the cloud-mottled sky and dropped mid-fairway forty yards behind Padraig's.

Padraig looked over as if he hadn't considered anyone could swing that way without ending up in the hospital.

"She's been through some things," Padraig went on. "Just be careful. Everyone likes you so far, Spencer. Don't make us have to kill you and bury your body on the moors." He looked at Spencer eye to eye. Then he laughed.

Spencer thought: so, they have moors here after all.

The two men shifted back into full cordiality, with some fist bumps following good shots and Padraig searching for Spencer's mishit balls when they drifted off into the marram grass.

Spencer was impressed with the *way* his new acquaintance raised the issue of his sister like a steep downhill putt, just getting it started and letting Spencer act as the features in the green that directed where this thing would go from there.

But Fox-trotting Jesus, he'd had it up to here with others telling him to be careful.

———————

The next evening Spencer and Trisha prepared dinner together at her cottage. While they drank French chardonnay on her flagstone patio as a roast cooked in the oven, he said, "How is it that a beautiful, drum-playing, lead-singing, only sparsely-tattooed ginger such as yourself isn't married in a small town like this?"

"So we're turning to the deeply personal now, are we?" Trisha said. "I'll bet my brother put a bug in your ear."

"Maybe a small bug. In just one ear," Spencer admitted.

"He loves me, my brother does," she said. "But it can be a bit inconvenient. Like having a drooling St. Bernard following you around, making a gooey mess of everything."

If Spencer had learned anything from the many women he'd dated, he knew to let this play out. He also knew that brothers could be inconvenient.

"He's always overprotecting," she continued. "Like a good brother. Or like a good father, might be more accurate. Which I've got one of already . . . "

"That puts you one ahead of me," Spencer said.

"Yeah, there's that. But I might as well get out with it all now, since he's opened the door."

She told him about her years in Dublin and London and Edinburgh and Amsterdam since university, chasing a guitar-playing novelist, a lovely woman who hurt her afresh in each new city they moved to. The freckled beauty from the photographs. It went on for a decade—until Trisha returned to Ballydraiocht to regroup, and then the job at Irish Heritage came up, and she began playing music with some of her old mates, and it was the right place to stay for a while. That was six years ago, and she was happy. And also sad. But happy part-time, which was a vast improvement.

"I loved her like a drunk little princess," she explained. "It was the first time I let myself go in that direction. I'd been with mostly boys before that. I let her become more important than the love I had for myself. She loved me back a little—as much as she was capable of. I wanted her to be someone different—and she could have been but she didn't want to, which I understand now. So I came home. To where they have to love me."

"Just so you know. I won't do that. Break your heart, I mean. Treat you like a drunk little princess. Like any kind of little drunk."

"Like the Meatloaf song," she said. "'You Won't Do That.'"

"I was thinking I would try a little tenderness. . . "

"For feck's sake, tell me you're not quoting from *The Commitments*? You know they're on a postage stamp now?"

"No, Otis Redding. The original version. If I was going to quote from *The Commitments* I'd imitate the priest who corrects the confessor who thinks that Marvin Gaye wrote 'When a Man Loves a Woman,' by saying, 'Percy Sledge.'"

"I *cannot* believe you know that . . ."

"I'm deeper than I appear," Spencer said.

"Yeah, right. And just so *you* know. I wasn't looking for a boyfriend when you came along. Or a girlfriend. I'm not likely to move to New York."

"Whoa," Spencer said. "Let's just get through dinner. And maybe have sex at some point, if you think you're back on your original team. Then we can go from there."

"Yeah, sex," she said. "I miss that. It's been a while." She put her wine glass up to her face to hide her smile. Her hair was a flame through the Chardonnay.

"I can help with that. Just let me know."

Which she did, later that night, with half the pink roast sitting out on the stone kitchen counter, the two of them halfway into the bottle of Burgundy they opened after finishing the Chardonnay.

"I don't take this lightly," she said in the bedroom, stepping out of her sundress. "And I've not been with a man in a while."

The day's final light bounced off the ocean in the distance. Spencer watched it out the window. Trisha slipped her tiny, bright green panties down her legs.

"And so you know. I rarely have sex with someone who's my half brother's half brother," she said.

"That's comforting," Spencer said. "It makes me feel special."

Afterward, sunk together into the warm memory-foam bed with the Irish linen comforter tossed onto the floor, she looked up at the ceiling, painted around the edges with wild roses. She stared out the window with its distant view of the sea.

"What are you thinking?" he asked, hating the question the second he uttered it: the question that bludgeoned relationships, especially early on. Was she regretful? Nostalgic? Did she miss her freckled princess? Was she riding a wave of post-coital endorphins?

"It's funny," she said. "I've always been a little more intellectual than most folks here. And more frugal. But tonight, I see it's true what the townsfolk have whispered: that I had a little Jew in me."

In the morning Spencer breakfasted at Lorna and Patrick's house as if he hadn't come home an hour before they woke.

"So you'll be moving over to Trisha's house then?" Lorna said, serving his oatmeal. He was grateful to be outside the land of full Irish breakfasts.

Spencer's instinct was to pretend he didn't know what she meant. Instead he said, "I may well be."

"We'll all be glad of it," Lorna said.

"While we're on about getting to know each other," Trisha said the next evening as they ate a broiled game hen, "Your ma must have been something. What was she like?"

Spencer picked up his tumbler of wine. He preferred drinking his wine from a tumbler. "She was the queen of misdirection," he began.

He put the glass down, poked at his food with the wrong end of his fork. "She invented fake news fifty years before it became popular."

"Were you close to her?"

"I thought so. For most of my life. But then the next thing you know . . ."

She grimaced. "Do *not* say, 'Bob's your uncle.'"

"No. I was going to say 'Old Jed's a millionaire.'"

"Huh?"

"It's from a ridiculous American TV show."

She shook her head. "Which is related to your mother . . . how?"

"It's not. It's just misdirection, which is related to my mother, since I learned it from her: avoiding emotion, making a joke when someone you care about is trying to be intimate. Lying about our father."

"I get it," she said.

"I have no doubt my mom loved us. But we often found ourselves thinking one thing was happening when it was something else entirely. We can see that now. My mom was the Mexican hombre."

"The what?"

"It's a puzzle she gave us when we were kids. There's this Mexican man who comes to the U.S. border every day with a wheelbarrow full of dirty laundry. The border guards have a look through the clothes each morning and never find anything other than clothes. This goes on every day. They know he can't be traveling to the U.S. to have his laundry done this often, he must be smuggling something. Our mom said we had to figure out what the Mexican hombre was up to.

"We devised theories: he was a cocaine mule who'd swallowed balloons full of drugs. He'd sewed currency into the lining of the clothes. Microfilm. He had something hidden in his gold fillings. He was transmitting information. She would not tell us the answer. She'd say no, they cavity searched him. They x-rayed the clothing. They checked his dental work. Whatever we guessed she had a reason why that wasn't it.

"Phillip had a fit one day, yelling that the Mexican hombre wasn't up to anything after all. He was just doing his laundry. He said he wouldn't guess any more, he was done with her stupid riddles. Breakfasts became very quiet.

"One morning we came into the kitchen before school. The table wasn't set. Mom hadn't made any toast or eggs or poured our orange juice. Phillip and I stood in the dark wondering if she'd dropped dead in the night.

"She came in and said: 'Wheelbarrows. He was smuggling wheelbarrows. You can make your own fucking breakfast.' That was our mom. *She* was a wheelbarrow smuggler. And the wheelbarrow was our father."

"That's a good one," Trisha said. "But she misled you to protect you, yes? She did it to make your life easier, right?"

"Sure, but maybe also her life," Spencer said. "The ground is shaky on that subject. The ground is like Jell-O. Like a green Jell-O mold that you can partially see through. You can see what color it is, what flavor—although I think we always referred to the color itself as the actual flavor, like green Jell-O or red Jell-O—but then there's also stuff suspended *inside* the Jell-O that you can't see as clearly."

He stopped to see if this was making any sense. He didn't know if they had Jell-O in Ireland. Was it possible only Americans were dumb enough to have invented Jell-O and consider it a food item?

"So you can see the stuff suspended in the Jell-O, but you don't know if it's fresh fruit or canned fruit cocktail or little Mandarin orange segments or I don't know, something toxic. Like diced mixed vegetables. Or salmon. Not that diced mixed vegetables and salmon are toxic, but they wouldn't be very good in Jell-O. Maybe more like stones or marbles or little colorful bits of soap or wax or shoe laces suspended in the Jell-O."

"We have Jell-O. But mostly it's for tequila shots."

"When I was growing up it was considered a treat—like: you've been a good boy so here's some cold, colored water with sugar and animal bones in it. Bill Cosby used to hawk it on television. Before he was a rapist."

"This whole Jell-O tangent," she said. "It's your own wheelbarrow smuggling?"

"Yep," Spencer admitted.

"Back to you mother, then. You loved her," Trisha said.

"Of course I loved her. She was my mother."

"But you feel she betrayed you?"

Spencer wouldn't have seen it precisely that way but Trisha wasn't wrong. Misled them, was how he might describe it. Because she probably thought it was for their own good.

"What are you, The Amazing Kreskin?" he asked, taking some satisfaction that she couldn't know The Amazing Kreskin.

"I'd say more like the amazing grace," she said. "Which is probably lost on you, not being Catholic. Or even Irish. But it's about forgiving people. Or taking time to understand their motivations. If your mother loved you that's no small thing. A lot of folks don't get that."

He loved the way she pronounced 'thing' as 'ting'.

"I've always had that," Spencer said. "And my brother. He loves me, too. Even if he's only half a brother to me now."

"I can see that. I may not know fuck-all about genetics or DNA tests," she said. "But folks loving each other—whether brothers or wives or men loving other men—that's something. It has nothing to do with science. It's stronger than biology."

"Chalk one up against science," Spencer said.

Chapter Thirty-Seven

David Schwartz

SPENCER EXCHANGED FREQUENT TEXTS with his brother. It became a morning ritual.

How's things?
All great here.
I ran into David Schwartz from the old neighborhood.
Please water my plants—oh, and I'm falling in love with Trisha.

On a Tuesday morning Spencer's cell phone rang while he was having coffee—coffee that *he'd* made: Trisha still wasn't to be trusted in that regard—on the front patio. Trisha had ridden off to work on her bicycle.

"It's 2:00 a.m. there," Spencer said after picking up.

"Couldn't sleep," Phillip said. "Wanted to talk."

"Not again with the sentence fragments . . ."

"Any idea when you're coming home?" Phillip asked. "Not trying to rush you. Just curious." Then he added, "Okay: I miss you. Maybe I am trying to rush you."

"No plans," Spencer said. "I'm going to ride this out for a while. You know—the girl. When are *you* coming back *here*, is what Irish folk are wondering? I might miss you, too."

Phillip was quiet across the ocean. Then he said, "Cousin Leah called me a couple of days ago. Aunt Phyllis is in the hospital."

"The regular hospital or the padded one?" Spencer asked. "The one where they provide helmets and take away your belt?"

"I think it's serious, for Leah to have called me," Phillip said.

"Why did she think you'd care? About her mother?"

"Don't be mean. You and Leah always loved each other in some weird way growing up."

"Yeah, maybe," Spencer said. "Until she didn't any more, because I have a penis."

"That's not what went wrong between you."

"We were close for a while in our twenties. But then she wasn't big on men in general. And I was high a lot back then. And for some reason Uncle Jerry didn't want us to be friends. He called me not long before he died and told me . . ."—here Spencer put on a thick Sephardic accent—'Stay away from my daw-ta. I am only gonna' tell you once.' That didn't help. He was politely implying he could have me whacked. Which is also what Padraig implied this week if I don't treat Trisha well. But he was at least half joking."

"I wasn't aware of that with Uncle Jerry," Phillip said. "I thought you'd want to know about Aunt Phyllis. We're not teeming with relatives."

"Well, *you* are. But okay, thanks for telling me. About Phyllis. Beneath my witty sarcasm I'm sorry to hear it. I'm sure you know that. It's sad. I hope she's okay. What's she in for, anyway?"

"Cancer."

"That reminds me . . . " Spencer said.

"Go on."

"My friend went to the doctor recently . . .'"

"Which friend?" Phillip asked.

"A friend. It doesn't matter. Jimmy. My friend Jimmy. And the doctor tells him, 'Well, Jimmy, I'm sorry to say. I have bad news, and worse news.'

"Jimmy says, 'Well, what's the bad news,' and the doctor says, 'I hate to tell you. . . . You have inoperable brain cancer.'

"'Well, what's the *worse* news, for fuck's sake,' Jimmy says, and the doctor says, 'You also have Alzheimer's.'

"'Oh, thank God,' Jimmy says. 'I thought for a minute you were going to say I had inoperable brain cancer.'"

Chapter Thirty-Eight

The Portland Timbers

A COUPLE OF DAYS later, Spencer moved to Trisha's house.

"Nobody seems to mind," he told Phillip on the phone.

"Why would they mind?"

"I'm sure I'll give them a reason," Spencer said. "What's happening there, in New York, anyway?"

"I'm looking at a property deal in Portland, Oregon," Phillip said. He pronounced Oregon as: 'are-ig-in'. "I'm considering going out to look at it. I'm driving myself nuts at home. I'm thinking too much. Like I'm trying to solve one of Mom's lateral thinking puzzles. Except the puzzle is me. Maybe a trip west would be good."

Jenny had taught the boys that travel provided perspective on the place you left behind. Phillip was convincing himself this was why he wanted to go to Portland. And that traveling would allow him to commune with the spirit of their mother. He also knew he was rationalizing his powerful instinct to flee. He was intrigued by his brother's idea that he could blame this on genetics—on the inheritable proteins that orchestrated the fight or flight response. But he also knew he was fleeing to Portland because he was back in New York. Just a few blocks from Marty. *That* was the puzzle *he* needed to solve. At least, he reasoned to himself, he'd made Marty the first priority of things he was running from.

Spencer listened to his brother's voice as it bounced between satellites and cell towers across the planet.

"I would note for the record," Spencer said, "that you have new family—and also old family—here in Ireland, which is east of you. All of whom are eager for your company at an exciting and confusing and disturbing time. And you're going to board an airplane and fly approximately the same distance, but toward the opposite compass

170

point under the premise that a trip might be a good thing for you? And—fuck me with a soft pretzel—you just got *back* from a trip! Congratulations. You have become a grand master of misdirection— *literally*. It's a feat worthy of Mom."

"I have a deal there. I'm not making it up. I still work for a living," Phillip said. "And what's the difference if I'm in New York or Portland, if I'm not in Ireland?"

"I'm just noting it. For the record. When you're shopping for a souvenir for me I might like a wild steelhead. Or a long beard."

"I'm shopping for apartments," Phillip reprimanded. "And since we're on the record, don't suggest I've established a monopoly on avoidance. You've done it your whole life. You completed your ten thousand hours a long time ago."

"Speaking of Monopoly," Spencer said. "Why don't you just put up a few houses on Boardwalk and Park Place instead?"

"You're just saying that because you won second prize in a beauty contest," Phillip said, referencing one of the Community Chest cards from the famous board game.

Despite Spencer's astute observation—and when did Spencer get so insightful?—Phillip did what he'd always done in emotional situations: like Harry Angstrom in John Updike's *Rabbit* series; and, usually, like his own brother: he ran. One more common trait that united them. As if traveling away from Marty would somehow propel him closer to her.

Phillip booked the Portland trip and flew three thousand miles to the eclectic city on the west coast. He stayed at a boutique hotel downtown because he loved hotels, despite the recent prevalence of homestays and airbnbs, which brought to mind crashing in a friend's parents' basement.

Phillip liked to walk through a lobby and have a young woman in a tight dress smile at him from behind the front desk even if only because she was paid to. He liked maid service and knowing the mini-bar was tucked beneath the television, though he never used it. He felt comfortable eating in a hotel restaurant where the other patrons were also displaced travelers from somewhere else; this was the version of intimacy he could allow himself.

At Phillip's hotel in Portland you could pay to have a Labrador Retriever sleep in your room overnight. Down the street he experienced a *perfect*, pristine sandwich: burnt brisket ends and local goat cheese (probably made from talking goats) and roasted peppers served on warm ciabatta bread, from a mobile cart. While eating in a park he watched a man in a Darth Vader mask riding a unicycle and playing a set of flaming bagpipes. He took a photo and texted it to Max 'The Factor' Feingold.

You couldn't make this shit up. If Portland were a person it would be Spencer. Which was another way Phillip convinced himself that by traveling away from his family, he was moving closer to them. Then he recognized the thought as total bullshit. Then he remembered a quote from Ben Franklin that he'd read in a history class at Vassar: man is a rational creature because he can rationalize almost anything.

Phillip woke early, drank a double espresso in the lobby coffee bar, and picked up a red BMW a block from his hotel that he'd reserved through a car-sharing app on his phone. He drove out to see the property, located across the Willamette River from his hotel. The onslaught of bikes coming at him on the Hawthorne Bridge made him wonder if he was in Tokyo or Amsterdam.

The project consisted of one hundred fifty-seven new market-rate apartments on eight floors in two buildings. The finishes weren't what he'd hoped for—developers had installed laminate flooring and hollow-core doors and cheap vinyl windows—but the neighborhood was booming, with new construction rising among the quaint brick industrial buildings and Victorian houses. Brew pubs and coffee shops were as ubiquitous as storm drains.

He'd examined the numbers on the airplane. The investment would fit nicely in his portfolio—a residential building in a hot West Coast location that should make for a solid five-year play. As Phillip focused on details he was able to shut out his emotional and familial strife.

He had a lunch meeting with three members of the project's ownership group at a sustainable sushi place on the east side. Phillip hadn't even known that sushi was endangered. The men wore Prana and Kuhl slacks and expensive, untucked dress shirts and outdoorsy shoes, as if departing for a sea kayaking expedition later in the day. They were casual and confident and good-looking young men who enjoyed themselves at lunch and didn't care whether he bought their building or not, which made him more interested. Phillip loosened his tie and unbuttoned the top button of his shirt when the second round of sake arrived.

After the meeting he took off his suit jacket and removed the tie entirely and explored the neighborhood, checking his Fitbit to make sure he got in his requisite steps for the day. There was no better way to assess real estate than to traverse the neighborhood you were buying into—and Phillip often hoofed past a potential purchase at different times of day before making an offer on a building to catch wind of a morning-only methadone clinic or a bar that played loud music at night, or a street where traffic snarled angrily at rush hour.

He always examined financials fanatically, as a basis for not rejecting a project; like any good forensic specialist, garnering additional information not obvious at first glance had always been key to his success. Even before this whole DNA kerfuffle, he assumed he'd inherited the organizational rigor from his mother.

The Portland opportunity also *felt* great—although he recognized the city around it was seducing him. That he was vulnerable and impressionable, owing to events happening at a five-thousand-mile distance. He didn't normally make decisions based on feelings, but things weren't normal at this time. Did he need to be more agile and flexible in regard to his feelings, as old Patrick had observed? As Marty had insinuated two decades ago?

That night, after eating alder-planked salmon at a renowned Portland fish house and spending an hour at Powell's Books—mostly in the science and travel sections—he wandered around downtown. Among the old cast iron facades and cobblestone streets near the river he discovered an Irish bar called Kells, which he thought of as a sign—though of *what* he wasn't sure.

Spencer would have loved that the bar was crowded with long-bearded hipsters, many wearing scarves from the Portland Timbers soccer club, which was playing a match that night against their arch rivals from Seattle. The game showed on screens around the room and the folks watching in the bar emoted like Italian opera stars.

Kells was loud with soccer fans of all ages and stripes, but lacked the requisite ancient career drinkers tottering on stools or leaning on the bar to hold themselves up, which he might have seen in an Irish pub in Manhattan; or any bridge and tunnel crowd from the suburbs—though Portland had eleven bridges. Phillip drank a grape-fruity IPA rather than his new-normal Guinness and considered going downstairs to the cigar room, but he didn't want to stink up clothes that would be traveling in a suitcase with other clothes, and which might prove a bad influence on the rest of his wardrobe.

When the Timbers scored off a corner kick in the second half, a large man wearing a leather kilt threw both arms around Phillip and lifted him off the floor in a bear hug. The man's beard brushed his forehead. The fellow roared something indecipherable. When he put him back down, a fresh IPA awaited Phillip on the bar.

A friendly town, if strange.

Phillip noticed that Kells was full of women of varying ages and sizes and coutures, and that tattoos were ubiquitous among them. He eyed a sleek, black-haired, middle-aged beauty with librarian's glasses and a full sleeve of colorful ink; another he might have described as a lanky sorority girl with blue Sanskrit letters visible across her back beneath a strapless party dress; and a pixie biker with neck tattoos of mermaids and porpoises. It was like a comic book shop where all the content was printed on people.

A woman appeared next to him at the bar—gray-streaked, wavy blond hair, fortyish, a winning, shy smile that she turned on him full force. A multi-colored sunburst in bright blues and reds and yellows decorated one well-gymed forearm.

He wondered about the smile but she turned away from him and he realized: simple, small-town warmth. As their shoulders touched he smelled fresh river air and candied pecans.

When the Timbers game was over—they beat the Sounders 1-0—she turned and yelled, "Are you a fan?"

"I like it," Phillip shouted. "Even though nobody ever scores."

"I just started playing in a co-ed league," she explained. "I've been a runner my whole life, but that started to feel so solitary."

Her voice, with a lick of western twang, sounded like fiddle music, pure and clear. She worked at Nike. Everyone here worked at Nike. Or for a company that worked for Nike. They ran marathons on their coffee breaks. She was from Idaho, originally, she told him.

"Are there really people from Idaho?" he said.

She laughed, guessed that he was from the East Coast. She'd spent some time in New York when first dating her husband, she said.

When her husband came into the bar in a Portland Timbers jersey they all shook hands and introduced themselves. The man was Phillip's age. Owned an ad agency. Played bluegrass and rode his bicycle everywhere. They raised bees and chickens in the yard of their one-hundred-year-old Craftsman home a half mile from downtown.

Was this shit for real? Had someone slipped a roofie in the IPA he was drinking only because the barman had recommended it—it was brewed just down the street, from hops grown nearby, and probably blessed by virgins camping beneath windmills on the solar roof deck, where more bees were tended by Buddhist carpenters who also alchemized mead. The couple invited him to a barbecue at their house on the weekend if he was still in town. They had a girl for him to meet.

Phillip couldn't help laughing. He'd been so enthralled by the city, imagining a life there, that he'd forgotten to collect his receipts throughout the day.

Later, he called Spencer from his hotel room.

"I ordered you extra baked beans this morning," Spencer said when he picked up.

"That's thoughtful. How goes it there?"

"All good. How's Poland, or Portland, wherever you went?"

"I'm thinking of moving here," Phillip said. "It's a magical land of friendly goddesses and soccer and fresh, delicious micro-brews. And possibly the best sandwich I've ever had."

"Hey, I have an idea," Spencer said.

"I don't need any more ideas." Phillip said. "I'm confused enough already."

Spencer recognized the line from the movie *The Brothers McMullen*. "How about coming back to Ireland to face your future?" Spencer said. "Trust me. You're not moving to Portland. You're over fifty and in some kind of crisis. You're a New York lifer. You have Yoo-Hoo in your veins. You still love the Mets, for fuck's sake, despite their ongoing mediocrity. You'd starve to death out there eating kale and spotted owls. There's no H&H bagels—what are you thinking?"

"I don't know *what* I'm thinking," Phillip admitted. "I'm running away. It's what I do."

"Of course you don't have any idea what you're doing. You thought you were on junior year abroad. But now you're getting clear again."

"I feel like I need a change," Phillip said.

"I have another idea; it's a lot like my first idea: how about a whole new family? In another country, far away? How about that for a change?"

"It's hard to explain," Phillip said. "That feels like what I need the change *from*."

"You're not yourself right now. We'll discuss this further when you're in your right mind," Spencer said. "When you're less delusional."

"I'm scared," Phillip admitted.

"Of course you're scared. Your whole life is unraveling. Our mother turned out to be a professional illusionist. Our father was an imposter. He wasn't even our father, that's how much of an imposter he was. Now all the characters in our movie have changed costumes and they're all someone else. Including us. We have to get to know them all over again. It's confusing. It's like somebody combined *The Life of Pi* with *Psycho* and *Atonement* and *The Great Gatsby* and made one film combining them all, where a tiger eats a pile of beautiful shirts then kills his mother in the shower and lies about it to Keira Knightley. It's like the Gaelic version of *The Sixth Sense*: I see dead Irish people. Dogs and cats are living together. There's underwear in the trees. And the surprise endings keep coming. Except they're not even endings. So of course you're fucking scared. But you need to come back and face it."

"I know. I'm going to." Then he added: "I miss Marty. I think I want a mulligan."

"I did *not* see that coming," Spencer said.

"Me either. But it makes sense. I had to run away to get close."

"Fuck me on a trampoline, that's it!" Spencer yelled. "That's the clue that was eluding me."

"I'm so glad," Phillip said. "Even though I have no idea what you're talking about."

"I finally solved something before you did. It's taken my whole life. It's an old Zen koan. Not to be confused with a Ben Cohen, who we went to junior high school with."

"Is it the running away to get close? You knew that already. About both of us. I've been waiting for you to tell me again how genes are responsible."

"When the mother dies," Spencer said, "the girlfriend appears."

Chapter Thirty-Nine
Molly

SPENCER MIGHT HAVE FOUND his brother's most recent misdirection to Oregon—Oregon? Really?—more confounding if he wasn't so caught up with Trisha. She took off from work and they rode bicycles out into the country and enjoyed a picnic with wine and French cheese, then had sex on a blanket on a deserted beach. Which was fecking cold and windy, but fun.

Another day Spencer borrowed her car and drove to the Bromore Cliffs and Ballydraiocht Castle and a couple of other ancient ruins nearby.

He played golf with Padraig and Patrick, who refrained from any further swing corrections. In the name of thoroughness, Spencer visited all the other pubs in the town. On Friday nights Trisha played music at St. Urants. He was developing a routine.

Then he played golf with Trisha. She suggested driving a few towns over to a quirky links course that tourists hadn't discovered yet.

"You've heard about my game," Spencer said. "You're not the first great-looking person who doesn't want to be seen with me on the golf course."

"It's not like that exactly," Trisha said. "But it *is* like that a little. There's no reason for everyone to know our business—they'll figure it out soon enough. Plus you don't want your half brother's half brother to see the whupping I'm going to give you."

"That is among the hottest things anyone's ever said to me."

On the first tee Trisha showed off her compact, fluid swing, finishing with the kind of exaggerated extension that distinguished good players. They watched her ball flight as it carried over a crescent of beach and landed in the fairway short of a pod of bunkers.

"Not a bad one, a'tall" she said.

Spencer took one of his patented hard-to-watch swings and also cleared the hazard, landing thirty yards behind Trisha.

"Jayzus, Joseph, and Ben Hogan, that's *got* to hurt," she said.

Trisha parred the first three holes and then chipped in for a birdie on the par-three fourth. She executed a double fist pump like a martial arts move.

"Your dad teach you that?" Spencer asked.

"The chipping?"

"The Kung Fu dance step."

"Nah. I learned that in rugby."

"How are you at board games?"

"What, like cards and such?"

"Monopoly. Scrabble. Cities and Knights of Catan."

"Can't say I've played much of those."

"Perfect. That's what we'll do when you're done dismembering me here. So I can show off *my* skills."

"It'll be some other skills I'll want from you," she said, bending to pull her ball out of the cup. She lifted her skirt in a curtsey, revealing her bare thighs. "*Now* try to concentrate on that putt," she said.

He made the downhill double breaker as if he'd never doubted it. He bowed like Pavarotti, sweeping his arms as if the rolling hills of tall grass were a stadium full of opera aficionados doing the wave.

On the back nine they smoked Hemingway Short Story cigars that Spencer pulled out of his bag, half joking, until he saw she was game.

"This is working out well," he said.

She dug in the pocket of her bag and produced a leather flask.

"Scotch?" he asked.

"If I wanted to poison you."

He took a small sip, tongue against the opening. He shook his head until his cheeks wobbled.

"What the what?" he said.

"They call it Poitín. Or Craythur," she said. "Irish moonshine. But don't tell anyone—it's illegal."

"What do they make it from? Gasoline? Diapers?"

"That's po-day-does," she said. "In the old times they used to hold it under the noses of dead people to see if they could be revived."

"Is it possible that's how they got dead in the first place?"

"'With a love of the liquor poor Tim was born, to help him on with his work each day he'd a drop o' the craythur every morn.' That's from *Finnegan's Wake*."

"*You're* the person who read *Finnegan's Wake*?" Spencer said. "I thought it was an urban myth."

"I read the first page, anyway. To write a paper at University."

He shook his head as if he'd just inhaled a full shot of craythur. "I have a feeling this is going to work out well," Spencer said. "But I said that already. I'm flustered. I'm too happy. Everything is going right. This has never happened before."

"Just wait," Trisha said.

After golf they went for a drink in the clubhouse. The small bar was carpeted in a light blue and gray Tartan. Behind the bar a black-haired woman poured their Guinness.

"Hiya, Molly," Trish said.

"Oh, Trish," the woman said, looking at Spencer. "This must be the American. So it's boys you're after again now?"

"I think I'm done with the other," Trish said.

"I'm sorry to hear it," Molly said.

———

Spencer incorporated calls with Phillip into his morning routine: make coffee and see Trisha off to work, read *The New York Times* on-line, catch up with email, keep an eye on his investments, and speak with his brother just after noon, when Phillip was first waking up in New York. Spencer looked forward to every new day with Trisha, and to each night when he would climb into bed beside her in her black satin boxers and Sligo Rovers jersey. He happily anticipated this being his life for some time to come.

At the end of his second week in Ballydraiocht Spencer's phone rang in the late afternoon.

Phillip said, "Okay, *now* Aunt Phyllis is officially a liar," and Spencer understood this was his brother's way of saying that there would *never* be any horseback riding: that their aunt was dead.

"Ach, I'm sorry to hear that. Not so much about the horseback riding, of course. I stopped counting on that when she turned seventy and had her hips replaced. And her tiny, shrivelled heart removed.

"No, wait. I take that back. I *am* sorry. She was Mom's sister. She cared for us in her way. I'm trying to be nicer about things like this.

More real. How am I doing so far?"

"Not great," Phillip said. "But wait; there's more . . . Leah also mentioned that Phyllis left you something. Something important. I have no idea what. She wouldn't give me any details. I told her you're on an extended trip and she said you should probably come home for this. The funeral is Monday. They're going to sit shiva at Leah's house in Westchester."

Monday; three days away. What to do? What was right—for him and for everyone else?

"I think you should come. To the funeral," Phillip said.

"Yeah, the funeral. Jay-sus the Redeemer, that's inconvenient. Things are going swimmingly here. Not that we've actually gone swimming. Although we have been to the beach a few times."

"I'm sorry Aunt Phyllis couldn't die at a more opportune time."

"Me, too. I need to think. Let me call you back."

He discussed it with Trisha that night. They spread out on the Moroccan rug in front of a fire that he built with long-dormant Cub Scout techniques, and Spencer told her about how his aunt and uncle seemed to hate him his whole life, while simultaneously loving him in a kind of grudging way.

"Like a rescue dog you don't have the heart to return to the pound even though he keeps peeing in the house," Spencer said.

"You should go to the funeral," Trisha said. "Isn't it what your ma would have wanted? That way you won't have regrets. You can come back straight away afterwards, if you like."

"I like," Spencer said. "But maybe you should come with. I'm afraid if I leave without you none of this will have happened. That I'll lose something. Well . . . you. We're on a roll, wouldn't you say? I rarely get this far. It's like a game show and I've reached the bonus round."

"That's very romantic. I'd rather not go with you under these circumstances—but some other time, yes. And you won't break the spell by leaving. I can promise you. For one thing, the band likes you. And they need a backup drummer in case something happens to me."

He called Phillip back in the morning.

"I'm coming," Spencer said. "I'm doing it for Mom. Even though she's dead. Which you already know. I'm not coming because of what

Leah said—just because Phyllis left me something."

"If Mom *wasn't* dead she'd probably appreciate the sentiment."

"But I'm coming back to Ireland straight away afterward. I like to say 'straight away.'"

"Yep. The girl," Phillip said. "Got it."

"I'm worried, though. About what Phyllis left me. I'm deeply concerned. It could be a bomb, or an envelope full of anthrax, or a recording of Aunt Phyllis singing Carol King's greatest hits. Still, it's the right thing to do—coming to the funeral. It's respectful to Mom, although I wouldn't expect her to appreciate it."

"You mean because she's dead," Phillip said.

"Partly that. But also because I'm uncertain about Mom right now. I'm not talking to her. I'm angry at her, too—although I know I'm always angry. It's the secret to my unceasing hilarity. But I'm hurt, too. Which is new. I see why people don't like it."

"What are you hurt by?"

"Let's start with her treachery. And deceit. And when she grounded me and I couldn't attend Donna Castellano's sixth grade graduation party. That she kept you from knowing your father—the one thing you craved your whole life and that was in her power to provide. And that she didn't leave any clues to who *my* father might be. I'm sure I'm leaving a lot out."

Spencer paused to catch his breath. Then he said, "What could Phyllis possibly have left me, anyway, do you think? A fortune in gold doubloons? A gift certificate for polo lessons? A rack of Dior dresses twenty years out of fashion?"

"It's impolite to make fun of the newly dead," Phillip said. "You should wait out a grace period."

"It's not like I didn't make fun of her when she was alive," Spencer said. "She was the original bobble-head doll. With jowls like Churchill's."

"She was family. Something you don't have much left of at this point."

"Speaking of family, I invited Trisha to come back with me. Is that weird? I don't think she's going to, but I wanted you to know."

Phillip wasn't surprised, but he didn't think it a great idea. But he wanted to support his brother.

"Hey, your friends are always my friends," Phillip said. "And your girlfriend is always my sister."

Chapter Forty

The Queens Rhombus

PHILLIP AND SPENCER DROVE out to the cemetery on Long Island, where they'd buried their own mother not long ago. It was early enough into autumn that you could feel spring in the air—from a certain gravity or in cloud formations or some factor too subtle to definitively identify. It was a weather phenomenon Spencer claimed only existed in an oddly-shaped area between Kennedy, LaGuardia, Newark, and White Plains Airports. He theorized it was related to unusual conversions of flight patterns, and called it the Queens Rhombus—to differentiate it from the Bermuda Triangle: the phenomenon was especially strong around either of the solstices or equinoxes. If you paid attention, you could detect aspects—temperature, air quality, the scent of tortilla chips and salsa consumed watching baseball or football—of the opposite season.

The boys were upbeat and cheerful despite the occasion. They were happy to be in each other's company. Spencer kissed Phillip on both cheeks when he picked him up at the airport.

"That's very European of you," Phillip noted.

They were sorry their aunt was dead, the generation before them all but gone now and them next in line. But it was difficult to focus on death on an afternoon where the very air around them presaged the changing season and another trip of the earth around the sun.

"At least they'll be together now, in adjoining plots," Spencer said. "Mom and Phyllis. Can't you hear them bickering, and imagine the guy buried across the walkway complaining to management?"

"I'm not sure we ever talked about this: where are you going after you're dead?" Phillip asked.

"To hell, I imagine—if there is one," Spencer said. "It's a restaurant run by gym teachers. The Bee Gees headline there, but they don't play any of the good stuff, like 'Massachusetts,' or 'How Can You Mend A Broken Heart'—just 'Saturday Night Fever.' Over and over again. Every item on the dessert menu is flan."

Phillip looked at his brother, then back at the road. Probably best to drop this line of inquiry, he thought.

"How is Leah taking this whole thing, anyway?" Spencer asked. "She and her mom weren't close after Leah went on her gender bender. But at least Phyllis got a grandchild. And could lord that over her sister."

Leah and her partner had adopted a young Syrian boy—possibly, Spencer theorized, to double-stack the odds in favor of the Jews by raising an Arab under the laws of Moses. Uncle Jerry would have appreciated the effort.

That would be a great test of nature vs. nurture, Phillip thought—of DNA vs. experience. He'd look forward to seeing how it played out. Would the boy grow up to hate them because they were Jews? Would he yell 'Allahu Akbar-mitzvah' when he turned thirteen? Or would his parents' lesbian nurturing turn him into an intellectual peace activist marching beside refugees in a knit reggae hat?

"It was weird, when Leah called me," Phillip said. "She said, 'Now *my* mother's dead.' As if it were my fault somehow. Or there was an epidemic of dead mothers."

"Phyllis's anger kept her alive for a long time," Spencer said. "It was unclear if she would *ever* die. Plus there was the preservative power of alcohol. But people get tired, even the angriest people. And people who hate people are the luckiest people. Maybe it wasn't the anger that finally did her in. Perhaps sheer crankiness was a contributing factor. And the misanthropy. Who's to say?"

They endured the funeral. Turnout was sparse, Phillip noted, because when you live that long most of your friends are already dead.

"A real skeleton crew," Spencer observed. Then he whispered, "I bet they'll have cookies from Walls' Bakery. At the shiva. It's why I flew in for this. If not, I'm getting back on the plane."

The gathering in Scarsdale at Leah and her wife Stephanie's house featured an amalgam of reformed Judaism, modified yoga-pants Buddhism, and the trappings of a Grateful Dead show if Jerry Garcia had been from the Five Towns and had gone into his family's jewelry business. The boys shook hands and exchanged hugs with distant cousins, friends of Leah's and Phyllis's and their mom's whom they hadn't seen in years, acquaintances from the old neighborhood. There was something comforting in the interactions and the memories they evoked; the brothers barely remembered they were there because they'd just dropped Aunt Phyllis in the cold, hard ground.

Leah was still a beauty in her fifties, with an intelligent lilt to her mouth, and chocolate brown eyes that seemed to radiate self-acceptance. Her dark hair was cut short, accentuating the high Jewish cheekbones she'd inherited from her handsome father. It warmed Spencer to see her looking so comfortable. She hugged him tightly.

"I've missed you," Leah whispered, her voice hoarse. "I'm sorry we didn't get to talk at Jenny's funeral. I've been thinking about you a lot since then. Even more, recently."

Spencer had come here knowing she had something for him—something she'd described as 'very important'—but he couldn't very well ask about it when she was in mourning, with a house full of friends and relatives descending on the platters of lox and bagels and smoked whitefish salad, some of them sniffing around the spacious house, everyone vying to be supportive of Leah, or at least appearing to be.

"We told everyone the shiva is until 6:00," Leah said. "If you boys can stay after we'll get a chance to catch up. And have a fucking drink. We have to talk."

"We can do that," Spencer said.

"Go look in the kitchen," she said, before disappearing into the teary embrace of someone he didn't know.

On the kitchen table were boxes of cookies from Walls', their hometown bakery—macarons stuffed with jam, scalloped butter cookies, almond crescents half covered in chocolate and colored sprinkles, tiny Linzer torts. It was what childhood tasted like.

"I am *so* taking a box of those home with me," Spencer said.

Most of the visitors cleared out before 6:00; a few stragglers remained until 6:30, pretending to say goodbye in a way that communicated they wouldn't really leave until threatened with water-boarding: Spencer knew Jews could spend two hours on their farewells following a half hour visit. He preferred the fabled Irish goodbye: sneaking out when no one was looking. Leah handled her guests with a no-nonsense, get-the-fuck-out-of-here strength but simultaneously with grace, edging them toward the door with a gentle hand on each shoulder. She's got skills, Spencer thought.

When the room was otherwise empty, Leah dropped onto the couch. She kicked off her shoes, revealing an immaculate pedicure, each toe capped in what looked like an orange candy coating. Spencer sat close beside her; he could smell the subtle sub-tropical jasmine breeze of her perfume. Phillip took the big leather club chair opposite. Stephanie had been thoughtful enough to excuse herself, leaving the cousins alone together for the first time in many years.

"Let me get the thing," Leah said. "It's in my study."

She unfolded her legs from beneath her like a giraffe getting up off the savannah and went through French doors to her home office—she and Stephanie ran a law practice out of the house. Judging from the size and décor they'd done well for themselves.

Leah came back carrying a 9 x 12 manila envelope with "For Spencer Elliot," written in faded marker in a flowing script across the front. It looked like their mother's handwriting, though Spencer assumed it was written by their aunt.

Leah sat back down without any indication she was going to give up the envelope.

"I have to preface this," she said. "I found this in Mom's safe deposit box. At the bottom. Underneath her jewelry and last will and testament. And, oddly, a pair of unused tickets to a Neil Diamond concert from 1968. She always told me to open the box the moment she kicked—her words—because she kept a broach in there she wanted to be buried in. A gift from her brother."

So Leah knew about the long-dead brother who fell off the produce truck, Spencer thought. Possibly a root cause of what had made their mothers the way they were, which might have passed down to them.

"I didn't know anything about this, ever," she said. "I just found out. It was a shock to me, too."

She gave the envelope to Spencer.

"Just tell me what it is," Spencer said. "I don't have the stones to open it right now."

Leah considered for a long moment. "It's a paternity test."

"So now *I'm* somebody's father?" Spencer laughed, calculating whether this was possible.

"No. It's *your* father's."

"Huh?"

"It shows who your father is—my father."

"Wait, your father or *my* father?" Spencer said. "You're not making any sense."

"They're the same father. Yours and mine. Jerry. Your uncle Jerry. My dad. Our dad."

The color fled from his face. "You have *got* to be shitting me," Spencer said.

Phillip couldn't help interjecting. "So, what, now you're our sister?"

"Well, Spencer's sister," she said.

"My cousin, my sister; my cousin, my sister!" Spencer yelled, purposely misquoting *Chinatown*. "For fuck's sake, you've got to be fucking kidding!"

"I am so not kidding. Bro." Leah said.

"I don't fucking believe this!" Spencer shouted. "All this time Phyllis really *was* a liar."

"But wait, there's more!" Leah said.

She opened the envelope and pulled out the paternity test and also a black and white photo of Jenny, Phyllis, and Jerry huddled into the frame together on a beach blanket, the ocean behind them. They were all smiling. Each of them had one hand on Jenny's belly.

On the back of the photo their three names were listed. Followed by a question mark on the fourth line. And then: 'Seville, 1964.'

———

After a couple of twelve-year-old Macallans, Spencer recognized it made total sense. He felt the relief that comes when a stomach ache you've had for a long time stops hurting and you're ready to get back in the pool again.

Or, in this case, the gene pool.

As Phillip drove them back to the city from Leah's house, Spencer went over the details.

"The whole Southern European thing, from the DNA test," Spencer said. "It adds up, with Jerry being Sephardic. Oh, and why everyone was so upset when Leah and I were fooling around . . . And the fact that nobody in this family ever gave up a fucking micron of personal information—they've all been hiding something. At least we can skip the trip to Seville, now," he added.

"But the weird part . . ." Phillip started to say . . .

"And that's why Jerry never acted like a father to me," Spencer said. "Because he *was* my father. And trying to hide it. That must have been hard for him, if he had a beating human heart somewhere in that muscular body. I'm more sorry for him than I am for myself."

"But . . ."

"Yep, I know. That *Phyllis* had the paternity test all these years: she knew!"

Phillip accelerated into the left lane, as if his driving were a metaphor for the increased speed of the utter craziness of their family. "I think it's even weirder than that . . ." he said. "It sure looks like they all agreed to it. Like they were all in it together. Like maybe Uncle Jerry was doing her some kind of *favor*. Maybe Mom *asked* Phyllis and Jerry. She needed a man to have another child . . ."

"You mean like a sperm donor? A little Spencer donor?"

"Exactly. Maybe she didn't want to sleep with a stranger. This whole scenario wouldn't have been beyond her."

"Maybe Mom kept *that* hidden to protect us? So nobody would know what twisted bastards we really are? And Phyllis kept Mom's wacky secret all that time . . ."

"Let me ask this again: who *was* that woman?" Phillip said. "Aunt Phyllis was *right*: It's not all about our fathers at all. We have no idea who our mother was."

"Now she's whoever we decide she is," Spencer said. "*We're* to say. It's our turn to determine who she was. She had her chance."

"There's one more thing," Phillip said. "Maybe Patrick Elliot being my father was no accident either. Mom could have planned that too. And not even Patrick would know."

Chapter Forty-One
Leslie Levine

SPENCER DELAYED HIS RETURN back to Ireland for a week, telling Trisha he needed to spend more time with his brother given their latest bombshell. He spoke to her every day around ten a.m. New York time, when she got home from work —now on the opposite end of the telephone space-time continuum. These calls reminded him of wooing his first girlfriend—Leslie Levine—in the sixth grade. They grew close to each other by speaking on the phone for hours each night, his homework spread across the bed and *All in the Family* or *Columbo* on the TV. It had always struck him as a fine way to get to know another person.

But it was disorienting, too, and hard to keep straight in his mind that he'd fallen for a woman he'd only known for a very short period of time, who lived thousands of miles away on an island in the frigid North Atlantic. Who happened to be his brother's new sister. And who might be a lesbian, which would be inconvenient. Weirder still, he had a newly-minted sister of his own. Everything felt tenuous, like he was a table setting and someone could come snatch the table cloth out from beneath him at any moment—not the trick where someone could do it while leaving the dishes and silverware in place. Someone who'd scatter it all to hell and back and shatter the crystal.

He struggled with the tendency for something novel and exciting to fade as he returned to daily routines of tinkering with his stock portfolio in the mornings, going to the gym, managing his unruly band, and ordering the Szechuan hotpot to be delivered from Mein Chow Palace on Sixth Avenue.

When he told Trisha he'd inadvertently found out who his own father was, she was ecstatic for him, but said, "What the feck, Spencer?

What is it with that family? Next you'll be solving the mystery of the jumping church of Kildemock."

"The what?"

"Never mind. It's an Irish joke that most Irish people wouldn't even get."

"I wasn't even looking for *my* father," Spencer remarked.

"Perhaps when the mother dies, the father appears, too," Trisha said.

He pictured her padding around the cottage barefoot, still in her work clothes, looking for her keys, which went missing most afternoons.

"Still, it doesn't change much for me. For Phillip, finding his father was a big deal. For me? Meh. But it *is* weird that my uncle was my father—that might take some getting used to. It explains a lot."

"Such as?" Trisha asked.

"I have to think he was maybe a not fully-willing participant. That my mom and aunt convinced him against his better judgment? So he was resentful, or he didn't know how to act around us. It made him awkward, so he shied away from connecting. He did what was asked of him, for his family. But then disengaged. It's tragic."

"By the way . . . I love you," Spencer whispered, his heart flexing and contracting in his chest.

"I love you too," she said matter-of-factly. "It sounds like staying longer in New York is best for you and Phillip right now. But get yourself back here soon as you're able. I won't keep forever. Bring your brother if you like. Bring any new brothers you've discovered—sisters, cousins, whatever. Bring them all."

"I'm hurrying as fast as I can," Spencer said.

The brothers got together every day—meeting near the chess players in Central Park, over lunch at Phillip's favorite noodle house in Chinatown, in Spencer's apartment.

"Let's talk about what we know," Spencer said.

"What do we know?"

"My Lactose intolerance, neither of us having a hairy back: genetic," Spencer said. "My incredible power to remember movies, your real estate prowess: pure happenstance. Your never being late: nurture. My gift of humor: God-given."

"Are you making a list?" Phillip asked.

"Yep," Spencer said.

"Don't forget to add that our ring fingers are longer than our other fingers; and that we can smell asparagus in pee," Phillip said. "Those are genetic, too."

"I'm trying to sort out root causes," Spencer said. "I'm getting to know myself. I'm something else! I have to admit relief at knowing who my father was. Despite not caring before. It's liberating."

"It changes you," was all Phillip could say in response.

The night before Spencer flew back to Dublin the brothers ate dinner at a trendy uptown eatery where Phillip scored a table because one of the owners was invested in his real estate fund. They dressed smartly—Phillip in a suit jacket with no tie, Spencer wearing long pants for one of the first times in a while, and actual shoes, and a guayabera shirt—what he called 'a third-world dictator shirt.'

"Where do we go from here?" Spencer asked over cocktails. "When do you think you might come back over? To Ireland?"

"As soon as I figure out a reason to."

"How about: you always wanted a father. Now you have one."

"That may be right. But it's like I just solved a riddle that Mom gave us forty years ago. Like the one about the couple lying on the floor in a puddle of water."

"Goldfish," Spencer said.

"Or the one where a naked dead man is lying on the side of a mountain."

"Hot air balloon," Spencer said.

"I feel that huge, gratifying relief of figuring out the answer. I don't know whether to think about the whole puzzle again with this new perspective. Or just forget it and move on."

"How *could* you know?" Spencer asked. "Ice. The car is on a Monopoly board. A parachute," he said, listing the answers to other lateral thinking puzzles their mom had made them solve. "You couldn't see any of these coming."

Menus arrived and the waiter recommended the two hundred-dollar tasting menu—of course he did, Spencer thought. He said, "Now we're at that part like at the end of a thriller where they've revealed who the killer is but still need to end the movie. They can't just run credits or fade to black. The characters are standing around. Somebody has to say something pithy."

"I have nothing pithy," Phillip said.

"On the other hand, sometimes at that point you find out there's one more surprise," Spencer continued. "Like in *Citizen Kane*. Or *Planet of the Apes*—the original, not any of the crappy remakes or sequels."

"That may be the first time in film history that *Citizen Kane* and *Planet of the Apes* were mentioned in the same sentence," Phillip said. He gulped from his Manhattan. He admired how the heat of the bourbon and the bite of the bitters warmed him through the ice.

"Speaking of film. Who do you think should play me in the movie of all this?" Spencer waved his hand around as if Phillip would see a medley of images: Jack Elliot smiling from the Vietnamese jungle; their mom throwing her rising curve with a Wiffle ball; Patrick and Leah and the rest of them, projected on the wall of the restaurant in a giant, spinning blue-light double helix.

"Matt Damon and Ben Affleck?' Phillip said.

"I was thinking the two Jasons—Bateman, for you; Schwartzman for me. Schwartzman is handsomer and devil-may-care. Like me. Bateman is repressed. He's perfect for you."

"I'll give that some thought," Phillip said.

"I've got one more surprise," Spencer went on, grinning like an eejit.

"I don't want to hear it," Phillip said.

Spencer kept smiling, holding back before the reveal.

"All right, then; just fucking say it," Phillip said.

"You might be my full brother again soon." Spencer offered a gleeful fist bump across the table.

Phillip bumped him back and said, for possibly the ten-millionth time since his brother arrived on the planet, "I have no idea what you're talking about."

"We've established that we're half brothers after a lifetime of being full brothers. But I have a plan to restore things to the way they were. To recoup the missing half. Two halves: full fucking brothers. Stronger than DNA. DNA is a pussy. Crick and Watson were pussies. They were drooling imbeciles. Eejits. Crick and Watson were liars. E.O Wilson was pathological."

"I don't know who E.O. Wilson is."

"He wrote about social Darwinism. How things other than straight genetics might be inheritable. Emotions, for example. Memories. Maybe it was Proust's *mother* who ate the madeleines. If your grandfather survived the potato famine it explains why you're hungry all the time."

"And what did Crick and Watson lie about? Did they promise to take you horseback riding, too?"

"No. They claimed there's nothing more powerful than genetics. But they were wrong."

"That's a lot to think about," Phillip said, hoping his brother would stop.

When he figured out what Spencer was talking about, and intended, to make them brothers again, Phillip smiled broadly. "That doesn't make any sense. But it's still fecking diabolical," he said.

Epilogue
Mr. Wizard

WHAT PHILLIP DECIPHERED FROM his brother's cryptic description of his ill-formed plan—which was like the kind of treasure hunt Jenny might have thought up—was this: biologically, he and Spencer were half brothers, despite their deep bonds, their shared history growing up in the same house, their love of college basketball, their penchant for thinking the same thing at the same time, their Morton's toes and unibrows.

Only half their DNA, at most, was the same—who knew how many pages in their libraries of encyclopedias of genetic code were different. Did their childhood mastery of Monopoly or their volumes of shared punch lines ('Paddy O' Furniture'; 'You have a drink named Ralph?'; 'It looks like you blew a seal.') matter any less than some unfunny chain of proteins?

But if Spencer were to marry Trisha—Phillip's half sister—then Phillip would become Spencer's brother-in-law. If you counted the actual half brother relationship and the new brother-in-law relationship each as half a brotherhood, the marriage would restore him and Phillip to full brotherhood. That he even comprehended Spencer's logic made Phillip more certain that Spencer was his brother. It made sense: if not genetically then at least Spenceretically.

"It's like a restoration comedy," Spencer said when they talked about all the swirling relationships on the phone one night. "It's like . . . The Taming of the Jew."

"Shakespeare was a little early for restoration comedies, if I remember right. Not that it matters," Phillip said.

"What about *The Winters Tale*, where everything goes back to the way it was at the beginning?"

"The restoration part of restoration comedies wasn't that the relationships in the play were restored—I used to think that, too. They were defined by the time period, which followed the restoration of one of the British Kings—a Charles or a George—to the throne, like in the mid 1600s. You would have loved that period—the plays were full of filthy language, drinking, and general befuckery."

"Okay, Professor. Name two restoration comedies for me." Spencer hated when Phillip's Vassar education paid off.

"Coincidentally, considering your upcoming nuptials, there was *The Country Wife* . . . oh, and *The Provoked Wife*! The first is relevant now. And can the latter really be far off? There's also one called *Love in a Tub*, about a man who loses his pants."

Spencer had never been one to joke about marriage, Phillip noted. Men were forever seeing a beautiful woman across a softly-lit restaurant or on a tropical beach and saying: 'I'm going to marry that girl.' Which usually meant: I'm not ever going to speak to her. But Spencer—rarely outwardly serious about anything—was an exception and always had been. Implying that he was going to marry Trisha was a dramatic new development for a man who'd stopped mentioning marriage a decade ago, and had never been unhappy without a mate.

"And by the way," Phillip added. "'All tragedies are finished by a death. All comedies are ended by a marriage.' According to Lord Byron."

"He should know," Spencer said. "He's been married *and* dead."

———

Trisha and Spencer's reunion was right out of a rom-com, Spencer thought—something that might have starred a young Lisa Kudrow. When he emerged from customs Trisha ran to him, with flowers, jumped into his arms, and wrapped her legs around him. He slipped his hands under her thighs to hold her up.

"This is the best car service I've ever hired," Spencer said." They're usually so taciturn."

"I've never heard anyone *say* 'taciturn,'" Trisha said. "I've read it in books but nobody says it out loud."

In the car she said, "I was thinking I want to slow play this. Is that what they say in Texas Fold 'Em? I've been reading about your card games."

"It's Hold 'Em," Spencer said. "You'd only fold them if you didn't have a good hand."

"Oh, I'm going to hold them, alright," Trisha said.

She drove them back to her house. They both talked at once. They went straight to her bedroom and made love with the windows open, a cold breeze coming off the sea. They went out to the kitchen and had tea and made love again.

"The barriers are down," Trisha said. "Funny that by your traveling away from me I became closer to you."

"Hey, that's my brother's trick," Spencer said.

"Which brother?" Trisha asked.

The wedding took place in October in Dublin in the intimate ballroom on the second floor of The Joyce, the hotel the boys had stayed in on their first visit together to Ireland. The ballroom looked out over the treed expanse of St. Stephen's Green. Spencer told Trisha he thought it was a good omen to get married in a place named after a woman.

"I think they meant to name the hotel after James Joyce," Trisha said, unclear if Spencer was having her on. She gave him the reprimanding wifely look she'd promised to start cultivating.

"I was bluffing about it being a good omen, anyway," Spencer said. "I really have no idea."

Spencer claimed to his brother that this time *they* would be the hipsters drinking mimosas in the hotel dining room in the mornings. During breakfast a day before the wedding, Spencer asked their server, "Is there any way in bloody hell I could get a fecking cheese omelette, no baked beans of any kind on the table? I'm highly allergic." Siobhan, the waiter, remembered the boys from their previous visit. He said, "I'm afraid the beans are required. As is the black pudding. But I can see if they'll put them on a side plate. But if you don't finish them there'll be no flan for you. Even if it is your birthday."

———

They held Spencer's bachelor's party at the Royal Dublin Golf Club—just Patrick, Padraig, Spencer, and Phillip knocking it around in the wind and sun in the short grass. At the bar afterward Spencer and Padraig went to get drinks. They intentionally took a long time, leaving Phillip and Patrick alone.

"I'm not sure what you want from me," Patrick said as they sat in the Lumsden Room.

"I don't know what you want from me, either."

"I lost a son," the old man said.

"Padraig mentioned it."

"They all think I'm trying to replace him with you. But that's not it at all."

"And I don't think I'm looking to replace my other dead father with you. But what is it then?" Phillip asked.

"I love being a father. To my own kids. Being fatherly to their friends. The role suits me. Even more so when I see those who crave fathering. Some had a bad one and need a better example for when they're fathers. Some only need a golf lesson. I'm trying to better determine which ones are which."

"I'm not sure which category I fall into."

"I'll aim to be whatever you need me to be—even if it's just the old man who's your brother's father-in-law," Patrick said. "We'll invite you for Christmas if you feel like coming. We'll miss you but carry on all the same if you don't."

"Jews always feel awkward at Christmas. It would be nice to have somewhere to go," Phillip said.

During the ceremony a day later Spencer and Trisha smashed a pint Guinness glass together with their feet in an Irish adaptation of the old Jewish custom. Spencer's oldest friend, Max 'The Factor' Feingold, played the wedding march on the bagpipes, which he learned for the occasion. During the hand fasting ritual, Phillip, as best man, tied the hands of bride and groom together using one of Jenny's favorite silk scarves.

Phillip started to explain in a whisper that this was where the phrase 'tying the knot' came from, but Spencer shushed him as they stood underneath the chuppah. The Irish officiant made a face like a cross between Mel Brooks and a leprechaun and Spencer laughed like he did when he used to get kicked out of Hebrew school. The rings that bride and groom exchanged were designed after a Claddagh ring that had been in Trisha's family for several generations—they made hers with a diamond that Spencer bought from an old friend from high school who had a jewelry store on West 47th Street in Manhattan, near where Uncle Jerry had worked.

At the reception—for forty people who were mostly friends and relatives of the bride—the newlyweds sat in on drums with the makeshift band, which included two members of TOWER of Haggis as well as the singer and lead guitar player from Gorsey Park. There was French wine and Irish whiskey and guests from both sides enjoyed the corned beef—both the Jewish and Irish among them smiling at what they considered a thoughtful nod to their own culture. The cake was a sculpted artwork of chocolate and meringue and almond shortbread with raspberries custom made by Walls' Bakery on Long Island, and flown in with one of the guests who refused to put it in the overhead rack.

Phillip was accompanied throughout the three-day festivities by Marty, who was pleased to be invited as part of the family again, despite how confusing it all was to her—including what this meant for her relationship with Phillip.

"Am I coming as your girlfriend?" she'd asked him after dinner one night back in New York, when they were cautiously making out in his apartment and talking about the upcoming trip.

He kissed her with a tenderness he'd not felt toward anyone in a long time, and knew she would take it as a sign. "I've decided that I'll go to Staten Island with you. Or Coney Island. Or any island you want," he said.

Marty decided to change up her hairstyle for the occasion, cutting her waterfall of unruly curls short and tinting her eyebrows darker, which highlighted rather than hid the shape of her face, which was like the work of a fine finish carpenter. The new look made Phillip feel like he was starting a relationship with someone who strongly reminded him of someone he already loved.

Their new aunt Katherine attended the affair, as well—traveling from her assisted living facility in Lynbrook. Phillip told her she was going to need a new bible to work in the names of the bride and groom. Spencer was happy to recoup all the aunts and uncles and cousins he and Phillip had lost on the day of their visit to her.

After the big event, Spencer and Trisha honeymooned in Turkey for two weeks because neither had ever been; there were no memories or preconceptions, only things they would discover together. They rented a car in Istanbul and drove down the Aegean coastline, across the Mediterranean, then slanted inland back north toward the capital again, renting an actual palace one night in Cappadocia through VRBO that included a cook and a maid who seemed confused that these middle-aged people could have just been married. They kept asking when the children would be coming and at first Spencer thought they were enquiring about babies. But then he realized that they mistook him and Trisha for the *parents* of one of the newlyweds.

When Spencer landed with Trisha back in New York before they headed off to Ireland for who knew how long, he realized it had been nearly a year since their mother's death. There'd been so much tumult he sometimes forgot that Jenny was at the heart of all of it.

Spencer and Phillip arranged for close family to convene for Jenny's unveiling—the Jewish ritual in which, within one year after a death, loved ones gather at the graveside to say a last good-bye and consecrate the new tombstone.

Old Patrick came back for the occasion to give the mother of his first child a fair send-off though he hadn't seen her in more than fifty years. He was proud of the son they'd created together. It was his first visit back since he'd left the states as a young man. He brought Lorna, too, using the airline vouchers Phillip had given them.

Padraig attended as well.

The new Irish part of the family spent a week in the city visiting museums and attending Broadway shows and getting to know the boys in their natural habitat. They took selfies in Times Square with SpongeBob and hoisted a few mahogany-colored beers at McSorley's, which the Irish didn't really seem to *get*, much to Phillip's disappointment. They found the gigantic margaritas at Muchos Hermanos, an upscale taqueria around the corner from Spencer's apartment, more to their liking. Trisha and Spencer went out to listen to live music almost every night.

On the family's next-to-last day in Manhattan Phillip hired a couple of Towncars to transport everyone to the cemetery on Long Island. He insisted Jenny would have loved the dark formality of the black limos with their lights on speeding down the L.I.E. Trisha had a chance to see where the boys grew up. They detoured past the old house on Harbor Stream Lane on the way to the graveyard. Barbara Linkletter, their old neighbor, was nowhere to be seen.

"It's so . . . American," Trisha commented as they sat in the long cars and looked through tinted windows at the aluminum siding, the tiny bedroom windows, the half sidelight by the front door with its patterned red plastic pane. The Japanese maple the color of molten metal beside the white house.

"The servants hated it," Spencer said. "They had to live in the garage and sleep on our bicycles. Phillip kept a grown lion in the yard and we had a tree that shed gumdrops all year, like acorns."

With the windows down they heard what sounded like the metallic chirp of a bird imitating a custom smart phone ring tone imitating a bird. Spencer said the tree next to the house always looked to him like the red wheelbarrow in that famous poem about stealing plums.

Trisha and Phillip looked at each other, shaking their heads. "I don't know how you do it," she said. "I do so wish I could have met your poor mother."

"You mean to thank her?" Spencer said.

———

At the cemetery, after Phillip read aloud from the Book of Psalms, and they recited the kaddish as best as they were able—Leah providing the lead, as she was still a practicing Jew—Spencer offered a few words. He stood in the wind in his expensive camel hair coat with the collar up.

"Hi, Mom. It's your family," he began.

"Spoiler alert: your old friend Patrick and his wife Lorna are here with us; you remember Patrick—your husband's brother, the one you had Phillip with? Oh . . . and I'm actually their son-in-law now, but more on that in a minute.

"Patrick brought his son, Padraig, too—one of his other sons, not Phillip, although of course Phillip is also here with us. As it turns out, Padraig is Phillip's brother!

"I'm here with my new wife, Trisha. If you think that's a surprise, she's also Phillip's sister! Go figure.

"Cousin Leah is here, too, with her wife Stephanie and their son Asher, who is a young Syrian refugee.

"And—surprising to us, but you already knew this—Leah is also *my* sister!

"And just for the record, your dead husband, Jack, would have been an uncle to, well, just about everybody. And uncle to Trisha on both sides. So double uncles! You don't see that every day.

"I know you'll also be glad to hear that Phillip is here with Marty.

"Boy, Mom, you sure made this all complicated. But we love you. We always loved you, more than you knew. Maybe more than even we knew. You did the best you could, and it was thoughtful of you to leave the clues to all of this, to bring us together.

"Phillip figured it out, but it was really all you. It was always you. Aunt Phyllis didn't lie about that. Phyllis is here too, but in a different way than the rest of us. You might be able to see her if you turn to your left. It looks like there won't be any horseback riding, after all. Oh, and we know about your dead brother, we'll put some stones on his grave. And Uncle Jerry—well, I still have some work to do around that one. But I sure am glad he paid for my bar mitzvah."

Spencer was crying, which made everyone else cry, too.

Phillip could not remember the last time *he'd* shed a tear. Marty wiped his cheeks with her hand.

"We're going to unveil your stone now, Mom," Spencer concluded. "We hope you like it."

He reached down to pull the cloth off the gravestone—a rough-edged tablet of black-speckled pink granite—which read:

Jennifer P. Bernstein
Born February 7, 1943,
Died March 10, 2017
Loving Granddaughter, Daughter, Sister, Wife, and Mother.
Oh, Yeah. And Wizard.

They left the gravesite and headed back toward the cars, some of them smiling a little, squinting at the sun breaking through in the winter sky, Spencer and Phillip each moving quickly to try to grab the front seat of their limo before the other one got there first.

Acknowledgements

THANKS TO THE FOLLOWING friends, family, and colleagues—many of whom were early readers—for their various kinds of support, including literary, editorial, culinary, psychic, alcoholic, cigarological, and moral: John Strawn, James Latham, Kieran Devine, Steve and Gina Wallach, Sue Hill, Brad Studstrup, David Fishman, Tim O'Leary, Maureen Sullivan, David Frost, Darrell Williams, Kym Croft Miller, Ed Reid, Leslie Jones, Brad Wellstead, David DeSmith, Karen Moraghan, Terri Cheney, Dan Pope, Bob Brigham, David Ross, Kelly Huddleston, and anyone else who is extremely important but I have inadvertently forgotten. Without the kind words and generous help of Michael Curtis, *Mr. Wizard* would likely have remained an unpublished short story. And of course, and above all, infinite thanks to The Reneé.